James, THE
IS THE BEST PART :

The Viking Pawn

A Novel
By
MICHAEL CARR

The Viking Pawn

Copyright © 2012 – Michael Carr

ISBN: 1470085836

ISBN 13: 978-1470085834

First Edition

This is a work of fiction. Names, characters, and incidents are either a product of the author's imagination or are used fictitiously. Any resemblance to actual people or events, living or dead, is entirely coincidental.

Cover Design by James McManus

Printed in the USA.

To Mom, Dad, and Ally for bringing me back to life.

And to Chelsey, for showing me how to live it.

For them too history was a tale like any other
too often heard, their land a pawnshop.

-James Joyce, *Ulysses*

Well now everything dies baby that's a fact
But maybe everything that dies someday comes back
Put your makeup on fix your hair up pretty
And meet me tonight in Atlantic City

-Bruce Springsteen, *Atlantic City*

[1]

All In

When plastic-coated casino cards snap against the felt, it's easy to tell that a bluff is imminent. A quick, two-card snap, the "machine-gun" snap, means that the player quickly saw paint in his hole cards and is probably on tilt to begin with. A slow, drawn-out snap where each card hits the felt with its own acoustic reverb means that the player sees rags but is working off a large chip stack, so he or she figures, what the hell, I'll take a shot.

I usually don't look at my cards until I'm forced to act. My hole cards leave the felt in one swift, sweeping motion. I reveal each quickly; their image sears into my mind like grill marks on a nice filet. If I decide to play, a chip drops on them immediately, and they don't get revealed again until there's a showdown. If my opponent folds, they go straight into the muck. I made it a rule to never reveal my hole cards. No use giving anyone a read. Life's full of mysteries and unsolvable puzzles, and it's no different in poker.

If my cards are deserving of the muck, I usually take my index finger and flick them forward into the dealer's waiting hands. I don't like to toss them for fear that in their fluttering flight downward they may choose to inadvertently reveal themselves, either through some freak updraft of casino wind or just general nuisance. My poker habits are fixed. They should be by now. I've been sneaking into casinos since I was seventeen. Tonight, I'm thirty-five with forty looming somewhere out there on the horizon like an impassable milestone. I hear things are downhill after that, but if you spend most of your life charging up hills, a reverse trajectory is welcomed.

My swashbuckling days are slowly fading into the twilight, the only reminders being aches and pains at night, too many scars and a tattoo that will eventually sag off my shoulder. But, I'll always have poker. Even when the ink of the eagle and trident wilts with my drooping skin once taunt with muscle, I'll still be able to play cards. That eagle will eventually look like a rooster and I'll certainly have trouble peeing, but I'll still be able to see flops. It would be nice to kick the bucket staring down at pocket Aces. Metaphoric "bullets" are certainly better than real ones. Don't get me wrong I did what I did back in those days for a reason. They dropped us into some terrible messes and we fought our way around, but it's the after that they don't tell you about. The after. Great swaths of time spent thinking about things done that can't be undone. Some guys paint toy soldiers or meditate. I play cards.

I want to live quietly, but sometimes in my line of work, you have to deal with a few unsavory sorts. Take this afternoon for instance:

A twitchy, pockmarked face was staring me down across my counter. It was the kind of face that oozes trouble, along with the seeping oil from clogged pores. This face and the thin body that it came with showed up in my shop looking to pawn an iron chest, scrawled with intricate latticework. He said his name was Leonard Leanos and he wanted two thousand dollars.

"What's in it?" I asked, noticing the chips and cracks near the lid. Somebody tried unsuccessfully to get it open.

"I really couldn't say," Leanos snapped stealthily looking over his shoulder.

"You never tried to open it?" I asked skeptically arching an eyebrow.

"I bought it from an antique dealer," he said hurriedly, "You want it or not?"

2

Of course I wanted it. The chest was sixteenth century from what I could tell. The ironwork and the nails: all hand-forged. It was worth far more than the two thousand he was asking especially if he had the paperwork, which he told me was conveniently misplaced.

Usually my theft radar would turn on at this point in a conversation, but something about the chest was mesmerizing, deserving of my attention even if I knew the hassle that would ensue when the Atlantic City Police department went through my back room and found no paperwork to accompany the chest. But, I'm a sucker for historical artifacts, always have been. My shop's full of them. I've got a golden sword pommel from Anglo-Saxon England, a set of Colt peacemakers, three Winchester '73s, a claymore from the Battle of Bannockburn, more samurai swords than Steven Seagal, and one of General John Buford's cavalry sabers hanging right next to my PhD from Boston University. Yes, I'm a pawnbroker with a PhD. Doesn't seem like the most obvious career choice right? Well, when you join the Navy after high school, get your ass kicked at Coronado before you're twenty-two and hitch up with a SEAL Team, the government tends to reward that kind of behavior with education. I took full advantage. Got my PhD in history five years ago. Pop died before graduation. I took over his pawnshop, but more on that later.

Right now I'm back in the cavernous Borgata Poker Room glancing down at my hole cards. Two Lovely Ladies are staring back at me.

In hindsight, I wish I had left the table earlier in the evening when I was ahead. It's been terrible action considering I sat down with two thousand in my pocket and been forced to re-buy for another thousand after the guy in seat three wearing Italian sunglasses rivered a flush on me. All the money I care to spend is on the table now, a measly thousand-dollar stack. Sunglasses looked down at his cards

3

moments ago and snapped them quickly as he's been prone to do all night. I can feel the bluff coming.

"Rik," says Phil the dealer, my friend and a regular customer, "your action."

I always liked Phil and he's known me for more years than I can remember. I helped him out with some cash last year when his wife was laid off. He's snapped me out of my trance. Replaying bad beats while thinking about the iron chest sitting in your office is not conducive to winning money. I see the action in front of me.

"What's the raise?" I ask Phil.

"One hundred to you, Rik," he says forcing a smile. His face is tired and sunken. It's easy to see that he'd rather be anywhere else than working the graveyard with a bunch of amateur cardsharps like the collection around this table. I don't blame him, but for some of us, late night cash games, surrounded by the stale air of a poker room, heavy with abolished cigarette smoke, still clinging for years after it had been outlawed, is as appealing as the satin sheets and stunning views of the villas upstairs. Poker makes sense to me. It's the ambience mixed with the adrenaline that keeps me coming back for more.

I look over at Sunglasses. He raised to one hundred dollars at a 10/20 no limit table, but he's been over-betting all night with small pairs and face cards. Two players down from him sits a drunk Undergrad, who after downing an entire can of Red Bull in two gulps, called the hundred. I'm last to act. Everyone else has folded.

Sunglasses takes the iPod buds out of his ears and curls his lips into a sneer. I haven't realized that my hand is covering my cards like I'm about to muck. My pockets are empty and if I choose to make a stand here and lose then it's going to be a long walk through the glistening halls of the Borgata and into the parking garage. The buzzing bells and electric lights, the chlorine smell from the resort pool, the cheers in the distance from the craps tables, will all be a cruel Siren song to me, the loser.

I'm putting Sunglasses on Nines or Tens. If he had Jacks, he'd push harder. The Undergrad has Ace-Rag suited and is hoping to get lucky. They both have me covered, so if I come over the top all-in and lose then it's goodnight Gracie. I check the screen on my Casio dive watch. Midnight is a mere memory. One AM is in the rearview mirror and three AM is visible in the headlights. Table's been hot and cold and I can't stop thinking about the iron chest. I didn't want to tell Mr. Leanos that I actually do know how to open it. I know it's been underwater for quite a while from the corroded edges and the patina. Someone did take great care to restore it. I'm assuming it wasn't Mr. Leanos, who seemed like a loud fart would send him through the roof. He had either just blown a few lines of coke or he was not supposed to be in my shop pawning that chest. Or it could have been both. I've seen all kinds.

He wouldn't tell me where he'd bought it. I ran it through my database of recent reported thefts and nothing hit. That doesn't mean that cops won't find something, but I covered my proverbial ass with the database search so I made the deal for two thousand cash. He's got ninety days to pick it up with my two thousand plus interest or I own it. That's a pawn transaction. I'm certainly going to get it open before he comes back. In fact, I may even attempt it this morning. The guy was in such a rush to get his cash this afternoon that I didn't think he'd care about the secret keyhole I knew to be camouflaged within the iron-lattice-work on the lid. I'm not sure why I didn't take a crack at opening it right after he left. I suppose I just got distracted. Life moves on even if someone does drop a treasure chest into your lap. I should probably get back to the shop and have a look and with that I've made my decision. I turned to Phil and crack a smile.

"All in," I say, causing Sunglasses to shut his gaping mouth.

I knew he would call. It was a quick call too. The Undergrad was not yet sober enough to realize his bad decision so he called; a three thousand dollar pot in the blink of an eye.

Sunglasses and the Undergrad check it down on the flop, neither one wanting to make a move after seeing a Queen, Deuce, Five, rainbow. No straight or flush draws, but my pocket Queens just made me a set. Fourth Street is a Nine of Spades, a great card for me. If Sunglasses is playing pocket nines he just tripped up. As if on cue, he bets. The Undergrad folds like a lawn chair, but not before belching and blowing some bad air across the table. His buddies should come back and get him before he pisses himself.

"Showdown gentlemen," Phil says with a yawn.

Sunglasses pulls back the five hundred dollar bet and smirks. He coyly turns over pocket nines, using one card to flip the other, an annoying slow roll.

"Your Ace-Queen's no good, Sir," he says as if adding the word "Sir" will somehow take the wind out of my sails. My read was spot on. But, I nod for a nanosecond making him think he was right, just because he needed to be taken down a peg. Nothing wrong with a little Hollywood to make a jackass think he's the smart one. I can hear his thoughts percolating. He's getting ready to rake as he sees my wince and then I toss my two smiling ladies on to the felt so they can cosy up next to his lonely nines and show them who's boss. The sunglasses finally come off as if he can't believe his eyes. Phil knocks on the table with his hand announcing the last card, the River. He turns over a Deuce of Hearts giving us both Full Boats. Unfortunately for Sunglasses, mine is bigger. I nod respectfully and rake my chips, tossing Phil fifty for the effort. Sunglasses gets up and heads to the can as

I make my exit from the table. Phil colors me up, tossing over two orange chips, the Borgata thousands, a purple chip for five hundred, four black chips, each hundreds, and two green, for twenty-five each. I then slide my chair out and make my way through the meandering maze of the poker room, happy to only be down fifty.

[2]

The Helmet

Half an hour later, coffee and an egg white omelet are processing nicely. I didn't eat dinner and after chopping back at the table, I thought I would treat myself to a late night snack. No good sleep for me tonight. The sun will be up along the Boardwalk soon. This is the time when most turn in for the night. The casinos don't stop, they just slow down for a bit. It's the quiet lull of gears relaxing and neon cooling. We're open all night, but every town needs a break.

Atlantic City's a nocturnal town. I learned this the hard way the first year I took over the pawnshop. My competitor two blocks down had a twenty-four hour window and I didn't. You'd be surprised how many people want to drive up and pawn some strange items at some strange hours. I had the window installed last year and our late night business is thriving.

I'm walking quietly down the Boardwalk past closed tourist kiosks and the Convention Center. I parked my Jeep behind my shop on Morris Avenue and walked over to Caesar's for the omelet and now I'm heading back, listening to waves crash along the pier. A thin veil of darkness covers the vast world out there across the sea. Soon, the pink and orange hues of morning will begin to poke out from the east. I do love watching sunrises. I've seen the sun rise on six continents in my thirty-five years. I do hope the magic of the morning will never fade.

My father came up with the name: *Pocket Aces Pawnshop*. He started the business before I was born and I took it over after he died. Alfred Frederik Rodriguez III, my Pop, was a terrible poker player but that didn't stop him from entering all the tournaments and floating from casino to casino. He never broke the bank, but let's just say I wouldn't have to work so hard if Pop saw Pocket Aces a few more times in his life. It's been five years since he left. I miss him every day. A heart attack got him right before my dissertation was complete. I remember calling him and reading him the first few chapters over the phone. If I was excited, so was he, even though he didn't care much about my topic: *Early Shipbuilding and Navigation from the Phoenicians to the Vikings.* He fell asleep on the phone when I started in on Viking sunstones and early astrolabe technology. He was good people, the best man I knew. I loved him a lot. I know he was proud.

I thought about entering the world of academia, but the lure of the old familiar pawnshop and my Atlantic City home was too much. Besides, I guess I felt like I owed it to him to keep his dream alive. I had as much time invested in our little home as he did. I was sweeping the floors when I was five after all.

Being home after being so far away for so long seemed like a good idea. People say that home is a state of mind and you take it with you wherever you go. I agree, but I've seen some cesspools in my life and it was hard to find home or humanity in their folds. And yet, a few miles up the road from those very same places I was treated with the warmth and hospitality of a prodigal son. I get mad at people who are quick to judge the world. There's the good, the bad and the in between. Most of us occupy that *in between* space. It's easy to cast dispersion on other people from far away, but sit down, have a meal with them and then make your decision. That's one of the many things I hated about academia. I think I liked living history more than writing about it. I disappointed a few people when I turned down teaching jobs, but sometimes you've got to do what's best for you.

And besides all that, I was really lonely. I needed something comforting in the world after all those isolated nights out amongst the folds of that darkest shroud. Being lonely and having plenty of nightmarish mental ammunition can send you off the deep end pretty quick. But, you work through it. You make it work for you. I still have bad days and nights, but they're fewer and farther between. I settled in to this world down here along the Boardwalk, full of symphonic crazies, whirling casino illuminations and cackling tourists and once I learned to tune all of them out, I've been pretty happy with a quiet life. That's how I became a pawnbroker with a PhD.

I turn the corner to Morris Avenue just off of the Boardwalk. I can see my late night window is alive and healthily producing. Ski is leaning out the window handing over an envelope to a rather anxious couple in a Camaro. My steps bring me closer and I realize that the guy is wearing a tux and the girl is decked out in her wedding gown. The thought makes me smile. I wonder what they wanted to sell at four thirty in the morning?

The May air is cool and comforting. My steps are soft and a bit weary. I haven't been sleeping much and the approaching summer makes me long for a vacation. The Camaro speeds past me and I can hear a gleeful cheer from the open driver's side window. Thoughts about marriage flicker like silent movies in my head; all exaggerated actions, no sounds.

There was a girl once. But, my younger self was certainly not in a position to settle down. I had an important job, but in hindsight it was just a job, not the all-consuming devotion that I made it out to be. The only things left over from that job is the tattoo on my shoulder and my love for diving. If I'm not working or playing poker, you can usually find me underwater. If hindsight's twenty-twenty I probably should have put more time into the girl. She was and still is quite perplexingly brilliant.

"I hope you won because it's been a slow night," Ski croaks as I amble through the door. The wood creaks. Needs some WD-40. Don't we all.

"And where's my coffee?" he adds indignantly.

"You didn't want any coffee, remember?" I swear the old sailor's losing his memory by the day. I certainly asked him if he wanted anything when I walked over to Caesar's.

"Oh yeah," he recalls after scratching his salt and pepper beard for a moment. "Well, shit I'm going to go make some coffee then." He ambles back to the office, his leg noticeably sore from the change in barometric pressure. He took a round in the knee on a PBR in '69. Pop was at the helm and Ski, short for Daniel David Szelingowski, was on the .50 cal. Some Viet Cong sniper cracked off an AK round that caught him in the knee. Surgeries and physical therapy never healed it correctly. He still walks with a limp, and it gets worse when the weather changes.

I hear him rattle around in the back as I stand in the middle of my store. I like to think it looks more like a museum than a pawnshop. I really am a sucker for history. There's a long glass case with firearms and jewelry; heirlooms all safely tucked away. There's a few Les Paul Fenders hanging on the wall, a grandfather clock in the corner. Some of these items are only visiting; earning me interest with each passing day. Some of them I own outright and are generating bids on eBay or other online auction sites. And some of them are just mine, on display because they're too magnificent to collect dust in my apartment upstairs. The pawnshop is my Louvre and my Smithsonian and it makes me happy every time I walk through the door.

I send Ski home to bed. He's tired and cranky. Mornings are usually slow. I'll be able to shut my eyes in the office for an hour or two. Cynthia, the pawnshop matron will arrive around eight AM, probably whistling "Hot-Blooded" even though I hate Foreigner, and my day will be in full swing.

I've poured a fresh cup of coffee from the pot Ski made into a clay mug that I picked up in Kenya. I only buy strong coffee. This particular blend comes from Sumatra. It's Indonesian rocket fuel and it picks me right up. I was in Jakarta for a weekend a long time ago, but it wasn't a sightseeing trip. Seemed like a fascinating country from the little of it that I saw. Pain in the ass to slog through rice paddies, though certainly not as bad as Pakistan. That really sucked.

This iron chest is intriguing me the more I look at it. It's sitting right in front of my desk. I pick up the forms that Leanos filled out just to remember if he left a valid address. His poor penmanship reveals nothing but a P.O. Box. I have a feeling that I'm never going to see this guy again. "Well, Mr. Leanos," I hear myself say. "Let's see what you've got inside this thing."

The ingenious bit about these particular chests is the fact that the key is usually hanging right on the handle, but someone, probably in a fit of frustration has pulled it off. Everybody tries the "mock lock" in front; a simple iron hole meant to fool a pirate or highwayman. Nobody bothers to look for the tiny crevice in the latticework on the lid. If you push down on the crevice, a latch lifts and exposes the keyhole. I do just that.

The chest is about the size of a carry-on suitcase and is covered in a blanket of age. This thing belongs in a preservation lab or in a museum display, not on the floor of my office, but like I said, I'm secretly hoping that Mr. Leanos will not return to claim it so I can actually do something with it. Anticipation churns in my stomach as I work my Leatherman tool into the crevice and apply a slight pressure.

The latches and levers click open inside the lid. I would've made a good criminal. I slowly lift the lid and the wood creaks with a moan.

No pieces of eight. No jewels, rubies, or emeralds. But what I find, carefully wrapped in burlap, is a forged-iron helmet, dented near the bridge. The eyepieces swoop down like two loops and the intricate inlay is gold or gold leaf. This was not an average warrior's helmet. This was worn by someone important. The earflaps are carved with complicated precision. Producing a magnifying glass, I begin to scan the carvings. Most are braided patterns but in the center of both earflaps, carved with care and exactitude is what looks like an "X". The magnifying glass reveals something different though. This "X" has a left-pointed hook almost like an arm and appears on both earflaps. A surge of electricity shoots through me. This is a rune. Runic writing was the early form of written communication amongst the Vikings, Anglo-Saxons, Frisians and could have even originated near the Alps with the Etruscans.

Pulling back from the miniscule rune I realize that this is probably a Viking helmet or even an Anglo-Saxon helmet. Thoughts run through my head about huge Anglo-Saxon gold hordes recently found in England. This is going to make my day interesting especially because I have no idea if that carving is a rune or not. The helmet looks too perfect to be old. It's probably a reproduction. But that rune: It looks like something I've seen before but no sense getting excited at five in the morning. Better wait until the sun comes up.

I got the intercom fixed so if anyone rings the bell I can come down from my apartment. I might send an email or two about the chest and the helmet later in the morning. My friend Victor Meek in Dublin might be able to help with authenticating the helmet, but right now, my stomach is growling. The egg white omelet didn't do the trick. I remember a box of cupcakes in the refrigerator and a fresh gallon of milk. Perhaps I will have a great epiphany with the help of some chocolate frosting.

[3]

Shadows

I've fallen asleep with a cupcake in my hand.

I'm dreaming.

Slow streams of warm water ebb and flow around me with the tide. I'm underwater above a palatial coral reef – there are thousands upon thousands of fish swimming all around. I can breathe. I have no mask, no regulator.

The sharks: Whitetails and nurse sharks. They dance around above me in harmonious splendor.

And now I'm alone, in the middle of the ocean. No reef. No sharks. Colder water. I can see the shadow moving toward me; the phantasmal wingspan of a ghost; a giant manta ray flying like an otherworldly monster of the abyss. The ray glides swiftly and I'm powerless. His wings flutter as the water parts in his presence. He flies over me, his jet wash sending me spinning wildly, tumbling in the water. And now I can't breathe and I'm falling.

The crash of the helmet against my new wood floors jars me awake. I am clutching the cupcake like a life buoy. I stare around, dazed, completely confused and then my TV comes into focus in my small living room. I must have knocked the helmet off the table with my elbow.

I'm in my kitchen. I glance at my watch and it's six-fifty in the morning. I slept for nearly an hour and a half. The milk is warm on the table. I see my refrigerator, the hardwood floor I replaced last month, the long book case in the den full of everything from Hemingway to Yeats and enough history to keep me occupied forever. My La-Z-boy.

This small apartment: my sanctuary, my fortress, passed on to me by my father. This is our heraldry, our coat of arms; a dusty apartment above a pawnshop. The Rodriguez clan lives on.

My hand is covered in chocolate frosting from the mangled cupcake. Cool water from the sink washes away the solidified sugar and completes my arrival back from the dream. I have a habit of trying to immediately analyze my dreams. This one is puzzling. Any good shrink (and I've seen a few) will tell you that it's a classic "performance" dream. The fall was my inability to see the task through to its completion.

I try to disregard psychobabble whenever possible even though I believe in analysis. Sometimes a dream about a giant manta ray is just that. I dove with them in the Sea of Cortez last summer. Sometimes they'll appear in my dreams. Anyone who's ever felt their presence will attest that they possess an ancient mystique. They are monstrous and beautiful, archaic and otherworldly. Manta rays are a glimpse back to times primordial and in many ways beyond our comprehension.

I stare at the hooked X carved in the helmet and consider the possibility that this rune might just be beyond our modern comprehension as well. I carefully pick the helmet up off the floor, hoping that I haven't damaged it. No scratches, no chips, which is relieving. The metalwork is understated yet brilliant. Each turn of the chisel: perfectly exact for the craftsman. The hollow inside where the stately head of a Viking or Anglo-Saxon chieftain rested comfortably remains empty after years spent secluded in the chest. The hooked X: the rune carved for reasons unknown, perhaps unknowable and yet I could be sitting here, fascinated, enthralled by a cheap reproduction, a knock-off. Something tells me it's not, but skepticism doesn't journey far away.

It's now seven in the morning and probably time to return downstairs to make sure no one's cleaned out my shop, but this X is captivating. The chest originally started out as the most interesting bit but now a sixteenth century chest has been usurped by an ancient helmet: origins unknown. History's great mysteries are usually contained in such simple packages. Hieroglyphics were so remarkably strange until Napoleon found the Rosetta Stone. Early man was a mystery until Leckie unearthed "Turkana Boy". This helmet, contained for centuries in an iron treasure chest, could be yet another breakthrough in the meandering timeline of man's existence. Or, it could be just another fake, like the many millions that came before it. However, I can't help but feel rather ecstatic about finding this particular helmet with a hooked X. I'm reminded of Jim Hawkins, half expecting old Billy Bones to amble up my stairs and tell me to beware of the "one-legged seafaring man".

The whole reason I began studying history was because I wanted to find a buried treasure – none in particular – any treasure would do. Then I met Rachel Hexam years later and realized that archaeologists spend more time in the dirt with specimen brushes than they do swinging over snake pits with a bullwhip and a fedora. I stuck to the water and the library, wreck-diving, and research. My adrenaline rushes came in other forms in earlier times. No director yelled cut after the bullets started flying and someone made a mistake.

The intercom buzzes with a grating sound and I hear a familiar voice: "Rik, get down here, they robbed the store," Ski croaks like a bored bullfrog.

He's used this ruse before and I take the bait to humor him pushing the intercom button on the wall. "That's good. I can finally retire to the Caribbean."

"I got some breakfast down here."

"Why didn't you sleep longer?" I say, knowing the answer.

"You know I don't sleep good in the dark," he chortles.

"Just during the day, while you're supposed to be working."

"You got it."

The treasure chest and the helmet fascinate Ski. I don't even get two bites into the Taylor ham, egg and cheese sandwich he brought me before he inundates me with any and all knowledge he has about the hooked X. Ski is a connoisseur of conspiracy theories. He, like my father before him, knew exactly who killed Kennedy, could tell you the location of most alien landings within the Continental US and had a nasty habit of relating everything and anything back to the Knights Templar. Why? Well, I suppose that they just liked knowing some things that were inexplicable.

"The Kensington Rune Stone! This symbol's from the Kensington Rune Stone!" Ski is shouting in the office. He's already got ketchup in his whiskers from the egg sandwich and his enthusiasm is sending little bits of partially masticated breakfast across the room.

"What's the Kensington Rune Stone?" I ask, genuinely curious.

Ski is channeling his best Walter Brennan as he flashes me a toothy grin. "See that Professor, it's nice to be the smartest guy in the room. I'm just going to revel in this for a minute and then I'll tell you."

"Don't leave me hanging like that, Ski. If we're sitting on Priam's gold, tell me quick." I know it's cruel to play this game, but I like to see him get excited. I made the connection before we sat down. That's where I recognized the rune. I am well aware of the Kensington Rune Stone and all of its history. In fact, I spent a good portion of the winter reading a fascinating book about the geology of that very stone. But,

I give Ski a moment. He still needs to teach me a few things. And I still need to learn.

He cradles the helmet in his calloused hands. I can see the genuine fascination on his face. "No gold, Rik," he says quietly. "Only the key to the early history of North America."

"Can I sell that?" I ask him.

He scoffs at my sarcasm and continues: "Kensington, Minnesota 1898: Olaf Ohman, a Swedish farmer, is clearing a tree stump with his sons and he finds this big block of sandstone wrapped in the roots."

Ski never fails to marvel with some theatricality. He's set the scene like Hollywood screenwriter forcing me to put my sandwich down and pay attention. I'm legitimately curious even though the curiosity is feigned. A good story should make you feel a little paradoxical. It's good for the soul.

"Carved into the stone are lines and lines of runic text including this little beauty right here," he holds up the earflap on the helmet like it was the secret of life. "This rune appears on three other rune stones scattered around America."

Here's where I have to pull back the curtain and contribute to the conversation: "I heard about the ones in Massachusetts and Maine. Where is the other one?"

"East Greenwich, Rhode Island. It disappears and reappears with the tides like a phantom," he says finally sitting in the chair in front of my desk. His excitement has gotten the best of him. He looks elatedly exhausted from those few sentences.

"So?" I ask just to piss him off.

"So what?"

"So, what does it mean?" I say persisting.

Ski shakes his head as if I were a child who wandered into the middle of a compelling film and demanded to know the ending before it was over.

19

"Nobody knows what it means, Doctor," he says. "It's thousands of years old and the inscription is being debated as we speak."

"Where?"

"Where, where, everywhere. That stone proves that there was a European exploration party in America one hundred plus years before Christopher Columbus. The date extract from the rune stone puts it being carved and placed in 1362."

"How did they date it?" I ask, knowing the answer already.

"I don't know how they deciphered the goddamn date," he says taking a frustrated bite from his egg sandwich. "I just know that somebody smarter than you or me figured out the thing said 1362."

I lean back in my chair smirking at him. I watch him chew, dissatisfied until he notices my tell.

"You know how, don't you? You pain in the ass, letting me ramble on like that."

I nod folding my hands behind my head. "It's called the Easter Table method. You would use two letters and a number placed on a runic table and then figure out your year. There's evidence on gravestones and in Churches throughout Scandinavia and Anglo-Saxon England."

Ski finishes chewing and takes a swig of coffee. "See the difference is, I learned all that stuff from watching the History Channel and you spent hundreds of thousands of dollars on a fancy degree."

I must concede to a valid point.

It seems that quite a few people lost last night, because the shop is jumping today. It started right around nine o'clock. Cynthia, the matron of the pawnshop, blasted through the doors like a wrecking ball and went right to work yelling at

Ski for the stains on his shirt. She sold a gold pocket-watch and a Winslow Homer print before she had her coffee and acquired two oil paintings that we can turn around for twice their value.

I snapped a quick picture of the Viking helmet with my iPhone camera before locking it in the safe, a closet-size enclosure that takes up the left side of my office. No sense leaving it hanging around. I send the picture to a former professor of mine, now retired in Dublin, Ireland. Victor Meek for years was the keeper of a plethora of medieval knowledge in academia. He could read runes and recite most of Bede's *Ecclesiastical History of the English People* from memory. I took a course with him at BU and spent a semester in England with him working on some Anglo-Saxon cemetery sites, but mostly, he liked talking baseball. He is an expatriate for sure but you don't lose Brooklyn and the lifelong love of the Yankees. I wasn't much of a medievalist, much to his chagrin, but we still kept in good touch over the years and if anyone would recognize an authentic piece it would be Meek.

It's noon now, and I've had a chance to settle in to my day. Paperwork, counting cash, trying not to spill countless cups of coffee on the new "Pocket Aces" golf-shirts I had made for the staff; Navy blue with gold lettering of course. I sprung for the full color "Aces" on the seal: spades and diamonds.

Cynthia is sitting in front of my desk and in all her whirlwind fashion is rattling off an inventory list of items coming up to the end of their pawn transactions. She's about four foot nine inches tall and speaks with a lilting Korean accent but her diminutive exterior quietly masks the tightened savvy of a gunnery sergeant.

"I am quite sure that we will at least acquire the Waterford crystal vase. His grace period is nearly up," she says crossing another item off her inventory list. If it were up to her, she would cancel the transaction the nanosecond that someone's grace period expires, making their pawned property our property. But me, well I'm a bit soft.

"Send him the email reminder anyway," I tell her. She rolls her eyes and departs with a fluctuating "thank you," indicating disapproval and sarcasm. Her words hang in the air for a minute along with the scent of her gardenia perfume before my office becomes mine again. I can see her through the window angrily punching away on the keyboard reminding the man who pawned a one thousand dollar Waterford crystal vase that his time is up. She and Ski have two desks set up behind the cash register with computers and various knickknacks scattered about. My office is behind their desks, but my father did the smart thing when he put up the partitions and the door. Sometimes you just need to shut the world out.

The activity outside and Ski's frustrated profanity have eased so I click through some emails. Nothing from Meek yet, eBay items are selling nicely, some spam and then one I'm not expecting. I have to do a double take when I see the name, bolded against my Gmail backdrop. A cloud passes in front of the sun sending a patch of gray through my window. The high noon shadows shift and I click on her name to open the email. *Rachel Hexam.* My eyes immediately go to her signature:

Rachel Hexam, MA, PhD
Princeton University,
Wildwood Underwater Research Laboratory
Beachcomber Drive North
Wildwood, NJ 08260

Memories like the shadows flittering across my desk creep back into my mind. An apartment in Brookline, she calls me "withholding", a wreck-dive in Mexico, hotel room with silk sheets, an empty closet and an engagement ring I had to return. Her signature irritates me. Why?

Unknowable. Maybe it's because I know she once plagiarized three passages in an undergrad research paper on the Spanish Armada? Maybe it's because I know she likes to eat Cheerios right out of the box with her hands? Maybe it's because after two apple martinis she becomes an amorous adventurer? For whatever reason it may be, I'm irritated and I haven't even read the message.

My eyes scroll through the one line of text:
Rik, call me. It's important. – R

I hate that she doesn't type out "Rachel" like I'm one of her graduate assistants. I could draw a detailed sketch of her naked body from memory and she types "R". And then, because Gmail has decided it, her signature is a watermark below the "R". Perhaps this is her runic, tantalizing inscription. If she tells me she's engaged to the millionaire she's been seeing I'm going to lose a lot of money in the casino tonight and I will not refuse the complimentary drinks, despite my abstinence from alcohol. I will be in a polluting mood if Rachel Hexam is engaged. I will definitely get drunk. I will definitely win for a little while, riding the buzz of beers, and then I will most assuredly lose when I'm too drunk to concentrate. It's irritating when you can't change the future, even though you can see a bad decision miles down the road. If Rachel Hexam is engaged, I'm getting drunk tonight.

Withholding. The word festers like an untreated wound. It hangs in my head like bad reverb. What a stupid word. Of course I was withholding. I don't want to go back to those places. I couldn't tell her that I once killed a man in front of his wife and daughter. He had a gun to the head of my Captain and I could not hesitate. He was dead before he heard the report from my rifle. These things we do either make us or break us. Rachel thought I wasn't confronting my issues, but the truth was that I confronted them by allowing myself forgiveness. Who could live knowing the things I knew? Who could sleep after wiping blood from a dive knife on a neoprene suit on some beach in a country I can't remember after killing people I can't remember? I told myself that I did it because I was ordered to do it and Rachel thought I was lying. I've seen the demons. I've confronted the shadowlands and I can sleep at night.

I took a bath on that ring. I had a moment to propose all picked out and then one day I came back to our apartment and she was gone. Just like that. A finger snap. No note, just gone. She told me later that she could never love me if I didn't let her all the way in. But, I promised myself after too many drinks and a fall in an alley that I would never bring anyone into that world, my shadow world, the world of enemies and submachine guns, destruction and death. That world is mine and I can live with it. I had to quit drinking after that night.

I need a minute. More then a minute actually. I need a shower. I bluster past my staff and head up the back staircase to my apartment. Rachel's email has sent me reeling and I sit and stare at the wall for a long moment, waiting, wondering, staring at the blank screen on the phone. Should I call? Should I ignore her email? It's all too much to comprehend.

The blaring ring of the iPhone in my hand wakes me from the dreamscape. It's Cynthia calling me from downstairs. I glance over at the CCTV monitor on the wall. She's irritated to have to call me. In the split screen, the Boardwalk view reveals the reason why.

"You have a visitor down here, Rik."

I can taste bile in my mouth. It's amazing that an ex can send me into such a tizzy, but Rachel Hexam is anything but ordinary.

"Yeah, who is it?" I ask.

"Joel Molitor," she scoffs.

But, I've already seen him standing outside. I certainly didn't want to see him this afternoon. "Tell him I'll be down in ten." I put the phone on the kitchen table.

It's 4pm and now I've got to go downstairs and see Joel Molitor. I wouldn't say I hate the guy. I don't really hate anyone. Maybe loathe? He's just a pain in the balls, but I keep up appearances with him because he collects a CIA paycheck. We worked together on an op in Afghanistan ten years ago and I taught him how to play Hold 'Em. Whenever he's in town, he usually comes by looking for a game.

The shower is welcomed. The night of feverish excitement and the stale stink of casino need to be wiped clean, especially if I have to deal with Molitor. I don't know why I make nice with the guy. Pop always said, "someday you might need a way to cross a river, so don't burn any goddam bridges." It's a rather simple aphorism, but still pertinent. Molitor knows some people. I'll humor him.

"Rik, you old sonofabitch!"

His shirt is dancing in the breeze. The tailored cut fits him well, but he puts too much gel, product, or whatever into his hair to make it stand up and shout. That's the best way to describe Molitor, he shouts with a whisper. He blends while he stands out; a walking contradiction.

He's standing on the railing of the Boardwalk when I walk out of the shop. He had ended the call on his Blackberry when he saw me, and he thrusts a big paw into my hand proceeding to shake it forcefully.

"How's it going, Joel?"

The afternoon sun is blinding me. Tourists are pouring all over the Boardwalk and I'm still completely perplexed about Rachel.

"Couldn't be better, Rik, seriously. It's good to see you."

"You want to talk inside?" I ask.

He agrees and a few moments later he's sitting across my desk sipping a cup of coffee and smiling superciliously.

"How's business?" he asks with a hint of sarcasm as if everything that goes on in my world, including the sale of a Warhol print for six thousand that I can see Ski writing up, is somehow beneath him.

"Things are good. How's government work?"

"I'm back Stateside for a while. Working out of New York and DC mostly."

"A domestic spy now?" I scoff.

"Not tonight anyway. In town for a little poker, you game?" He shifts his weight forward.

"You got something lined up?" I ask, slightly curious.

"Fifty thousand dollar pot over at Harrah's."

I'm interested. "Yeah? How did you swing that?"

"Friend of a friend. A couple of whales are getting together in a villa up there. Could be really easy money. You feel like playing? They need one more. The buy-in is five thousand."

For fifty thousand I definitely feel like sitting in, but it means a whole night of sitting with Molitor.

"Say," he continues, changing the subject mid-stream, "how's Jay Brown? You still talk to him?"

I certainly still talk to my friend and SEAL teammate Jason Brown. And if there's one person that dislikes Molitor more than me it's Jay. "He's one of yours," I respond. "Surprised you haven't run into him."

"Company man? Where's he stationed?"

"Well, if I told you that Joel, wouldn't I have to kill you?"

He laughs at the jibe, but laughs too hard to be genuine. Something's not right with him.

"Well, when you talk to him again, tell him I say hi, wherever he is."

"Sure," I say, now allowing him to drive the rest of the conversation. All the while, my peripheral vision is drawn to the wall safe where my latest acquisition is resting comfortably. I really want this guy to leave so I can figure out what to do with the helmet and so I can figure out what to do about Rachel's email.

"So, about that game, you think you could come up with five thousand?"

"And if I could?"

His eyes scan around, almost preoccupied, almost jittery. "Then you should put it on the table tonight."

I nod. It's as if we're already in the game. I can see in his reptilian gawk that he's not telling me something and he can see that I know there's more to this visit than a friendly pop in.

"What time?"

"Nine o'clock at Harrah's. Meet me in the lobby at eight forty-five. If you're not there, I'll know you're out."

"Fair enough, Joel," I say standing up. He makes his way to my office door.

"Say, you get anything interesting in here lately?" he asks almost as an afterthought. I feel a flash go toward the wall safe. The hair on the back of my neck stands up, almost protective of my new piece. But he couldn't possibly know what I've got stashed in there?

"Why don't you browse around a little before you go?"

He laughs again, that nervous laughter of someone with a secret and then he shakes my hand. I shut my office door and sit back down in the vinyl chair, spinning slightly towards the window and rocking slowly back and forth, the annoying creak enough to drown out the doubts and misinterpretations in my head.

When you make a decision, stick to it. Pop used to love to drill that in my head. The Boardwalk is bustling as the sun begins a slow descent. Up and down, the hoard of humanity: winners, losers, and all of us in between pound the planks and listen to the waves cresting and breaking a few feet away.

Metallic pings and whirs of the penny arcades wash over me as do the smells of cheesesteaks, frozen custard, saltwater taffy and the cacophony of carnival life that is my home. Caesar's is coming up on the left. All over, people whiz by eager to get somewhere, anywhere. The Wild, Wild West is lit up with a thousand lights and the giant billboards of the cowgirl dancers hang gracefully over the sides of the boomtown façade.

Rachel wants me to call her. We haven't exactly spoken in quite a while. She thought it better that we sever all ties, which meant that she found someone else. Quite honestly, I don't want to talk to her, even if this ridiculous turn of events does have something to do with her. Last I heard through the grapevine, meaning the last I heard from our mutual friends, Rachel was working on some pre-Columbian dig on Lake Champlain in addition to running the Underwater Research lab in Wildwood; a busy woman as always. This could easily be some big happenstance, neither the helmet nor her email having anything to do with the other, and yet something is telling me that I should call her. *Call her you idiot, call her*! I can hear my Dad's voice screaming in my head.

The phone is in my hand. All I have to do is press send. But somehow, I get lost in the crowd on the Boardwalk, swept away by the grand tide of the City: *always turned on*. Then, as if I'm through a wormhole, it's dark, and I'm in my Jeep driving towards Harrah's to take Molitor up on his offer.

I hired a kid named Chris Rhodes a year ago to work the night shift. He's twenty-two and massive, nearly four hundred pounds. He gurgles when he talks. His tattoos and menacing mustache scare the daylights out of anyone thinking of robbing the place, but he's a teddy bear. Most mornings I'll come in to find fast food wrappers and chocolate bars all over the back room and I'll know that Rhodes had a productive night. I like the kid and I'm happy to hear his voice when I call the shop from a few blocks away.

"I sent Ski home, Rik," he says. I can tell he's eating, probably mini-Snickers bars. Those are his favorite. Cynthia keeps a stash for him in the fridge, but I keep telling him to cut them out. He can't afford the calories.

"Was he cranky?" I ask.

"Yeah, but his wife called and said she made him lasagna so that perked him right up."

I smile as I drive, headlights whizzing by: anxious to arrive or depart. For those of us living and working these streets, the hustle and blur of a night in AC is like any other. Our normalcy is heightened. Rhodes played guard for the Atlantic City High School Vikings, so I liked him already. He's a good soul.

"That's all right then. I'm out driving around. Might make a stop before I come back. You'll hold down the fort for me?"

"I got it, Rik. No problem. Win some money tonight. Bring me a burger from Harrah's."

"Sure kid, no problem."

Chris Rhodes, like everyone in my small circle of life, knows me too well.

[4]

High Stakes Poker

Every time I gamble at Harrah's it feels like I'm one step closer to the World Series of Poker Main Event in Las Vegas. Their entertainment group sponsors the tournament. It's on my list of things to do. I don't know if I'm good enough, but some day I'd like to try my hand.

The Resort is wide and sprawling, so much so that it, like the Borgata, warrants its own exit off the Extension. The crowd for The Pool nightclub is starting to arrive as I take the escalator down from the parking garage. The dresses are too high and the shirts are too tight, all stereotypes are covered as uncovered skin reigns supreme. Not that I'm complaining necessarily. Some of the talent walking around this casino is extraordinary, but all the glitz and glamour is for show, an illusion, like most things in a casino. The house always wins, except if you're a good poker player.

It's eight forty-four and I can see Molitor, standing, eagerly checking his watch and scanning through the sea of humanity. I don't like the fact that he wants me in this game so bad. But, against my better judgment I grabbed a wad of cash and drove over. Ski barked his disapproval. Sometimes a gamble isn't a gamble. You never know who could be sitting around the table in that villa. The experience alone might be worth it. Sometimes these whales get big names to sit in with them, guys like Ivey, Hellmuth, Brunson, Greenstein, bracelet winners, cardsharps and straight-up gamblers. It could be fun or I could get my ass kicked on the felt. That's why it's called gambling.

"Game still on?" I ask walking up beside him.

"Hey Rik," he says, ecstatic. "Game's still on, follow me. You got cash or you need the ATM?"

I look at him with disgust. Anybody who's ever been to a casino will tell you that drawing money from an ATM on the floor means one of two things: you're at the end of your rope or you're a tourist. I'm neither.

"I've got cash."

"Good. Then let's go."

I notice my friend Bobby Cusano, one of the casino executives, on my way to the elevators. He's one of the good ones, easily available for a favor. He reassures me that the game is on the up and up. Molitor shrugs off the meeting, anxious to arrive at our destination – the villa elevators. Molitor quickly swipes a key card for the villa floors. We step in and then we're going up.

"Lord Lucan, allow me to introduce Rik Rodriguez," Molitor says almost giddy. He's led me into a penthouse suite in the *Water Tower*. Floors below us, the nightclub is bumping with a hormonal surge and I'm shaking hands with:

"Matthias Lucan, Earl of Bingham," he says in an ash-coated British accent. He's dressed in a five thousand dollar Armani suit with black onyx cufflinks and a gold ring. The ring is garish, etched with some kind of cross. If feel like I've seen the symbol before. Molitor has been playing Fredo from *The Godfather*, trying to make me feel at ease. The whole way up he assured me how legitimate this game would be. "Everything on the up and up." The suite behind him is a buzz with seven other players milling around and helping themselves to a buffet table of food sent up from McCormick and Schmick's restaurant.

"Nice to meet you, Mr. Lucan," I say as he releases my hand.

"It's Lord Lucan, actually," he intones shaking my hand forcefully. His smile is piercing as he scoffs, "but it couldn't matter in the slightest."

31

My hands are big, his are bigger. He's got broad shoulders and sunken cheekbones, carrying what I imagine to be sixty-five years like a gaunt wolf.

"Mr. Molitor, will you get Mr. Rodriguez all checked in?"

"Sure, sure," he says like this isn't the first time he's taken the Lord's orders.

Molitor then escorts me to the Harrah's employee serving as banker/dealer where we deposit some monies, collect some chips and before I know it, there's ten players sitting around an oval table and the dealer is tossing cards my way. We drew cards for seats and my King put me on the button first, sitting immediately to the dealer's left. The small blind has a shaved head and a full handlebar mustache. He's introduced himself to me as Omar and his accent sounds Venezuelan, although it's been a while since someone paid me to notice things like that.

The big blind is Omar's brother Tuco who's wearing dark sunglasses and a teal blue sport-coat. First to act is Kristoph, a Dane with a *Tapout* tee-shirt and bulging artificial muscles. I watched him polish off half a dozen king crab legs at the buffet in two minutes. In fifth position, directly across the table from me is Lord Lucan. In sixth position is Molitor. In seventh position is Jules Montgomery, just got a name on him, except he's got a diamond pinky ring on that's worth more than the pot. I think he's Haitian, judging from his accent. In eighth position is Montgomery's cousin Esteban. He's pushing fifty and his open shirt buttons are showing me the top of an elaborate tattoo adorning his chest. Twin brothers, Henrik and Tor, occupy ninth and tenth positions. I think their last name is Magnusson but I can't be certain. Both of them have blond hair cut high and tight, probably ex-military. The dealer announces that the blinds are twenty-five and fifty to begin and we're under way.

On the button, I look down at pocket Deuces, not a terrible hand to start with, but not great either. Action goes around the table and nearly everyone mucks. Tor Magnusson in tenth position limps in for fifty so my pocket ducks don't look so bad. I raise the action up to one hundred dollars. Omar folds. Tuco folds. Tor checks his hand and then folds. And just like that, I'm up one hundred and twenty-five dollars. I rake the chips and catch Lucan smiling.

"So you came to play then, Mr. Rodriguez?"

"Just a couple of ducks," I say turning over my Deuces. I break my own rule to show them my bet was half a bluff.

"Well done then," he says.

"Where is Bingham located?" I ask, stacking my chips.

"Just outside of Norfolk actually. The old kingdom of East Anglia. Are you familiar with *Beowulf*?" he asks, taking a draft of a deep raven stout, thicker than a chocolate shake.

"I've read the translation. Why?"

"Hopefully Mr. Heaney's version?"

"Yeah, that was the one. Why do you ask?" Is this guy kidding, talking literature at a poker table? I've been playing poker a long time and I don't think I've ever discussed Seamus Heaney while cards are being dealt.

"Only because they believe the poet was from the area in and around Bingham in Anglo-Saxon East Anglia."

"Interesting." I say as I muck my hand.

Molitor chimes in, "You should see the library he has at Bingham House, Rik, it would knock your socks off."

Lucan glances at Molitor with quick precision, almost so I didn't notice. He gave him a stare like the swift strike of a venomous snake. Now I certainly have a read. Molitor knows this guy as more than just a whale. Where have I sat down? Who are these guys? Lucan quickly changes the subject. I suppose I should have asked these questions earlier in the night.

"How about you, Mr. Rodriguez? Atlantic City born and bred?"

"Yessir. Haven't traveled too far from home." A lie, but I already showed them my pocket ducks. No use giving telling them the truth.

Omar shuffles his chips in front of him. His voice is grating and discordant. "What's your business, Rik?"

"Pawnbroker."

Lucan's eyes brighten. "Really, how extraordinary. And where is your establishment?"

"Pocket Aces Pawnshop," I hear Kristoph, the Dane, say matter-of-factly.

"That's right," I say. My suspicions are heightened. I know I've never met this guy before. Molitor told them who I was? Am I being set up?

Instead, I retort: "Have you been in my shop?"

Kristoph shakes his head no. "It's on your shirt." I forgot I was wearing my lucky blue golf shirt with the shop's logo like a medieval blazon on the chest. Kristoph continues, "I also know a guy who went there. He told me your name in case I ever have any business. I put one and one together."

"I'll make sure I give you a card then," I quip. My radar is on now. This is all a little bit too, well I don't know yet. I can feel a "burn in" coming. The "burn in" or parachute malfunction usually led to a bad case of dirt poisoning. That's why I would never jump without a triple check of my gear. I try not to believe in luck.

Three hours can fly by at a poker table. The Magnussons went bust and decided not to buy back in. They've been sitting behind the table the whole time just watching the action. It's rather disquieting having two guys on the periphery awkwardly gawking like they're waiting for something extraordinary to go down, but hey it's not my game. I rivered a flush on Montgomery sending him to rail and Tuco lost trips against trips on the last hand heads up against Lucan. There are six players remaining. Lord Lucan has the overwhelming chip lead. I'm sitting in second place and it's just about even through the other four.

I take a sip from the water bottle I grabbed during a break and look down at my next hand, Ace-Jack of spades. I'm sitting in the big blind and we're now at five hundred/one thousand dollar blinds. My thousand is in and it's up to Omar to act.

He calls.

Esteban calls.

Kristoph calls.

Lord Lucan looks down at his hand. "Raise gentlemen." He counts out five thousand in chips. "Five to play." Now it's getting interesting.

Molitor looks down at his hand. He's got about three thousand in front of him. He's been playing sloppy all night, overbetting the pot, calling with dogged hands, but from the expression on his face, I suppose he figures that this is the time to make the move. "All in," he announces.

Now, the action comes back around to me. I've got twenty thousand in front of me. It's been a fantastic night to say the least. Lucan is staring at me, as are the others. There's an old expression in poker that if you look around the table and can't tell who the sucker is, then it's you.

"Call, five thousand," I say and toss my chips into the middle.

Omar calls for five thousand putting him all in. Esteban calls for three thousand. Kristoph calls for five thousand and he's got about five behind it. The dealer divides out the side pots and it's three-way action to the flop. Molitor and Esteban can only win the pre-flop side pot.

I was hoping for a couple of spades but I never thought in a million years that I'd be looking at Queen-Ten-

King all spades. I'm holding a Royal Flush, the best hand in poker. I have a wonderfully elated feeling that I'm going to rake all their money with this hand and then I catch a glimpse of Omar's right hand out of the corner of my eye. He's had his hand in his pocket for most of the night, playing with what I thought was a cell phone but now I'm not so sure. It's elongated, so either it's his dick or a knife.

I'm first to act and I check my Royal flush to Kristoph. He pushes. "All in," he announces. Five thousand more to Lord Lucan.

Lucan looks at his cards. He thinks he's sitting on a monster. I'm guessing pocket Kings giving him three Kings on the flop.

"Well, you have to gamble sometime," he says feigning weakness. "Fifteen thousand on top," he states with a smile thinking this is all good sport.

Molitor looks terribly nervous.

It's back to me. It will cost me all my chips but there's no hand that can beat me. I have to sell it a little bit. I never look at my cards once the chip's on top, but just this once I have a look and then recap them.

By now, I'm certain that Omar's got a knife. I'm thinking switchblade or stiletto, which means the Magnussons probably have guns, which means I'm sitting in the middle of something baleful with the best hand in poker.

My iPhone buzzes. I can't answer. I can feel a little sweat starting to form under my arms. My jeans suddenly feel heavy and my Merrell boots are tied too tight.

"I call."

Lucan puts up his hand stopping the dealer from asking us to show. He leans across the table and looks right at me.

"What's say we play for the rest of my stack here? Side bet."

Omar stirs in his chair. Kristoph looks straight down at the table. Molitor annoyingly cracks his knuckles.

"What's the bet?" I ask.

Lucan's smile fades into a coldly ferocious expression, "My chips and your life for the chest that Leonard Leanos brought into your shop."

So, here's how it will play out: Omar is going to reach into his pocket and try to stab me in the chest with that knife. He's not going to want to kill me yet, because I haven't told them where the chest is. The Magnussons and the rest will most likely pull guns and knives and then I'm surrounded. Molitor sold me down the river. I'm staring at him, seething. My iPhone buzzes again in my pocket.

The only way out of this is to turn over the table. I'll have to deal with Omar's attempted stabbing and then flip the table and make for the door. The dealer has already started backing away from the table. She's not stupid. She knows what's coming too. I'm just mad that no one is going to see my Royal Flush and I'm out another twenty-five hundred.

"How about it, Mr. Rodriguez? You want to bet?" He stares malignantly, eager to do violence.

Molitor won't even meet my gaze.

"How much is he paying you to sell me out, Joel?"

"Jesus Rik, just tell us where the goddam chest is! These are serious people. Leonard Leanos found out the hard way!" Molitor yells. He's broken character. He hasn't sold the bluff completely, whereas Lucan remains calm and collected. Leanos is dead. That takes a moment to sink in.

I glance to my left for half a second to see Omar, wound like a spring ready to pounce with the knife in his pocket. He's just waiting for Lucan to give him the green light. He's a fighting dog straining against a metal chain.

"Come now, Mr. Rodriguez," Lucan says patronizingly, "We've been playing for three hours and your tells are worse than your raises." He leans forward across the table. "The chest you have in your possession is one more clue in the greatest treasure hunt in human history. Do you know that?"

"I've been using it as a doorstop," I quip.

"Your friend Joel here has told us all about you, Rik. Ex-Navy SEAL, PhD from Boston University. Studied under world-renowned medievalist and reclusive genius Victor Meek. Nobody wants to see all that promise gone in a flash. Why don't you be reasonable?"

"What's in this chest?" I ask buying some time. "And how do you know Victor Meek?"

"Well, Professor Meek and I are old friends you see. But, I seem to have misplaced his address," Lucan chuckles. "So perhaps you might be so kind as to hand it over when you give us the chest?"

"I don't know where Victor is," I say instinctually and without hesitation.

"And the chest?" Lucan presses.

"What if I sold it already?" I ask with ease.

"This is no time to bluff, Mr. Rodriguez," Lucan says with a snarl. Molitor already has one hand inside his coat, ready to pull a gun. There's only one thing left to do now, show my hand. I flip the Jack of Spades over with the Ace of Spades showing the table my Royal Flush.

"No bluff," I say. "I win."

Omar blindly thrusts forward with a stiletto. I have to break his wrist with my left hand, while my right hand flips over the table. I see the dealer already out the door. Cards and chips are flying everywhere and I hear the familiar pop of silenced rounds. Omar and I crash to the floor along with table and I kick him in the side, breaking his ribs. Half a crawl, half a roll later my hand grasps the door handle and I'm through as bullets hit the wall outside. I slam the door home and see the dealer rushing on to the elevator, she's screaming as the suite door opens and Kristoph and Molitor take aim behind me. I sprint down the hall toward the elevator. I dive head first as the doors close. The world goes black. Then, I'm going down

[5]

Wildwood

My eyes are shut and the ground is moving. I feel like I just got hit with a giant wave while wading into shore. Thoughts are coming in and out of focus: a royal flush, Rachel's email, a Viking helmet, guns and a room full of people wanting to kill me. Molitor: snake in the grass. Did that just happen? By now, Lucan and his friends are on the move. No sense staying around a hotel when you've been shooting holes in the walls.

I open my eyes slowly and see the terrified face of the dealer. She lets out a scream and now I'm back. I hit my head on the wall of the elevator when I jumped and I can see Molitor's errant slugs lodged in two gaping crevices. They destroyed the sign for the five-dollar food court buffet.

"Relax," I say, "it's over. What's your name again?" I stand up in the moving elevator. We're flying past floors heading toward the lobby.

"Jane," she says panting.

"Ok Jane, listen to me, when this elevator stops I'm going to have to run fast. You get off the elevator and go right to security and tell them to send the police. Tell them everything you saw. Don't leave out any details." I put my hand on her shoulder. "Don't go anywhere tonight without someone you trust. You were just doing your job."

She nods frantically as the elevator slows and the doors open. I take her hand. "You're going to be fine. Just do exactly what I said." And now I'm running at a dead sprint through the lobby towards the parking garage.

Three minutes later, my Wrangler is peeling out of the parking space and heading towards the exit signs. I feel bad for Jane. I inadvertently chose this particular insanity when I took that pawn, but she was just working. Calm in a crisis is key. Hopefully, she'll follow my instructions to the letter.

I'm an idiot for going up there. What kind of scummy deal must Molitor be running to set me up like that. I'm pissed and scared. Two bad emotions when you're trying to escape. I'm not following my own "calm in a crisis" advice. The lights of Atlantic City are dull in the eerie black sky. It's very early. There is a dense haze hanging over the city. Rain will surely follow.

I pull the iPhone out of my pocket, ignoring the missed call and voice dial the shop. Chris answers.

"Chris, I want you to lock up right now and get out of there."

"What's wrong?"

"Don't ask. Just close the doors now and go home. Don't hesitate, don't stop for anything, hang up the phone and go."

I end the call, flying around the curves of Harrah's Boulevard. Voicemail is next. It takes a moment, but after a quick burst of static Rachel's voice echoes around the cab of the Jeep. It's soft and endearing, but rests on a stone foundation:

"Rik, why didn't you call? Listen, I'm in to something serious. I need you to get down to Wildwood tonight. I found something you're going to be interested in and well, I'm in…I'm in trouble too."

There's a pause in her voice. She doesn't know how to finish.

"I didn't know how much until a couple of hours ago when I found out that someone I know had been murdered. Listen, call me or just meet me at the lab. I'm not leaving here tonight."

She hangs up. The desperation in her voice is heartbreaking.

Chris has closed up. The shop is dark. I'm moving at a breakneck pace. It's fifty minutes south to Wildwood. It's nearly two thirty in the morning. I'm jumping the back steps wildly, taking three at a time to get back into my apartment. I figure I've got about ten minutes on them, but only ten. Molitor is CIA. God knows what he's got at his disposal. Another watch check as I rattle the lock and burst through the door: five minutes to get in, get out and then get back in the Jeep – Go.

I unzip a green backpack, descend into my office and retrieve the helmet from the downstairs safe. Gingerly placing it inside, I lunge back up the stairs and begin to stuff some clothes on top of the helmet. I twist open the mini-safe in the bottom of my bedroom closet and quickly pull out my Sig-Sauer P229 and stuff it in the small of my back, remembering to take three extra clips and jam them into the backpack. I also tap into my cash reserve. I've got about five thousand in small bills and I take most of it. I check my watch: three minutes in, time to move. Clif bar to ease my growling stomach, then I'm out the door. I lock it tightly then proceed to jump down the back steps three at a time.

The Clif bar is a welcome relief as I inhale it in two bites. Adrenaline quenches hunger pangs, but once it wears off, the empty stomach roars back with a vengeance. Unfortunately, I happen to glance down at the gas gauge on my Wrangler as I speed toward the Expressway. Never enough fuel when you're trying to make a hasty escape.

The gas stop on the Expressway gives me a chance to call Rachel and tell her I'm on my way. The connection rings and rings and I hear her voicemail – *"Hi it's Rachel. I'm away from my cell phone. Please leave a message after the tone and I'll get back to you."*

"Rachel, it's me. I'm on my way down." Cars are whizzing by on the Expressway. Anyone could be coming to end my life or even worse, Rachel's life. The metallic lumbering of a tractor-trailer, slamming and gyrating towards destinations unknown, fills the hazy night air with something foreboding. "I'm in this thing now too," I pause, trying to reassure, "I'll be there soon." I end the call. The gas nozzle clicks full. I'm still alive.

Garden State Parkway at three o'clock in the morning: a man drives alone contemplating a lost love and the mistakes he's made. The neon lights of Atlantic City sparkle over the tidal swamps and salt marshes on either side of his tiny Jeep. Lights streak by overhead. He glances around this once familiar landscape, now alien. His weary eyes can only see foreign ground in front of him and dangerous ground behind him.

This monologue runs over and over in my subconscious, varying each time. I keep trying to hum a few Springsteen lyrics, anything to quiet the sounds on the highway. I don't want to actually listen to any music. I'm too engrossed in what I'll say to Rachel when I finally see her. It's been a few months since we met up at one of our friend's lectures, and then two years since she walked out on me. Still stings. But, I think it was Pat Tillman who wrote: *it's much better to be sad than calloused.*

I'm not wild about the fact that bullets are now bringing us together, and this cryptic nonsense about her being in trouble is upsetting. How could she be involved? She's an underwater archaeologist. When they're not underwater, they're in libraries and laboratories. Her facility in Wildwood is state of the art. They've explored wrecks all over the world and she is preeminent in her field. She was also the only person I ever met who was a far better swimmer than me. I can swim. I can swim very well as a matter of fact, especially with seventy pounds of gear on my back, but Rachel was born in the water. She's lithe and graceful and dances through the ebbs and flows of the ocean like she has always been there and will always remain.

I'm doing ninety and I have to make myself ease off the gas pedal. I'm thinking about Lucan and that cast of characters and I cannot fathom how all of these moving pieces are connected. Why Molitor? What's he into with these guys? Money? Drugs? Why would Lucan, an obviously wealthy British lord want a possibly fake Viking helmet? And why would he be willing to kill over it? And what's this treasure? And how does Rachel know a shady character like Leanos? I can only assume that's the murdered person to whom she was referring, unless we both know people who were murdered in the last twenty-four hours, in which case I'm getting the hell out of Jersey.

The lights start to fade the closer I get to Wildwood. No light pollution. I feel lost as I drive, lost on a familiar road heading towards a familiar destination. I can't help but fear that a stranger is going to be waiting for me when I get there. It won't be the friend and confidant I grew to love over the years. It will be some distorted, scared version of her former self. And she in turn will look at me, full of adrenaline, ready to act – any bravado, a clever mask for the fear hidden below the surface.

Wildwood Underwater Research Laboratory sits atop a bluff overlooking Beachcomber Drive, North. The road is the only separation between the lab and the Coast Guard Beach, a wide sprawling shore used by students from all over the state for research and privately operated by the US Coast Guard. It's pristine, because it's untouched. No Staten Island tourists to come and destroy it. No coolers full of bottles and cans to be strewn about in its wading pools, only habitats for horseshoe crabs.

The wide glass doors of the building's foyer offer a breathtaking view at sunrise, which will be upon this fair seashore in a few hours. The lab buildings attached to the visitors lobby look dark but I can see Rachel's blue Prius parked near the walkway in the front. She always hated that I drove a Jeep. She's right that they get terrible gas mileage, but there's just something about the feel of a Wrangler in the summertime. I recycle everything. I have fluorescent bulbs. I've started timing my showers. My carbon footprint is dwindling by the day. But, I do love my Jeep. I kill the Wrangler's engine and take the Sig out from the small of my back, it's loaded, but I make sure the safety's on. I really have no idea what I'm walking into. The gun is now in the front of my waistband for easy access. Backpack over my shoulder, I shut the Jeep door and start forward.

The intoxicating, May salt air is drifting in with the early morning breakers. The haze is gone down here; only crisp clean air at the tip of New Jersey. The sound of the ocean is so serene it almost makes me forget that someone tried to kill me tonight. I could fall asleep right there in the parking lot. Coursing adrenaline is keeping me going but yet the tranquility of morning is hypnotic on the dim horizon. Splendor and hazard have agitated together in agonizing juxtaposition many times in my life.

The burning fires of Iraqi oilfields choking the atmosphere with their poison were magnificent in early morning sunrises. Exquisite images of destruction are cruel castigations of human existence. I can't admire the splendor in something horrible and yet every ounce of my cognizance wants me to. I suppose it's the burden of seeing many appalling still-lives and yet somehow not feeling guilty. I've lived and seen and experienced and now with wolves at my heels I can only see the majesty of the coast and sense the expectation of an anticipated meeting.

My steps forward meet the pavement with determined zeal, but the path to the front entrance is made of seashells set in concrete and is awkward under foot. Approaching the glass door, I wonder if Lucan's men used the extra ten minutes I took in my apartment to get here.

But, how could they? Why would they? I'm cautious as I try the door. Surprisingly, it's not locked.

The lobby's dark, but the moonlight off the ocean sends a pale aura through the great glass windows. I can see the crest of the W.U.R.L and the Princeton seal on the wall. I swallow hard and start to formulate the word, "Rach-el..." But, I'm on the floor before I can finish. My jaw is throbbing and I can see a Campbell's soup can rolling next to my face. Then I shut my eyes. The smells of coconut sunblock and seawater are wafting around me like a phantasm appearing from that pale moonlight. And then I hear the muffled words...

"Oh shit, it's you."

I would like to live in a world where not so many people have had to use the phrase, "Oh shit, it's you" in reference to my arrival in a room. I'm not saying it's happened often, but often enough so I can count the times I've heard it.

The room slowly comes back into focus. The ghostly-shape begins to take form. She's mouthing words. Her hair is shaking wildly. It's still thick, like matted sea rope and it hangs down toward me. Suddenly, the floor is rocking. An earthquake? Up and down. Undulating like a bobber on a fishing line. The room is spinning again. Muffled sounds: "Get up!" "Come on Rik, wake up!"

She's screaming at me, which is nothing new. All I can hear is a deep echo, and then like a light switch in a dark room, my brain flicks on. The room stops spinning. Her blurred face now comes into focus. It's oblong in shape with a high forehead and a slight, dainty chin. Her full lips are still screaming at me. Her hair is being tossed around wildly in her frustration. Her eyebrows are arched and I can feel her hands grasping my shirt.

"Stop yelling!" I finally interrupt. She releases her grasp and I fall back on to the linoleum, hitting the back of my head in the process. My wince causes her to put her hand on her mouth in quiet sympathy, a passive expression that always annoyed me.

"Are you ok?" she asks, her voice like a high note on a panpipe, lilting with strength.

"Do I look ok to you?" I say holding the back of my head.

"Well, I didn't know who you were," she says as she flicks on the lobby light. "You could've been anyone."

My head is throbbing as I sit up. She comes into full view now. The sound of a faint trickle of water forces me to turn toward the great glass windows looking out on the sea. It has begun to drizzle outside. Turning my head back, I'm confronted with the figure before me, Rachel, the mysterious, problematic lover of my past. She's wearing a pair of tan clam-digger pants, with fresh salt stains and a white tee shirt with the Princeton crest. I can faintly distinguish the blue bikini top underneath. She pulls flaxen hair back into a ponytail and watches me try to get my bearings.

"Good to see you, Rachel," I finally say, opening and shutting my eyes trying to dull the pain. The Campbell's soup can rolls near my leg. I pick it up with a smirk. It's "Select Harvest", half the calories of normal soup.

"Use Chunky soup next time. It'll hurt more."

"It was the first thing I could find. I thought you were one of them."

Now I'm standing in front of her. She's as beautiful as I recall, down to the tiny scar on her chin from where she fell on a dig in Greece. I begin to recall all the reasons why I loved this woman. They spin in front of me like the wheels on a slot machine.

"What's going on Rachel? What did you get yourself into?"

47

Her expression changes to a look of concern, my question: loaded like the gun in my waistband. Faint hint of blame, but she knows. She knows that she could ask me the same question and be perfectly within her rights. The backpack on the floor next to me. The helmet in question. Again I'm withholding.

She's about to open the floodgates and reveal all the secrets hidden a brain that's been actively, never passively thinking for thirty-four years. There was a time when she would reveal everything to me. I always had problems reciprocating. Before she would unveil, her face would formulate this very expression. It is the expression of genuine desire to share her unbridled excitement with another but yet she knows that practicality dictates a certain care in delivering vital information. This was one of a thousand reasons why I loved her, because in that moment we were the only two people on earth. Her news is the only news that matters. Whatever she is about to tell me exists only in the short space between us. The world outside the glass doors, the world of guns and criminals and my withholding subconscious is quiet as she says:

"Rik, I found *La Dauphine*."

The waves on Coast Guard Beach lull the surroundings with their constant sound and I can hear my mind shouting, screaming, wanting to pick her up and spin her around in the intense jubilation of discovery. Instead all I can say is,

"Where?"

[6]

Rachel's Story

Shattered glass. The world is coming apart at the seams. Pops, and ricochets echo through the now open lobby as we dive behind the visitor's desk. No time to discuss the gravity and significance of the revelation, only gunfire destroying our moment.

My Sig bursts bullets back in the general direction of the errant assailants that don't even seem to be aiming their weapons. Their shots explode over our heads and I can hear Rachel screaming as she clings closer. When the glass doors exploded, I had to almost tackle her behind the desk and she's been wrapped around my midsection for the last few moments. Then, as suddenly as it started, the shooting stops and I hear the Danish accented voice of Kristoph:

"Give us the helmet and you live!"

Rachel is panting now. She looks up at me and whispers, "Don't give it to them."

"How about this," I yell back. "You put your guns down now and I *won't* kill *all* of you!"

"RIK! RIK!"

A slap in the face. The lobby is quiet again. Rachel is holding my head, staring into my eyes.

"Who the hell is Kristoph?" she asks puzzled.

"What?" I ask, still dazed and confused about what happened to the bad guys.

"I think you've got a concussion. One minute you're talking to me and the next you're staring off into space muttering about guns and a Royal Flush."

49

"I had a Royal Flush."

Her cool hands are a salve to my agonized head. The pain shot through swiftly. She must have thrown that can hard.

"Come on," she says leading me down the long hallway past laboratories and offices. Before I know it, I'm sitting on the couch in her office with an ice pack on my chin. Her walls are adorned with pictures from her many different explorations. There are a few I recognize, one in particular. The blue Pacific is sparkling in the late afternoon and there we are holding the rusted, oxidized remains of a pirate cutlass brought up from the depths near Puerto Vallarta. It's the only picture where I appear, but it's hanging right next to her diplomas in what I'd like to think is a place of prominence.

Rachel is sitting behind her desk sipping what is now a cold cup of coffee. She's clicking through photos on her desktop and I'm overcome by a memory. It's just the way the light from the desk lamp hits her face. My stomach tightens up, flushed with jubilant sensation. She's in my arms softly swaying to "Drive All Night". The antique record player spins *The River* with quiet reverence and our apartment in Brookline is filled with the gratification of a finished thesis and a profession of love. The halogen desk lamp under which she now sits is replicating the dim light against her face that night.

Moonlight through a bedroom window. Contented, satiated bodies wrapped in cotton sheets and she breathes sweetly, quietly and regularly, infantile, un-phased by the troubles and tribulations right outside the glass windowpane. Lying awake next to her, thinking, my mind racing like a thoroughbred.

"Hey, you still with me?"

Sitting in front of me now. She softly removes the ice pack from my chin.

"You want to see it?"

She leads me by the hand over to the computer monitor. I see the photo plastered on the full screen. It's the ghostly outline of a ship's hull, crusted and entangled within the ocean floor. The faint outline of the once formidable carrack is clearly visible amongst the debris. Nothing more than boards and planks, a disentangled mess now, the stern portico: remarkably still somewhat intact.

"Where is it?"

"About ninety miles southwest of Cape May, give or take. Out in the trench. Six hundred or so miles from Bermuda."

"That close?" I'm amazed. "How do you know it's *La Dauphine*?"

Fifteen steps from her computer finds us in the main research laboratory. Before me is a brass cannon sitting in an electrolysis tank. It's covered in barnacles and sea scraps. Rachel flicks on a light on the bottom of the tank and leads me over to the glass. The stock of the cannon is etched with a familiar crest and inscription of Francis I, and the faintest etching still visible on the stock: *La Dauphine*.

Rachel smiles softly as she sees the excitement building on my face.

"Oh my God, Rachel."

She stands back very dramatically and recounts the story. "1524: Giovanni da Verrazzano explores most of the eastern seaboard under the French flag including,"

"Narragansett Bay and New York harbor," I add with flourish. Our intellectual fencing matches were legendary.

"Verrazzano sailed on the flagship *La Dauphine*, which disappeared," she chuckles pointing to me.

"Sometime after Verrazzano was killed and eaten on the island of Guadaloupe in 1528. It's morbid to laugh at a guy getting eaten, Rach."

"Can't help it, Rik. I found a ghost ship that was involved in one of the most extraordinary voyages in history. I'm a little giddy here."

51

"Yeah, it's pretty amazing, but what the hell's going on? How are you in trouble?"

Rachel gives me a glance, slyly and cool, wondering if I know exactly why she's in trouble, but won't give it up.

"I found an artifact on the ship. It was stolen from me," she says quietly then continues, "A chest with something inside of it that I couldn't explain."

I show my hand: "*You* pulled up the chest? The chest was from *La Dauphine*?"

"Yes. You know it? You've seen it?"

"A guy named Leonard Leanos came in and pawned it in my shop."

"Oh, now I get. It makes perfect sense," she says with a sigh.

It's been a whirlwind of an evening and my original query about Rachel's involvement still hasn't been answered. The hour is starting to affect me and I can feel myself yawning. She walks around the tank, beginning to formulate her explanation. I cannot fathom how this all connects, but sure enough Rachel begins to glue it together, like pieces of a broken vase:

"Rik, have you ever heard of Matthias Lucan, Lord Lucan?

"We're acquainted."

"How?"

I scratch my unshaven chin, and calmly add: "He tried to kill me tonight."

"What?"

"I happened upon a high stakes game at Harrah's," she'll pick up my dripping sarcasm. Oh, I just "happened upon" a den of thieves and murderers?

"Oh Rik, you're not still playing poker?" She flashes a disappointed look in my direction as if my playing poker has something to do with our current predicament.

"Still with this? You're not allowed to criticize the person you walked out on."

"Where's that written?" she mocks.

"It should be, somewhere." It's just like her to try and drag me into an argument. I guess I kind of broached the subject, but that's not the point. My jaw is throbbing and I'm getting impatient.

"It doesn't matter," I retort, "just tell me what the hell's going on. I just got sold down the river by and obviously corrupt CIA agent, shot at and no one saw my goddam Royal Flush! I need some more information please,"

Rachel sighs, secretly enjoying that she managed to get me flustered. She continues: "Lucan built this place, Rik. He was the principle investor through Princeton. He's a big time alum and he was really interested in the work we wanted to do."

"So, why did he and his goons try to kill me over Leanos's treasure chest?"

"Stay with me now," she says mockingly, "You *know* Lucan. You're just thinking out of context. You've heard of the Redstone Security Group?"

"The government contractors? The mercenaries. That's the Lucan that tried to kill me?"

She nods and I'm even madder than before. Lucan's mercenaries were cowboys and made Special Forces' job that much harder in Iraq and Afghanistan. He recruited anyone and everyone, didn't matter who you fought with before. A couple of those assholes are evil, pure and simple. Redstone, Blackwater, they were all one in the same: guns for hire. No rules, no consequences, just a mess.

"Lucan's under investigation in England for their work in Venezuela. They're going to bring charges this week or something right?" Yesterday's *New York Times* had a whole expose on the company. It irritates me that I didn't make the connection before I sat down tonight. What was I thinking?

"Yeah, they were contracted out to protect a government enclave that turned out to be a cocaine factory," she says, "and nobody knows what happened to the money or the drugs."

"Their US headquarters is out in the Pine Barrens," I say remembering the tour I once had at the facility. I'm not going to mention to her that these particular assholes once offered me a job shortly after I left the SEALs.

"Well, either way, last year, Lucan got really interested in our *Dauphine* project and the stuff we doing up on Lake Champlain. And then he got even more interested when we brought up the chest. Leonard Leanos was his intermediary. He handled all Lucan's day-to-day affairs. He was the one who came with a few large gentlemen and took the chest from me three days ago. I take it you saw the helmet inside?"

"You know me too well."

"A treasure chest, come on. You couldn't help yourself. Anyway, I can only assume that Leanos decided to run when he thought the indictments would start coming, which is why he took the chest from Lucan and ended up in your shop. "

I hate coincidence and this story seems all too fortuitous. "Why would a guy like Leanos think he could run from these guys and get away with it?"

"I have no idea, Rik. He didn't get away with it, that's all I know." She's looking at me now. The fear on her face is palpable. "Rik, I don't know what to do. I mean, I never thought this would get so out of control. But, I guess that's naïve considering all that money's on the line."

"What money, Rachel?"

"Gold, silver, artifacts of unbelievable value. Basically, one of the most important finds in history if the accounts are true."

"Ok, I'm listening."

She gets animated, swinging back and forth, ticking through an imaginary checklist in her head: "Between the site off Lake Champlain and now *La Dauphine* we may have stumbled upon the historic origins of Viking Vinland. And if what I'm finding out about Verrazzano is true, a history of the Knights Templar expeditions and possibly colonization."

Deflation. "So you've got nothing?"

"I've got Verrazzano's lost flagship and a chest with a elaborate carved Viking helmet on which is inscribed a phantom rune that no one yet has been able to translate. By the way, where is my helmet?"

I unzip my pack and produce the helmet in question. She turns it over and over in her hands, inspecting it with the zeal of diamond dealer.

"You thought it was a repro, right?" She smiles big. "Good restoration work by yours truly."

I nod sheepishly and realize that the mystique of this conversation is being rapidly replaced by rationality. The severity of the situation snaps home in my skull like a rubber band. "I'm just thinking, it's probably not a great idea to be hanging out here discussing theories and conjecture when guys with guns know where you work."

"This is almost ironclad!" she screeches. "I found *La Dauphine* with a Viking helmet aboard!"

"Ok, can we talk about this somewhere else?"

"How about the dive site?"

"You want to go back to your dive site, when Lucan has *killed* people. Does he know where the site is?"

"No. There's another piece we have to pull up that we haven't found yet. And now that I know Lucan is out for blood, we've got to get going."

"You need to start thinking clearly. We've got to get to a *safe* place."

She smirks slightly. "I've already got a boat waiting in Cape May, Rik. The salvage boat from the lab is out of commission. I was going with or without you. Now, you want to help me or not?"

"I suppose your plan is to find whatever this leads to before Lucan can, right? I mean why go to the cops or anything?"

"Good, you're in. Come on." She turns and walks toward the door with the same quasi-impish grin that I've always loved. She's got me hooked. If she ever knew the power that she still possessed over my decision-making abilities I would be in quite a bit of trouble. However, it seems that she does know. If I follow her through that door I'm going to get in quite a bit more trouble. These are the decisions we look back on with disgust or great admiration. Choices. Lives trapped by moments that make them great.

"This isn't going to be like Mexico, is it? I don't want to get dysentery again!"

I cross the threshold. She's taken the helmet from my charge. She's already back in her office, packing up her dive bag.

[7]

Shipping Over

"You haven't traded this thing in yet?" she asks climbing into my Jeep. "Nope," I respond. "Still got a few good years left, just like me."

We drive out of the parking lot. She's holding the helmet as we meander down Beachcomber Drive. We pass the long stretch of Coast Guard Beach and my curiosity gets the best of me.

"All right, so tell me a story."

She's still staring at the helmet, and finally looks up with grin: "It's a good one."

"Tell me."

"1000 AD: expeditions from Greenland arrive in North America, set up permanent settlements and explore most of the eastern seaboard. They fight wars with the Native Americans, make peace, intermarry, it turns into a colony, and then one day, gone with most of the evidence of it ever existing. Mid-thirteen hundreds, crusaders, Cistercians, Templars, whoever make trips over here to try and reestablish the colony. Prince Henry Sinclair, remember all that? They called it New Jerusalem, but it failed again. Probably plague, but we don't know."

"How does Verrazzano fit in?"

"Verrazzano, Columbus, they're all connected to the Knights of Christ in Madeira. Knights of Christ were the offshoots of displaced Templars after the roundup in 1307."

"Kind of thin."

"It's thin, but it's there. These guys were all looking for Vinland, New Jerusalem, Arcadia, whatever you want to call it. It was a new colony, a refuge. We dug up the remnants of a Norse encampment on an island in Lake

Champlain a few months ago. And then when we found *La Dauphine* and the chest with the helmet aboard, everything kind of molded together, so much so that I don't even know where this is going yet, except that there's gold at the end, I know that."

Her crescendo. Now, it's my job to question.

"What about the X with the hook on it?"

"The *hooked X*," the appropriate stress falling on the words in Dashiell Hammett fashion. She puts the helmet back in the pack. "The hooked X is a runic inscription that has many ins and outs, interpretations and extrapolations and basically we have no idea what it means."

"Nice."

Her eyes light up with adventure. We share a moment.

"We found a couple of artifacts at the Lake Champlain site marked with the hooked X, but when we opened the chest and found the helmet you can imagine I did a few cartwheels."

"You got a theory?"

She sighs. "Well, Verrazzano met with a Wampanoag delegation and supposedly exchanged items. If the helmet was part of it? Well, I don't know. I mean there's a thousand and one possibilities."

The lights of Cape May harbor appear in the distance. The turn into the lot is easy, uneventful. Up ahead a car is flashing its high beams in the Harbor parking lot. This private Marina is not terribly big and I follow Rachel's directions toward the car. Behind the car is a seventy-foot luxury catamaran bobbing softly next to the dock.

"This is your boat?" I ask as we pull up.

"No," she replies and then I see him step out of his car. He's tall and peculiar in shape. His head is too big for his body and his wide grin and mussed hair make him look slightly unstable. He's a gawky, arrogant, technocrat, software magnate, and a titan of industry.

"Oy, Rachel. Is that Rik you've brought with you?"

The Irish brogue slams it home as I see him walk over towards my Jeep. It's Nile Donovan, inventor of Stinger 2000, data collator and Rachel's current flame. I look over at Rachel who's smiling like she just robbed a bank and got away with it. Then she opens the door and steps out into the waiting embrace of a sanctimonious, pompous, pain in the ass.

I now wish Rachel had killed me with the soup can.

The catamaran is slowly lumbering out of the harbor as the incandescent light on my digital watch reads four-forty AM. The sun is pondering its rise in the eastern sky and Nile Donovan has set us a course for Rachel's wreck on the open ocean. Soft salt spray wafts around the deck. I only wish that I didn't hate this whole situation so much. I probably would be enjoying this brief moment, this quiet before the dawn.

"Aye there, Rik, so these bastards had a shot at you?" His voice is jovial and irritatingly likable. He steers with ease like a nautical prodigy. Rachel sits curled up beside him. The guilty smirk has never left her face.

"That's right," I reply, avoiding eye contact.

"This is worse than you told me, Rachel. Heading out to the trench doesn't seem like such a good idea anymore."

She sits up assertively next to the helm.

"No, it is a good idea because we've got to bring up the astrolabe if we're ever going to find anything. That is, if it's there. "

"Astrolabe?" I ask, turning toward them.

"That's right," Nile says with a smile. "The St. Clair Astrolabe was supposedly on board the *Dauphine* when it sank and you need the St. Clair Astrolabe to find the treasure in New Jerusalem. Of course, we don't know it's down there for sure. Could be collecting dust in museum."

Grimace. A skeptic's smirk and Rachel sees my disbelief. *We're here to do what?*

"You get all that from Wikipedia or something, Nile? Somebody send you an app with secret treasure maps?"

"Rik, stop it. He's serious," Rachel says indignantly.

"Serious about what?"

"The gold, mate. *The* Treasure. The Vikings buried all their plunder there and then the Templars came along and buried what was left of their gold in Vinland and called it New Jerusalem. That's what Verrazano was looking for." Nile's confidence is grating.

"The Sinclair family in Scotland has been trying for years to prove *actual* history not stories about treasure. There's more evidence against Henry Sinclair leading an expedition to North America than there is for it. And this Viking stuff, well…"

"Well, what?" Rachel snorts. "You've read the Sagas just like we have. You held the helmet. You know it's real. I know there's more out there, Rik. You've got to believe me. If this astrolabe is another piece in the puzzle then we've got to get it."

Desperation. She looks at me with quiet distraction. Already in the water. Already searching the murky wreck for the key to a lost lock. I can't fight her eyes.

"Have you got anything more? Anything from the site on Champlain?"

She looks longingly at Nile who produces a smartphone, a Droid, and clicks a few clicks, scrolling through data. He then leans over handing me the phone.

"Read that, boyo."

A pdf file. *Translated from the Latin.* - *Archivum Secretum Apostolicum Vaticanum*: The Vatican Secret Archives. By Papal permission. Most scholar's dream about examining the Archives.

"Which one of you broke into the Vatican?"

Nile smiles superciliously. "I pays to know people."

"You drop wireless in Vatican City or something?"

"No," Rachel pipes in. "But I played soccer with the Archive curator's niece in college."

"That's a big favor to call in."

"Not after you helped her cheat on a final essay."

"You're quite the academic badass."

"Just read it."

Back to Nile's phone. I move the document aside for a transitory moment and see the wallpaper. Two lovers wrapped in a warm embrace; the Manhattan skyline glowing in the background. Rachel in a black cocktail dress, cut just so, pearls dangling down her neckline. Nile in custom made tuxedo. Blissful. I miss this.

I return to the document, the Latin text, followed by the English translation, there buried amongst the dying recollections of a knight, calling himself Stephen St. Clair, descendant of the famous family and the earls of Orkney is the following sentence: *Prince Henry traveled west to the realm of the Vinlanders to settle New Jerusalem at Thorvald's Cross.*

"What's Thorvald's Cross?" I ask recognizing the name, albeit out of context.

"Keep reading," Rachel says intently.

"I only know Thorvald Eiriksson, Leif's brother." Professor Meek's seminars. *The Sagas of the Greelanders.* His exultant bearded face at the mention of Vinland.

"We think they're one in the same," Nile intones.

My eyes return to the tiny print on the cell phone as it brings to life a story, a failed expedition to stay and settle:

Months we stayed in the land of the vines. Natives in hide-skinned boats keeping distances and watchful eyes. Then Prince Henry made peace with the Narragansett.

Prince Henry sent expeditions north and west from Thorvald's Cross. I led the northward journey, using a brass astrolabe, plotting points on land as if it were sea. Our goal being to find the land of the Long Lake and the remnants of a Vinlander fortress and encampment where the great war chieftain Ragnar once ruled. We found the site in ruins, burned and pillaged. The westward party, we learned was never heard from again. Prince Henry abandoned hope and we made preparations for a return. We prayed at Thorvald's Cross and left our wares in his care. Prince Henry stayed. We will never know what became of him.

The text is smudged. Ink on vellum worn after so many years. Stephen St. Clair's testimony ends. Thousands of more questions.

"Ok, to start with, are we looking for St. Clair's astrolabe? And what are these 'wares' they left at Thorvald's Cross? And where the hell is Thorvald's Cross or Cross Point or Krossanes or whatever you want to call it?" Meek taught me well. I'm pulling names from *The Sagas of the Greenlanders* out of thin air, while also trying my best not to play devil's advocate, but it's been a horrendous night.

"I don't have those answers for you, Rik," she says delicately. Looking away now. I can't face her. She knows what I know and she moves over to sit next to me. Her leg brushes against mine and for a moment I remember what it was like when *we* were all that mattered. Now brushing a strand of hair out of her eye. Now looking through me with great sincerity.

"I don't know where this is going to go. Why did we get into this? To find something so extraordinary that it would rewrite history."

"I got into it for the girls," I mock.

"You need to listen to me now and focus," she says, unfazed by my stupidity. "You are the best wreck diver I know. You've done every deepwater salvage dive that I've ever done and then you've gone deeper. I need you down there if we have any hope of bringing this thing to the surface."

"This astrolabe is going to tell you how to get to Thorvald's Cross?" I ask pointedly.

"No," Nile chimes in turning the wheel of the catamaran. "The astrolabe is the last piece of the puzzle. You need three other bloody runic inscriptions to find Thorvald's tomb."

"Thorvald's tomb?" I ask.

Rachel picks it up, "Yes. You remember in the Saga when Thorvald was killed in Vinland, they buried him at Cross Point and erected a monument in his honor? The inscriptions regarding his tomb, its location and how to find it were on two runic carvings and a suit of armor. At least we think so."

I nod. A mystery straight out of fiction and I'm in the goddamn middle. So much for quiet. Losing business. Losing time. More bullshit that I don't want to deal with, but I'm here now and there's something on the bottom of the ocean that needs finding.

"I've got to make a call," I say and she knows and we're going to dive.

Moments later, I dial the one person I can implicitly trust. He answers with a grunt and a snort.

"Where you been, dummy? Rhodes got me worried sick?"

"Ski, write down these coordinates and fire up the boat. We've got a dive today."

[8]

La Dauphine

Agonizing sleep only wears on an already worn soul. I'm dreaming again and I'm lost alone in the sea, swirling through a vortex, the maelstrom surrounding me, cloaking me in terror and then it stops. I open my eyes underwater but the salt doesn't sting and then the serenity of the quiet ocean is destroyed by the sucking power of some imaginary cyclone, dragging me down further until I reach the ocean floor.

  The sand kicks up around my feet. It is a lunar surface, barren and mysterious. Then the amazing jet wash of a manta ray flying past sends me spinning once again. Now, I'm directly in front of the hooded phantom's trajectory. He flies toward me great with flaps of his wings and just before impact I fall and land with a thud, pain streaking through my bruised body.

The floor of the stateroom feels foreign but I can feel the familiar rocking and lurching of the boat swaying through the Atlantic chop. It's seven AM according to my watch and I slowly begin to raise myself off the floor after falling off the bed. The bruise on my hip from the elevator dive still stings and my head is still swimming from the traumatic evening.

  I can see a faint glimmer of light piercing through the windows of the stateroom as if a laser sight was pointed in my direction. My shuffling steps along the carpet toward the window give me a chance to completely regain my bearings. The boat is still swaying, but my footing is sure from many years at sea. Curtains are drawn and morning greets me like a left cross from a heavyweight. We're in the middle of the ocean now, nothing but Atlantic surf and salt spray for miles around. The blinding light reflecting off the water sets me wincing and I quickly close the shades again.

My backpack is near the foot of the bed and I need to get out of the clothes I've been wearing for the past two days. A welcome trip to the stateroom's toilet for a quick change and some washing up and I feel like new. I pull on swim trunks and a SEALs hooded sweatshirt. I know the deck will be bright so I remember the pair of Oakleys I have stashed in the front pocket of the pack.

Morning illuminates the horizons in every direction and the brisk wind off the Atlantic has a hint of Gulf Stream humidity. We're about fifty miles off the coast of New Jersey heading towards the trench. Tuna fishing out here is exquisite, but diving is hazardous. The trench is a deceiving name for the natural depression on the continental shelf, which then drops into the abyss a few miles later as the continental slope takes over. The trench is eighty feet down and hazardous. The light begins to get spotty there and you need a deepwater "Pyle stop" in addition to the normal decompression stop at six meters. It's certainly not going to be a terribly hard technical dive considering the hours that Rachel and I have logged in the water, but the trench has some strange updrafts and tidal patterns. It's not a recreational dive by any means.

The polarized Oakleys do a good job of letting just enough of the bright sun into my retinas. I can see Donovan still at the helm. Rachel is standing on the starboard side railing drinking coffee.

"Morning there, Rik," Donovan calls over. Rachel turns to see me. She nods her head wearily and tries to muster a smile. The wind whips through her hair and I can't stop staring at her. She looks like Calypso, standing, staring off in careful survey of all her domain, the vast expanses of sea. Donovan's hand slaps me on the shoulder in a friendly gesture. He's set the autopilot.

"How about a coffee then?" he asks, energetically as if he was solar-powered.

"Thanks," I say quietly and he disappears below deck behind me.

Rachel gestures me over to the railing and I'm grateful for a brief moment alone with her without the lively interjections of the replacement man.

"Seriously, Rachel, what do you see in this guy, besides dollar signs?" I ask standing next to her, feeling the wind on my face.

She takes a long sip of coffee, eyes fixed on the horizon. I press for an answer. "We had some good times, though. Does he make you laugh like I could?"

She turns to me. I can see the passionate ferocity in her eyes. Her words are marked and meaningful. "He has a good soul, Rik."

Almost on cue Donovan walks back on deck with a hot cup of coffee for me. He thrusts it in my hands with excitement and stands next to us by the railing.

"Going to be a great day, don't ya think?"

Rachel's smile returns. "We're going to make some history, Rik."

They both share the same enthusiasm and it swirls around on deck with the morning wind. I'm trying to stay practical.

"You want to show me the gear?"

"Come on," she says almost exploding from the railing, nearly skipping with caffeinated excitement across the deck toward the stern.

Donovan hasn't let the catamaran go under sail even though it's the perfect day for it. It seems he has a bit of a practical streak in him as well. Sailing to a dive site would not be conducive to hitting the precise location. He keeps the vast boat under engine power as Rachel and I step down into the dive launch, which is a tiny alcove underneath the helm with two dive lockers and a gate to jump off the back. This isn't a salvage boat, but it will have to do until Ski arrives with his iron-hulled clunker, the *Gina Marie*.

"Ski's on his way with some salvage gear. I called him a couple of hours ago."

"Good. We're probably going to need more help, especially when you see the mess down there."

"It didn't look that bad on the picture."

"The stern is still somewhat intact, which is where I'm putting the astrolabe," she says.

"If it's there at all."

"I think it's on the wreck and I'm sticking to it."

"I just don't want you to be crushed if we don't find it," I say half-mocking.

"Fifty bucks says it's down there," she says tossing a dry-suit my way.

"Just fifty, Dr. Hexam? You take a pay cut from the Tigers or what?"

"Fine, one hundred and you have to make an effort to like Nile."

"No way. That's going too far," I say with a scoff.

"That's because you know it's down there," she says pulling out a dry-suit for herself. She pulls off her sweatshirt revealing a lime green and blue bikini top that perfectly accents her form and I can't help myself from saying: "You've been working out, Doctor? Looking fit."

"Shut up," she says with a sardonic smirk, secretly loving my noticing.

"What else do I get when it's not down there?" I ask.

"You get to hear me admit I was wrong."

"Sold," I say pulling my sweatshirt over my head.

She scoffs, "You've put on some weight, huh, Rik? Too many cheeseburgers." I can only shake my head in defeat, bested by a smarter and more capable opponent.

"We could wait for a grid. I mean this is a really important find, Rachel."

"You think I didn't drop a grid already? Wow, I guess I really haven't seen you in a while."

"This is pretty amazing, that's all. Astrolabe or not." She believes. I'm not there yet.

The two hours running through the equipment disappears in minutes and before I realize it I hear Nile yelling down to Rachel that we've reached the coordinates and the buoy marking the wreck site. Take to the ocean once again. Find things hidden amongst the wreck. Hidden history. Shadowlands. Make her happy.

We're diving with Trimix: a mixture of helium, oxygen, and nitrogen, ideal for deep-water dives. Our re-breathers have been checked and rechecked. Rachel is bulky in her suit. She's carrying extra tools because if I'm going for deeper incursion I can't have anything hanging on my side. Donovan gives her a kiss, longer and drawn out for my benefit and I can only turn away in disgust, preferring to jump off the back into the water before Rachel can turn her head.

Underwater. At ease. My mask and fins are snug and my dry-suit feels like second skin. It's quiet all around. I can barely hear the lapping of the water against the hull above. Rachel disturbs my calm as she jumps in.

Slow descent. Our air supply will give us just about an hour underwater before we would be really pushing the limit. It's going to take fifteen minutes to get down there slowly so we'll have twenty minutes on the wreck before we have to begin our slow ascent, with a three minute deep stop and then a decompression stop at six meters. These are not the best circumstances because they didn't have enough Trimix on board, but when Ski arrives with more tanks we'll be able to take a second dive. Hopefully though, I can find this astrolabe quick so we won't need a second dive.

The re-breather produces few bubbles. It's similar to the Draeger we used in the SEALs and works well for delicate wreck diving. A single air bubble could disturb a vital piece of a find. I'm carrying a dive line, uncoiling the spool as we go to make our ascent that much easier. We're intrepid explorers of a forgotten world, sent to retrieve a piece of history and we float through the abyss calmly and quietly. The visibility is not great, but we brought lights along with us to guide us through the haze of sediment.

Hearing tides now. Rushes of water on every side, the silence of the deep, alive with organic harmony and yet deafening. Only our breath in our own subconscious. We cause the disturbances in the ocean. Flutter kicks, twitches, rolling pitches, faint clanks of tubing and tank. The ocean hears us. We intrude on the calm, but like a gracious host, we are welcomed to the briny depth where secrets sleep.

Hours of anticipation are finally assuaged as the specter ship appears out of the haze. Sunlight strains through the surf to light our surroundings but the flashlights are doing most of the work. The gnarled hull is covered in barnacles and anemones. Rachel flashes me the thumbs up as she leads the way around the hulk of wreck towards the stern.

The carrack: once formidable, outfitted by Verrazano, is decaying, destroyed, as I glide past the starboard side. I can see her beauty. She is nearly one with the trench floor, a mere shade of her past glory, slowly returning to the natural condition from whence she came. Rachel's grid carefully dissects the wreck, like scaffolding around a collapsed building; each coordinate easily catalogued and marked.

The stern is before me. The ocean floor and the wood are together in a tangled menagerie, but there's a vague semblance of structure to the stern quarters, which is where I'm supposed to search. Quick glance to Rachel. She flashes a quick thumbs up, turning the flashlight on the wreck.

Anything could disturb this ruin. Flutter kicks. Too quick. Frog kicks. Can't be done. Nothing left but coast forward with the tide. Swift breath. Slow forward. Sediment, sparkling like moon dust. Flashlight, scanning, searching the wreck. Remnants of barrels. A buried rapier. The cabin where Verrazzano slept, now fallen in upon itself. Charts and maps gone for eternity. The hard work of resolute voyagers gone with time, laid waist by era. Forgotten, now remembered by the woman I still love. Here with LED light in a ghostly cavernous room of a once noble explorer I admit to myself that I am still completely in love with her, but she, like history to Verrazzano, has forgotten me.

The heavy plastic goggles allow a full peripheral search both above me and below. There's nothing. All wasted away, washed clean by nearly five hundred years of currents. It's astonishing that any kind of structure remains to this hulk. Another long draft of gas. Check the watch. Time to move. Air supply getting low. No astrolabe. Exit.

Thumbs down and she nods. We move away from the vaporous shell, guarded by archaeological framework, resigning the St. Clair astrolabe to hopefully be found at a later hour.

Our Pyle stop lasts three minutes and is meant to further acclimate the body to the deep water so that upon slow ascent the body can make adjustments with each new depth and decompression sickness is avoided. We time three minutes near the wreck and then begin slowly fluttering toward the surface, following the uncoiled guide rope like Hansel and Gretel. At six meters, we stop again and get acclimated for five minutes. Our breathing gas is nearly spent and the last few meters are welcomed. The shadow of

70

the catamaran looms, but there is also a second boat. It wouldn't make sense for Ski to have arrived already and when we breach the surface I realize the awful, unfettered, and ridiculous truth.

Retreating to the water is no use, our gas is almost spent. I pull off my mask only to be greeted by the smiling malevolent face of Lucan standing on the dive platform. Kristoph is holding a gun to Donovan's midsection and the Magnusson brothers each have submachine guns fixed upon Rachel and me.

I'm forced to spit some seawater and I look at Rachel whose face is sickly white. Next to the catamaran is Lucan's hundred-foot yacht. The Venezuelans are on the deck staring down at us. No Molitor. That asshole didn't even bother to show his face.

No words. Nothing but lapping ocean water against expensive boats. Rachel. Terrified. Nothing to be done now. These men with guns decide our fate. I die before she does. Only thing I can control. Silent voices before violence. It's how it used to be. The world would explode right after everything quieted down. An engine, silent before the ignition switch. Sparkplugs flashing against petroleum leading to motion. The physics of violence. Bullets piercing the air at velocities of incalculable precision. And they've got all the guns. And I spit seawater again, staring at evil. Donovan: looking only at Rachel, with the petrifaction of true love, knowing he would do anything to protect her. And they've still got all the guns.

Wind whipping. Salt spraying. Malevolent smiles and submachine guns.

Lucan steps forward smirking. He smashes silence like wrecking ball.

"Dr. Hexam, Mr. Rodriguez. Did you find anything?"

We look at each other, each too exquisitely shocked to find words.

"I didn't expect you to. The astrolabe in question is safely behind plate glass in the Pitt Rivers Museum and has been for quite some time now. My family donated it."

"So, what are you doing out here, Matthias?" Rachel snarls.

"You know very well why I'm here, Rachel."

"I think she's out of your league, friend," I quip.

"Rik," she snaps. "Don't provoke him."

But, he's made up his mind already. I can see it in his face. I'm a non-entity. This whole thing is broken. Nothing for him to do now but fire, finish the job he started. Gun drawn from holster and I dive to my right. 9mm slug. Rachel shrieking.

The hot tearing of my shoulder's flesh sears through my entire body and then I'm propelled straight downward, hurtling through a vortex, a rocket shooting me straight down. I can sense Rachel lunging toward me, but the escaping gases from my damaged tanks have turned me into a hurtling projectile cutting through the water in tangential swaths. I catch a final glance of two giant shadows moving away in the distance as I strain back toward the surface. Frantically pounding the release strap with my one good arm, but the harness is stuck. I've got no air, I'm being suffocated, but with one final effort, I manage to unhook the plastic clasp and come free of the harness as it hurtles downwards. The chaos of the deep takes over and I kick skyward with all my might, my lungs burning, my cells pleading for air. I'm at least twenty meters below, hurt and disoriented. Blood is seeping from the wound in my shoulder and I'm forced to jam three fingers into the cavity to quell the bleeding. A hole on the top of the biceps. I'll never pitch for the Yankees. A lucky miss for Lucan. Movement made him miss the mark. Or he's a shitty shot.

Rachel's screaming still echoes in my head as I break the surface moments later kicking furiously from below. Dizziness overtakes me and I began to fade. Things are growing darker. The two boats are five hundred yards away now under full power and I'm left rocking in the surf, my shoulder bleeding. Glancing up to the clear blue sky, I say a quick prayer of salvation to God and my Pop. Hopefully, they can keep the sharks at bay. I close my eyes and wonder, the pain worsening, the hour waning.

[9]

S.N.A.F.U.

Undulating gracefully among the breakers, bobbing as if I were attached to some long imaginary fishing line, the blood from my shoulder the bait, I wait for the first shark to attack. Blood loss is clouding my already troubled mind. The pulsing blast of the emergency beacon on my suit stings my already seawater stung eyes with each beaming, photonic burst.

Kicking wildly below the surface, trying to keep myself afloat. Staring pleadingly at the sky above, wishing for one more moment and then one more hour and perhaps more days and weeks, I wait. Forty minutes by my watch. Then an hour. Then an hour and a half and the pain is unbearable and my fingers can no longer keep the blood at bay, my legs give out and I'm falling again. A mirage on the horizon.

A boat.

My dream.

I sink.

I can think only of Rachel. I allowed myself to love her. The world showed me bitterness and pain, violence and death. I wore a uniform to stand for right and true and yet I compromised. I allowed myself to be all-consumed by the basest human emotions and so I now accept my fitting end, here below the waves. My sins roll out before me like a giant scroll and the last breath of air escapes my body. No explanations for my deeds, dastardly and kind, only the hope that I might walk amongst the clouds with my Pop and Mom too, and hear the truths resounding in the sky like orchestral songs. I pray that I may know true love and once and for always let the phantasms that haunt me disperse here amid the millions of particles; my watery sepulcher.

Seeing is certainly not believing, but seeing the past makes it true. The village is chaotic behind me. I'm a twenty-four year old junior at Boston University and Navy reservist who's been called back to the Teams for the invasion of Afghanistan. I knew six guys in the Towers. I didn't even get to go to the funerals. It's November 2001. I got out for good in May '03.

The snaps and crackles of AK-47 rounds are exploding all around us and there I am, standing, staring into the cold dead eyes of a Taliban zealot who's holding a giant paring knife, the kind they use to skin ibex, to the throat of Dave Chakrin, my team leader. Behind him, his wife and daughter are standing in the doorway screaming at him. But, he is all ablaze with hatred. The girl stares at me with piercing blue eyes, beseeching me to make this all stop. The truth is caught somewhere between the bullets and the pain. Our eyes lock and my countenance turns mineral.

The killing is easy. He dies before he even sees my finger squeeze the trigger. The pistol coughs the bullet and explodes his skull before he could even register that I fired. We turn and run, the stabbing screams of widow and child ricochet through our ears.

One slip of many. One shot in the dark. Moving now, somewhere between here and there. Somewhere the cool blue waters of the Pacific are lapping. In the North Atlantic, the icy chop cradles swordfish. The water is untainted and antediluvian. It has seen and known and remembers all that we trespassers have brought before onto, into and under it. And then, the primordial lands of the earliest men and women welcome the first weary travelers to make their home and force us, the contemporaries, to brood over the questions of derivation. Who are we and where did we come from? Who was first, second and third? When will the chronicles forget? When does clemency actually take hold?

MICHAEL CARR

My self-exculpation is a clever camouflage so I never have to tackle those things that disturb me when I not looking. Rachel called it withholding and I know that wounds can sometimes open up, even when they're stitched.

Examine.

Trust in the things known:

I am Alfred Frederick Rodriguez IV, born August 12, 1975 in Atlantic City, New Jersey to Alfred Frederick Rodriguez III and Diane Haggerty. I am of Guatemalan and Irish ancestry with a hint of Italian for good measure and I spent much of my life as a non-committing human being. Oh, I did many things and saw many places, but did I ever actually embrace the life I was given? Did I live for others? Sometimes. Did I sacrifice for the good of humanity? Yes. Did I love another wholly and truly…well definitely truly, but not wholly…NOT GOOD ENOUGH!

"Not good enough!" I can hear my own voice.

"Rik! Hey Rik!" I'm getting slapped in the face. I can feel pain. I don't want to feel pain in death. It's not supposed to be that way.

"Rik, open your eyes!"

A light. Finally the light.

My eyelids open and instead of incandescent radiance, there's a penlight. Why is there a penlight? Why can't I hear the choirs of angels?

I can feel. Fingers, toes, body, eyelids, arms, legs. I can see…Ski.

"Rik! Come on, asshole, wake up." His voice disturbs my calm, my serenity, my peaceful afterlife.

Awake. Taking waking slow, like Roethke.

And then laughter. Then Ski's face, bearded, disheveled as always. His eyes are sunken. I can see tears forming. He rubs a drop away quickly hoping that I won't see; a simple sentiment for the son he never had. I can feel an oxygen mask on my face and an IV tube in my arm. My

76

neoprene dry suit has been cut up the arms and down the torso. The pain in my shoulder is searing like someone sticking hot irons on the site at regular intervals. Lying supine, I look up and recognized the rust on the ceiling of the *Gina Marie*. The tiny cabin, as familiar as a second home, is adorned with photos of past dives, dive charts, maps, a broken barometer, and the remnants of snacks and beer bottles; a sailor's salon, a parlor of nautical integrity.

Rhodes must have her at full throttle because I can feel the breakers blasting against the hull. I see him at the wheel, loving to take the old girl for a spin. The cabin holds the elevated platform where Rhodes stands grasping the wheel now and staring out towards land.

"You let the kid drive?" I ask as Ski, slowly helps me to sit up. His corpsman training and volunteer EMS skills have brought me back from certain death.

"I'm a good driver," Rhodes says in his slurping way as the *Gina Marie* careens off a wave in a trough.

"Keep your eye on the road there." Ski barks like a German Shepard. He turns back to me. "You gave us a scare you pain in the ass."

"Thanks for the help. I'm pretty sure I had it under control though." Guffaws from both. Sarcasm my only defense.

"Who did it?" Ski asks.

"Long story," I say hyperventilating. "Bad men with their eyes on gold. Rachel and Nile Donovan are gone and I don't know what to do now." My shoulder, now searing, a reminder of frailty. A small boat. A big ocean. Where to go from here?

Rhodes turns his head, his girth, endearing padding, "Nile Donovan, the millionaire? You know him?"

"Yeah, kid. I know him. He's been kidnapped by Matthias Lucan."

"Lucan!" Ski yelps, "The Redstone guy. He's been all over the news. Missed a congressional hearing. *He* kidnapped Rachel and Donovan?"

"Yeah."

"So, now what Boss?" Rhodes asks with a hint of adventure in his voice.

"Back to base," I say mimicking the *A-Team*, and Rhodes hits the throttle. Ski hip checks him out of the way and takes over the wheel. I sit back and let the pain sink in.

Regroup. Refocus. Plan next move. Pitt Rivers Museum, Oxford. Call Victor Meek.

Close eyes. Almost home.

[10]

Kiss the Camel

The dock, Ski's car, then a blur and I'm sitting at the kitchen table in my apartment, shoulder bandaged and taped. I refused the hospital. The tiny CCTV screen just off to my left on the shelf near the window. The morning air has done nothing to revive me and the pain is worsening. My gear is gone. Phone, wallet, everything. Rhodes has leant me his iPhone to try Meek and I'm scanning through a shoebox full of paper scraps to find his number. Shot in the shoulder, and now all I can think about is frying some eggs and calling a professor in Dublin.

Ski ambles up the stairs. Rhodes is still down in the shop. We're closed due to attempted murder and an ancient mystery. This is the first time we've closed the doors since Pop opened them all those years ago.

After two tries on Victor's cell phone I give up for the time being and try to slide through some web entries about the hooked X, Verrazzano and the Pitt Rivers Museum in Oxford with the iPhone. Logic would dictate that Lucan would head back to Britain with Rachel and Donovan in tow, but nothing up to this point has been logical.

Ski sits down across from me, glancing wearily at the bandage work he's done on my shoulder wound. "You're about to bleed through again."

Scarlet protrusions on the gauze. The damn thing hurts, but I'm lucky. Should have been a killshot. Saw it coming. No, I was lucky.

"I should get you to a hospital."

"No hospital," I say refusing again. "I've got to figure out what's next? Smart money says he's taking Rachel and Donovan back to Oxford to get this astrolabe, but they told

79

me they needed three separate runic inscriptions and then the astrolabe to find whatever's at the end of this. Hell, I don't even know where you would start looking for this Thorvald's Cross. Vinland could be any one of a dozen places."

"Let the cops sort this one out. This is way above our pay grade," Ski says leaning back in the chair. "And, while you're up, make me an omelet."

"I was just thinking that," I say opening the fridge. "But my shoulder's really hurting," I say mockingly.

"Shut up and make me eggs, dummy. I pulled your ass out of the ocean this morning like a goddam tuna."

Fair and valid point. I turn on the stove burner.

Burning rubber, brakes screeching to a stop, the jangle of my front door bells. I can't hear what Rhodes said, but I see him clearly turn his back and move toward the stairs. The black and white CCTV camera picks up every movement.

Gun.

Raised toward the back of the kid's head. He doesn't hear the shot. Nothing we can do. Dead before he hears the report.

Molitor.

Rhodes, bloodied on the floor behind the counter where he worked so hard for me.

Frantic leaping down the stairs without regard. Terrified, searing anger welling up. Ski, light years behind.

Now, standing face to gun with a man I thought I knew.

Molitor.

Hatred on my face: blazing, searing. Ski, somewhere behind me coming down the stairs.

Three words: "Where's Victor Meek?" The machine-gun emphasis. His suit, newly pressed. His hair slicked back all the way, pulled taut like a rope on a docking ship. Meek? What does he want with Meek?

Repeat: "Where's Victor Meek?" Hammer drops on the Beretta 9mm. Now they want Victor Meek, my friend. What could he possibly have that they want? Information? Artifacts?

Rhodes's body in front of me, the blood escaping from the wound. His mother, a waitress at the Tropicana, probably just coming off the graveyard shift. What will I tell her? What answer could she possibly accept? Your son was murdered because some rich fucker wants a treasure.

"What are you into Joel? How did they get your soul?" I ask. The question, both pertinent and necessary. Molitor, a man I once knew, now a shade, a hallucination in a murderous act.

"A lot," he answers; the agitation of homicide beginning to take hold inside of him. He's strung out. His eyes are bloodshot and burned. Maybe it wasn't money, just cocaine that pulled him in. The killing: I've been there, Joel. It doesn't go away. You can't take back what you just did.

A third time, with emphasis: "Rik, where's Victor Meek and maybe I won't kill your other friend there. I know you know. Lucan's going to find him with or without your help. Turns out that Rachel and Donovan are useless!"

"I always hated you, Joel. I just want you to know that now."

A snicker. A sneer. Tightening his hand around the gun, ready to pull the trigger. Action now or inaction.

My hand. An egg. One I didn't crack as I watched the horror unfold in the shop below. I can smell the burning yolks and now I'm caught again in the in between space. Action. Inaction. I've been here before. It's like falling. It's like kissing the camel, what we used to call falling between a docking ship and the wood planked bumper on the side of the dock: certain death either way.

At my feet, the body of my friend. He was a good kid and now he's dead. I can see the wound. His mother will have to bury him with a closed casket.

Molitor.

The egg in my hand.

Throw.

The egg splatters on the mark, right between his eyes and the rest happens tornado-like, all a blur of development. I move swiftly forward and knock the gun away. Two quick punches to the chest, bend his arm back and then thrust him down and forward into my display case, all hatred and energy channeled into throwing him south. The explosion is epic. The glass shatters in brilliant spectacle. I pull his bloodied body out, the jewelry and watches inside ruined by his betrayal. I toss his body on the linoleum and see Ski panting, kneeling over the kid, his lip quivering. My forearms now cut, I step back and survey.

Molitor. Dying: head and neck trauma. He gurgles his last earthly sounds. Dead.

Rhodes. Dead. Gunshot from Molitor.

Me. Alive in the center of my shop, my sanctuary, the calm destroyed by the events of the past two days. I move past Ski dripping rivulets of blood. Ski, bewildered, cannot find words.

Phone. Cops. Ambulance. Be gone before they get here. Go to Dublin. Find Victor Meek before they can. No stopping now. Must follow wherever this leads now. Upstairs, I pack a few things in a bag. Passport in hand, I book tickets with Rhodes's iPhone, AC to Boston, Boston to Dublin, then come back downstairs to find Ski still back on his haunches next to Rhodes's body, sobbing.

"Both dead," he whimpers.

I dial 911 on the iPhone. "Hello, there's been a double homicide at the Pocket Aces Pawn Shop. A man shot and killed an employee in cold blood. The security tape will prove it. Send an ambulance." Hanging up, I toss the phone to Ski.

"I'm going to find Meek and then Rachel and Donovan." Ski nods, unable to do anything else.

"What'll I tell them about this?" he says regretfully.

"I was never here." But I was there and will always be there, my actions recorded not just by the security camera but also by history. I'm on the Expressway driving Ski's car before I hear the first siren screech past. Never there. Never here. Keep saying that. Between the ship and the camel. Between here and there. Go to the Airport, then to Dublin. Call Rhodes's mother before you get on the plane.

Find the words.

[11]

The Valley of the Black Pig

Atlantic City to Boston. Dusk now. A whole day gone.
Logan Airport is full of humanity waiting to board
international flights that will carry them into morning. I left
Ski holding the bag. Hopefully, he thought of a good place
to put me. If not, Homeland Security will arrest me before I
can board the Continental flight to Dublin.

I killed a CIA agent. He killed an innocent kid. Their
blood on my hands.

The bookshop though is relatively tranquil, library-
like. People mill about abstemiously, wanting to speak but
restraining themselves. Across the threshold of the store,
travelers fly by on a conveyor walkway, but in here things
stop, the moving machine temporarily in sleep mode. It's a
simple volume for which I hunt, thin, printed by a big
publisher and yet possibly containing some of the most
important revelations of this entire ambiguous sequence of
events. It's a collected edition of *The Vinland Sagas* and
surprisingly I've found it tucked away near Bede's
Ecclesiastical History of the English People and *The Saga of the
Icelanders*.

The clerk rings me up and I take the change with my
left hand, trying to get some use out of the shoulder. The
pain still sears white hot, but I keep reminding myself of
what's at stake. Rhodes's mother thankfully didn't answer. I
don't have the words yet anyway. I thought I'd find them on
the short flight. But I haven't found them in thirty-five years,
what the hell made me think I'd find them on a puddle-
jumper to Logan?

On the plane to Dublin now. Taxi. Stale, recycled air.
Takeoff. Homeland Security was not looking for me after all.

Ski's story must have been a good one. What if they arrested him? Not possible. His sincerity and solemnity around death is unmatched and besides they'll watch the security tape once Ski downloads it for them. They are probably in the police station on Atlantic Avenue right now watching me kill Molitor. They'll see his crime first, but I'll have to answer for the justifiable killing sometime later. Why did he do it? Why did he kill my friend and then turn the gun on me? Horrific answers to terrifying questions.

Cramped in an airplane bathroom. My shoulder bandage seeping crimson fluid. When you feel dead inside it's hard to recognize your own blood because anything natural is unnatural. Painstakingly, I rewrap the shoulder with some Tefla bandages, a new combine pad and some tape I picked up in the Logan airport drug store. The blood wipes away easily. It washes clean from the countertop. My reflection in the mirror is hollow and two-dimensional, almost terrifying. It takes a few minutes back in my seat to calm the welling panic attack, but it subsides with some overwhelming will power. Will it to stop. Make it alright. Make something positive out of this destruction, all of it.

Now, I'm enrolled for this particular mission. Find the origins of European settlement in North America and save three people before a British mercenary decides to kill them. I need a drink. The flight attendant offers, but I pass. I won't break the pact to myself. Besides, I need to focus or else the bloody images from this afternoon will overtake my thoughts. It won't be like it used to be. I won't let it. Make it work.

The Vinland Sagas are short and to the point; their authors preferring to give information in a matter-of-fact manner as opposed to using a literary filter. The plane is soaring over the vast Atlantic, the same primordial ocean traversed by the explorers of the past. Their apprehensions are now mine as I make the reverse trek. The book has produced a few interesting passages worth noting. I bought it to jog my memory of Meek's early medieval history lectures at Boston U and then again in England on our research dig.

I see him sitting in the middle of a circle. He never liked to stand and lecture. He preferred the desks around in a Socratic style. Most of the students with me are fresh from undergraduate work, now on to master's degrees and doctorates. My tour in Afghanistan brought me nightmares and a bronze star. The University was accommodating and let me make up courses online and during the summer of 2003 so I could maintain my status.

It's Fall 2005: I'm a twenty-eight year old undergraduate senior with permission to take a graduate course called *"Early Explorations of North America"*. Meek spoke plainly and to the point, commending original thought. When he was puzzled he would scratch at a black beard and adjust his spectacles. He laughed with buoyant boom and encouraged all of us to question the things we thought of as foregone conclusions. He introduced me to Rachel, one of his doctoral candidates. He bought me a beer the night before I graduated and told me to pursue a PhD. He shook my hand years later at my father's funeral like he meant it. Whatever he knows or whatever they think he knows is going to stay with him as long as I'm alive. I don't know what to do about Rachel and Donovan yet, but Meek is going to enjoy his retirement in Dublin without getting killed. When I can, I'll call Jay Brown in London. He'll at least give me some direction and probably call me a dickhead in the process; of those two things I'm certain. Maybe he knew about Molitor's dealings. Maybe he'll be happy to find out.

Too many thoughts swimming around. Focus on now. Back to the book and the passages of note. The first deals with the naming of Vinland. In *The Saga of the Greenlanders*, a man named Tyrkir, a German, is the one who discovers the wild grapevines and relays the news to Leif

Eiriksson. In *Eirik's Saga*, Leif finds Vinland and then a second expedition with two Scottish servants led by Yule Karlsefni explores further south from Vinland and it's the Scots who return with handfuls of vines. It's Karlsefni who also discovers the land of Hop, which at one point was put as far south as New York harbor.

In *The Saga of the Greenlanders*, Karlsefni, years after his return from Vinland, is approached by a man from Saxony. The man offers to buy a carved decoration that Karlsefni keeps on the prow of his ship. Reading a note at the back of the book, I found that this prow decoration may have been an early mariner's astrolabe made of burl wood. Perhaps, the astrolabe we're looking for is made of wood and not brass?

But, the most interesting episode from the *Sagas* is the story of Leif's brother Thorvald. Thorvald went back to explore lands around Vinland and was killed by Native Americans. His crew agreed to bury him under a cross because he had converted to Christianity. It doesn't say how or where they buried him. I'm reaching back in my memory to try and place all the different native confederations in their locations. These natives must have been Eastern Algonquin, but were they Mi'kmaq, Wampanoag, Narragansett? Thorvald's Cross or Krossanes, a name that I pulled dramatically out of my ass this morning, is set in at least five different places according to the notes. No help. More questions. No archaeological evidence. I'm nowhere.

Fleeting lights. My mother. Diane Haggerty. An actress, raven-haired and bright-eyed as a doe. I'm staring up at her. Three years old. I run into the hydrangea bushes near the saltbox we used to own in Sea Isle City. She picks me up and pulls me back, laughing. I run back into the bushes. "Find the man," she yells and I shriek in delight.

Capture the gnome, the tiny man who lived in the hydrangea bushes. He was painted with a multi-colored palette. I see him there, clear as day and I see Diane, my mother. The woman I know only from photographs. She was gone before I was old enough to leave the gnome alone.

She's face to face with me now. I'm thirty-five years old. She's younger than me. Only twenty-seven when she passed. Now, we're standing in the shop. Rhodes and Molitor, both alive and standing next to her. Things are tightening up.

She's gone.

They remain. I watch it live, again, and again and again.

Molitor pulls the trigger and kills Rhodes. The kid's head snaps away like it's been belted by an imaginary hand. And I can't stop it.

My mother, there again. Rhodes and Molitor gone.

She speaks: *The dews drop slowly and dreams gather.*

Bewildered I try to hold on for one last moment, one more transitory glance of this stranger. She breaks into glass shards that fly up all around me.

Alone. Cut by glass.

I can't respond. Tightness again. Rage wells, anger at her senseless cancer, then every time I pulled the trigger, then Rhodes, then Molitor. Death, uncontrollable, incalculable. Finished. Asleep.

Awake. My teeth sunk into my lower lip. Blood. I hold a tissue to the self-inflicted wound and lean back in the plane seat. The window, lightly cracked reveals the brilliant sunrise over the Atlantic and the notion that soon I will have to act again. Soon, I will have to find things in more complicated places than Sea Isle hydrangea bushes. I wish it were easier than this. I touch my shot shoulder. Yup, still hurts like sin. Time for another Aleve.

Before the pill can take effect I'm walking through the Dublin airport, backpack over my good shoulder and fighting the piercing sun cascading through the window like rolling ribbon candy. It's blinding.

The customs agent checks my passport, stamps it and I move through, once again avoiding the certain detainment to come. I will have to pay for Molitor, of that I'm certain. It's just a matter of where or when. Now I move like a wraith amongst these people. Climbing into a cab I rattle off an address, the last one I have for Dr. Victor Meek, "717 Temple Lane South, Temple Bar." Hopefully, I'm not too late.

The sun is low over the River Liffey sending sparkles dancing across. O'Connell Bridge is passable. No traffic yet. We passed the General Post Office. The cabbie was quick to point out the bullet holes from British guns. A terrible beauty is born.

I could use a coffee, but they like tea better over here. I've never been to Dublin and it's a pity I have to make my first trip under these circumstances. Once I find Victor, I'm not even sure what my next move should be. Thoughts again whisk through my mind. What could he have that they want? What does he know? Does he know where New Jerusalem is?

Hunstanton, England, six years ago: I'm sifting through a box of dirt. Granted, I only went on this dig because of a fetching doctoral candidate named Rachel Hexam and because Victor wanted to make one last attempt to guide my doctoral thesis away from the sea. The moor was cold and the bogs were nearly impossible to sift through. We had good luck in this site during the previous week and Victor thought for sure that we had stumbled upon a ceremony bog, one of the first to be found in England. Apparently, when the ancient Germanics vanquished an enemy it was common place across the board amongst the Jutes, Frisians, Angles, Saxons and even the Vikings to some extent to take all the armor, gold, swords, spears, everything from your enemy and cast into in a bog as an offering to the gods. That's what Victor thought he had in Hunstanton and all of us just went along for the ride.

So, I've got this dirt, perfectly ordinary dirt and as far as I see it, particulates falling this way and that through the sifter. Rachel is cataloguing a few spearheads about fifty yards away. I remember the way she glowed that day, her hair wrapped back in a French braid. The night before we made love for the first time. It was awkward and original. Ours. Naturally, my mind was elsewhere as Victor looked over my shoulder, into the sifter as I shook and shouted, "Stop!"

Gingerly, with the care of a thoracic surgeon, he extracted a circular piece of metal, round and caked in dirt and whisked it away before I even had a chance to ask. Later, he showed me the piece, cleaned up and sitting amongst other Anglo-Saxon artifacts. It was a brooch and it was carved with a hooked X. Memory flashes with the quick snap shut of the cab door. Anglo-Saxons carving a hooked X. Why?

My boots hit the cobblestone. The cab pulls away. Alone again. No helo to call in when things get bad. Temple Lane. Empty, save the swirling papers and traffic in the distance. Left is the Liffey. Right is Dame Street. Straight ahead is a Georgian row house with a purple door. 717. I roll up my sleeves. The button-down Oxford is now suddenly too hot for Dublin in May. Adrenaline surging. What if they already got here? Victor dead like Rhodes. Another ghost to join the cavalcade. My skull is splitting, shoulder aching, vision cloudy from no sleep, but I inch forward. Knock. No answer. Try the knob. It's open. Why would he leave his door open? The light of morning has not penetrated yet. The tiny alcove smells like garlic. Calling out, "Victor." Silence. Stasis. There's an umbrella in a can at the bottom of the stairs leading up to the main landing. Something, just in case.

One foot on the stairs. Creaky Irish wood. Then another. And another. The top landing. I'm waiting for a woman I don't recognize to appear. Joyce's Gretta; her Micheal Furey. Rachel; her Donovan.

"Rik?" The voice, guttural and jowly, easy-going and kind.

I turn with the umbrella raised, unable to make the connection. I jump. Someone's got the drop on me. I'm ready to be shot. Turning, there's Victor in the doorframe, morning tea and Irish Times in hand.

"Victor. Thank God."

"What are you doing with the umbrella?" he asks with a smile. "It's beautiful outside."

*Unknown spears suddenly hurtle before my dream-awakened eyes...*Words. The middle of a poem, repeating in my head like an overplayed hit. Victor walks me around his home, a shrine to medieval history, full of oil paintings and artifacts. On the wall in a gilded frame is a giant map of "the known world", probably drawn around 1100. It's fascinating in the mistaken details. Dragons at the end of the world. Perhaps it wasn't so wrong?

Then the fallen horsemen and the cries of unknown...

A broadsword on a wall rack. Crusader era. Victor blustering around, shirt half-tucked, putting the latest news on a stack of old papers strewn about the dining room table. Current news holds no sway with this man. He pushes his glasses back against the bridge of his nose and nervously takes a long draft from the tea, the bag string swirling under his chin. He wipes his mouth with his right hand and looks over, seeing me staring around the room. His collection is much better than mine back on Morris Avenue in the shop.

"Do they know where to find me?" he asks breaking the silence, his reflux finally getting the best of him. I can see him grasping his sixty-five year old stomach in nervous expectation. I wasn't expecting this question. My answer formulates slow, especially slogging against poetic words, left over from the dream on the plane, stuck to the bottom like coffee grounds or tea leaves. *We who still labour by the cromlech on the shore,*

I'm staring at the sword, thinking, reasoning and words come tumbling out in a whisper, *"The grey cairn on the hill, when day sinks drowned in dew,"*

He's puzzled and ruffles his eyebrows. I shake my head,"sorry."

"What was that? Yeats?" he asks.

Yahtzee. "That's it. Yeats. I couldn't think of who wrote the poem." *The Valley of the Black Pig,* Yeats' work that tells the tale of the Irish mythological Armageddon. Strange poem for my mother to quote in a dream. I think I've still got one of those shrink's numbers in a drawer back home. Might be time to schedule another appointment after all this is over.

"You show up in my house at seven in the morning quoting Yeats and tell me Lucan and his thugs are probably on their way here right now to kill us?!" He's getting more agitated. Obviously he's well aware of all that dealings with Lucan imply.

"So, you know then, about Rachel and *La Dauphine* and the helmet and Lucan?"

He gets that misty look in his eyes. He can't dive. He gets claustrophobic. There's nothing in this world that would have made him happier than to find a Viking helmet on Verrazzano's flagship.

Giddy chuckle and a chortle replacing the agitation. He's beaming, then he catches himself. "Rachel sent me the picture once they restored it. The same helmet that you sent me yesterday. This is extraordinary, Rik. Do you know how many Viking helmets were ever found during excavations anywhere?"

I shrug, having no idea.

"One!" he shouts, nearly jumping out of his shoes with excitement. "And now Rachel finds one on Verrazzano's lost flagship. I mean this is really happening. This is real, honest to goodness breakthrough archaeology."

"They kidnapped Rachel," I'm forced to say, derailing his thoughts. His face drops. Gravity hitting home for him. He covers his mouth, perhaps expecting me to tell him news like this, perhaps out of genuine shock. On his ring finger, he still wears the wedding band even though Margery passed three years ago. That's when he pulled his stake and moved to Dublin. Forgetting or remembering. Either one. It seems like a settled household.

"How? I mean, what happened?" he asks.

"Rachel brought me out to the dive site to try and pull up the St. Clair astrolabe. She thought it was on *La Dauphine*. But, it turns out it's not on *La Dauphine* but in the Pitt Rivers Museum in Oxford? She said you needed the astrolabe to find a tomb once you got to New Jerusalem."

"It's in Oxford? Damn. It's been there the whole time?" He stands up scratching again at his beard.

"Apparently. But, she still found *La Dauphine*. I mean Verrazzano's flagship is certainly not a minor discovery in underwater archaeology. I'm surprised she kept a lid on it this long. The grid she had down there must have taken a month to lay."

"Verrazzano's just another piece to this crazy puzzle," he says with half a smile.

"Victor, tell me what you know and you've got to do it quick, because I don't know what's going to happen here. They could kick down the door any minute," I say glancing over my shoulder toward the landing. "Did you remember to lock it this time? It wasn't locked when I walked in, obviously."

"Yes, Yes I locked it and you're right. You're right." He sits down and takes another drink of tea. "Do you know where they took her?"

"Oxford probably. Lucan's estate is out there."

"That makes sense. They're not going to hurt her. They need what she knows about Lake Champlain and New Jerusalem if they want the treasure. She did all the real research on the Templar angle," he says under his breath and then continues: "Alright so, Lucan asked me to work for him last year. That's how this all started. He thinks he has in his possession one of the three inscriptions that tell you the location of Thorvald's Cross. And Thorvald's Cross is where the Viking kings supposedly buried the wealth of Vinland. Might have been where the Templars decided to stash their loot too."

I nod. "That part I got."

"Right, right. You remember reading the Sagas with me. Once the Templars get involved, everyone starts to have delusions of grandeur, especially a guy like Lucan. Now, obviously I didn't want anything to do with him, but I did look at a photo of the carving he had and it's definitely authentic. It's an amulet about that big," he holds his two hands together forming a circle about the size of blueberry pancake from the CHEGG on Long Beach Island. "And then Rachel with Lake Champlain," he scratches at his beard a little bewildered then shifts gears, "are you two still together or is she with that millionaire?"

"Victor…"

"Because I was always rooting for you."

"Victor we don't…" but he continues on:

"Anyway she got in touch about six months ago about a site on Juniper Island in Lake Champlain and she thinks that's the most logical location for Ragnar's outpost, which would lead to the third and final inscription about

Thorvald's Cross. It's supposed to be on a suit of armor that he wore, well at least that's what I read in a manuscript in Uppsala."

"Victor, I don't think you're understanding me. Lucan is killing people. He shot me in the arm yesterday morning and a guy I've known for years held a gun to my head, asking me where you were right after he killed a kid that worked in my store. Rachel hasn't told them, so they sent that asshole looking for you. He probably thought he would have got it out of my people in the shop. I know he probably wasn't expecting to see me. But, who knows how long she will last? This guy needs you to figure out this treasure hunt for him. And he's not only been compensating with violence. He said he killed his own right hand man, the guy who pawned Rachel's stolen chest!"

"Jesus, Rik."

"We have to get you out of Dublin."

He pauses. He's not ready to concede yet. This is still esoteric for him. He hasn't seen blood. And then he says: "Not before I show you the second inscription."

"We don't have time." Of course there's no time. How can he even be entertaining this?

"Well, you were pretty good with runes at one time, don't you remember? You wasted that talent with the maritime studies, I'm serious." He's right about the runes though. I had a minor infatuation with Anglo-Saxon futhorc. Elder and younger futhark, the Norse versions were completely bewildering but something about reading futhorc always came easy.

"I wasn't any good with the Norse, don't *you* remember? Just the Anglo-Saxon."

"Oh you're gonna love this. You came all this way and if this is actually, I mean if we're really going on a treasure hunt, we're going to need this clue."

"I hope it's close by."

"You ever been to The Brazen Head?"

95

"You mean like from *Ulysses*?"

"*You get a decent enough do at the Brazen Head.*" He quotes Joyce with a wry smile.

"You mean there's a runic inscription in a pub on the Quay?"

"In the cask cellar," he says proudly, moving past me towards the door while adjusting his glasses. "Everybody thought they were pseudo-runes, but I think they're a hybrid. I've been working down there for about a month. The owner's a buddy of mine. Got him Yankees tickets when he went to New York with his kid. Now I've got carte blanche in there. He even gave me a key. But, you'll see for yourself." He's already up and past me.

"Then I guess I'm buying breakfast," I say, once again at a loss. Victor chuckles throatily as he walks out the door. Against my better judgment, I too walk out a door. I walk out a door towards trouble and the promise of "breakthrough archaeology". It seems, at least with Rachel and Victor, I'm the only one feeling the stress of impending doom. Hell, if I still wanted that kind of stress I would have stayed in the Navy. Victor shuts the door, remembering to lock it this time. He leads me west, through Temple Bar toward the river.

The Liffey. Merchant's Quay. Water rolling in rippled swirls. The first raiders arriving in the Black Pool where Dublin gets its name saw the potential of the river port. Of course they burned out a few Celts that were living on the banks, but they settled, they stayed until a better offer enticed them away.

Victor walks at a frantic pace when he's excited and I find myself taking great strides to keep up with him. The sun is warming the Quay as we walk south along the banks of the river.

"I don't think they know where to find me, Rik. I mean Lucan knew I lived in Dublin, but my address isn't listed. I think we're fine. Besides, Rachel's tough as nails." He looks at me for reassurance. I don't want to tell him that actual torture is nothing like the movies. Most people break in minutes, not hours. The idea of Rachel being tortured sends shivers down my arms. My scarred subconscious is too hardened to entertain that notion for one more nanosecond.

"Victor, it's not that hard to find a person that doesn't want to be found, especially for someone like Lucan with unlimited resources and his own private army. Believe me, eventually he'll be coming for you."

He stops, takes off his glasses, and wipes them on his shirt. "You know, for someone coming here to provide reassurance, maybe even a rescue, you're doing a shitty job keeping my morale up."

I throw my hands up, shaking my head and keep walking.

"No, I think we should talk about this," he says catching up to me. I can't help but crack a smile.

"How about you tell me what the hell these inscriptions mean? Maybe fill me in on this particular mystery?"

He readjusts his glasses and takes a breath of morning air. I can feel his indigestion as we walk. He didn't expect to be here. He didn't expect all this.

"Sorry," he finally says, "you're right. I should explain this all a bit better," He scratches his beard tautly again. I can see him pouring through years of lecture notes and bullet points, trying to distill complicated history down so that I can understand. This is his profession. He's made hundreds of people "understand" things over the years. It takes a special breed.

He clears his throat: "So, you remember that there's only about twenty people in the world that can read runes right?"

"I remember," I respond. "And I'm not one of them."

"Give yourself more credit. It's not always about accuracy with runes. It's about creativity. Nobody knows what these things actually meant. Scholars will tell you fifty different things about the same rune and none of them will agree. Your opinion's as good as the next. It's about the spirit of the thing. We're not dealing with Roman letters." He points around to the left. We turn with the bank of the river.

"You're near the top of that list of twenty, Victor," I remind him. "You're footnoted more than you think."

"I wish I saw a few more royalties for all that damn work, but anyway," his pace slows a half step as he begins to paint the story with words. "I translated this document from the Old Norse last year while I was in Uppsala at a conference. It was kind of like a schematic regarding the Vinland settlements. Look for the book this fall. Some Swede is taking all the credit for the work we did. He's a moron, but I can't afford a lawyer. Basically, what this document said was I order to find Thorvald's Cross, which is actually Thorvald Eiriksson's tomb, you have to have three directional markers. That's not going to be in the book because the agreement amongst the experts," he holds up some air quotes around *experts*, "is that any kind of Vinland treasure, tomb, anything besides an outpost, especially when you include the Templars, is bunk. They're so close-minded it makes me sick. As if five guys in a room can make a decision about what these ancient peoples intended." He's talking wildly with his hands. The flare for the dramatic is what used to draw students into his classroom. I can see a stone portico coming up on our left.

98

"So, this astrolabe is what connects the Templars and the Vikings?" I ask.

"Well that's if you believe the Templars got there. It's a two-part story, see. You've got Thorvald's Cross or tomb and then Templars from Orkney and their expedition. The astrolabe is theirs. Supposedly, they got to Thorvald's Cross around 1399 or 1400 and found that the Viking settlements had been abandoned. Then they built a temple or church on the original Viking site and moved Thorvald's tomb to an undisclosed location. One theory says that the astrolabe had the directional coordinates that you could use to find where they moved the tomb, but you have to know where the original tomb was first."

"Wait a minute, wait a minute. They moved the tomb? Does Rachel know that?"

"Nobody *knows* anything, Rik," he says getting excited, "This whole thing is rumor and hearsay until you start finding things, like the second marker I found in the Brazen Head."

"Second marker? So the amulet Lucan has is the first?"

"That's right. And Ragnar's inscription is the third. So, now you have three Viking inscriptions and one astrolabe and then you find the treasure. See, not so complicated." He continues: "The whole thing was this. There was no GPS back then, right. So, these guys would carve things so they wouldn't forget. You remember from the Hunstanton dig?"

I do remember. The brooch I found. Rachel and I in a stuffy attic room, sweating with each other, lustful, exploring our own treasures. I teased her by flipping on the lights at one point. She shrieked self-consciously. I never could figure that out.

"I remember the brooch with the hooked X now that I've got some kind of context to put it in."

"That's right. That brooch is still in Norfolk, probably collecting dust somewhere. My field notes are buried under three piles of manifests. Damn archaeology. Anybody who thinks it's friggin' Indiana Jones should come live my life for a day. It's saddle sores from sitting in a library chair for twenty hours and then having all your hard work lost because an undergrad intern mislabels an artifact."

My lips are pursed in confusion. Rachel used to call this the "confused dog look".

"You done?" I ask, playing along with his cynicism.

"Just getting warmed up," he blusters. "So, back to the story. The runes, right? See, most of the time it was an inscription that only they and few of their compatriots could read. Runic code if you will, because there was no standard until the thirteenth century and even then it's debatable. You remember how Thorvald died and was buried in Vinland, well after that he becomes venerated and future chieftains of the Viking world want to make pilgrimages to Vinland. We get this idea in some of the Sagas. The amulet Lucan has is supposedly from the family of Leif Eiriksson. Now, could I verify that? No. But, the runic inscription looked real enough. Unfortunately, the picture he sent me was blurred and then I never heard from him again when I told him I wouldn't come work for him full time."

"But didn't they exhume Thorvald's body a few years after he was buried and take it back to Iceland?" I ask, remembering the book from the plane.

"Ah, you *do* remember my lectures…" but I don't have the heart to correct him. He presses on:

"…See, that's one translation. But a second translation says *worship* not *move*. It's a clever loophole for scholars to argue. Did he stay in Vinland or was his body moved? You decide. Obviously Lucan's made up his mind."

"And what about the Kensington Rune Stone in Minnesota where they found the hooked X? Doesn't that date to 1362? Was that a Templar job? "

"The Kensington Rune Stone is a whole other Pandora's box of theories. Now, it certainly has medieval characters and I know that Scott Wolter, the geologist out of Minnesota definitively proved it wasn't a fake, but you have to think that there might have been more than one group of medieval Templars or Christian monks who wanted out of Europe. Perhaps you're dealing with two expeditions? And the one from Orkney with the Sinclairs was meant to pick up where the Kensington folks left off."

"Makes sense," I say, but with a twinge of skepticism.

Victor stops. We're standing in front The Brazen Head, advertised as Ireland's oldest pub, founded in 1198.

"1198? That's a lot of pints over the years," I say.

He puts his hand on my shoulder. "What they don't tell you in the brochure is that before it was a tavern, this foundation was part of the palace of Hasculf Thorgillsson, the last Viking king of Dublin."

"I thought Dublin Castle was built on the Viking palace ruins."

"That's what they sell to tourists. Come on." He waves me through the castellated archway and down a cobblestone corridor to an open courtyard. He pulls a skeleton key out of his pocket and before I know it, we're going down a windy stone staircase past old liquor boxes.

In the basement, the ceiling is low. The cold must hangs in the air. Keg refrigerators hum in the corners as Victor flips on an overhanging bulb. We're in the bowels of this pub. Rubber tubing snakes up all the walls, feeding the taps up above. I can just imagine Victor asking his friend the owner to come down and examine some old stone carvings on the walls. The owner, happy with a set of Yankees tickets, would've let him do anything he wanted in the basement. Victor pulls a small flashlight out of his pocket.

"Have you been down here already this morning, Victor?" I ask.

"Slept here last night," he says without taking his eyes off the walls. He's scanning the stone, searching around amongst the boxes and empty kegs.

"Hah," he says, " there it is." He shines his light on a hole in the foundation below the electrical breaker box. The cement is falling away. It's a jagged entranceway, cut into the masonry probably by a rookie electrician who was installing the box and hit a loose chunk of wall. Victor kneels in front of the hole and shines his light inside.

"In there?" I ask. "You slept in there?" I can see a sleeping bag and a satchel on the dirt floor inside. There's a footstool with an empty tea thermos and a lantern.

"Yeah. No mice. Jim, the owner has a whole squad of cats that roam around here. Asleep now, probably. Come on, I'm going to make a medievalist out of you yet," he says shimmying through the hole and inside.

I have to sigh. I take one last whiff of musty basement and slide through the entrance. I'm not expecting the drop. It's four feet down and I land with a thud. There's a small stepladder where Victor gingerly stood. I was unaware.

"Dammit, Victor. You could've warned me," I say standing up and dusting off. He flicks on the lantern bathing the tight space with amber light and suddenly, I'm staring at stonewall. The stones: intricately placed with mortar form an arching rounded ceiling that curves slightly backward on to the foundation wall of the pub. It is literally a buried wall and the little pocket where Victor has been studying is no more than seven feet across.

"How did you find this?" I ask slightly marveled.

"Jim had some electrical work done and they knocked through that inner wall. When they looked inside they found this other stonewall. He called me up and asked me to take to look, and this is what I found," he clicks on the flashlight and points at an inscription, carefully etched and preserved by time. I step over cautiously. The wall is made of sea stones and mortar, anciently simple. A chisel has etched out a complicated arrangement of runic letters, above which is a cross, delicately carved in the circular Celtic fashion. In the middle of the cross is a familiar symbol: the hooked X.

"You recognize it?" Victor says with a smile.

I nod, fascinated by these ancient cuttings. The runes take shape as my fingers brush through the inscription like Nordic Braille. The runes are feelings, expressions of ideas and their surge is still palpable all these centuries later. Excitement wells in my stomach. Perhaps this might be real after all.

"What does it say, Victor?" I ask turning away from the runes. He steps over picking up a leather-bound journal that was resting on the footstool. He flips back a page or two, holding the pen that was serving as a page mark between his teeth. He finds a passage, shuts the book dramatically and says, "I have no idea."

"What?" I scoff. "You've obviously been down here for a while and you've got nothing?"

"Well, I don't have nothing," he says. "I'm retired, I'm not dead. I've got theories. But in academia a theory's like an asshole…"

"Everybody's got one?" I say finishing the bad pun.

"No. It's usually full of shit."

"Right," I say. "Why don't you tell me what you've got considering we're under a bit of a time strain?"

He puts his hand on the wall, in the same reverent way that I touched it a moment ago. He has been awed by this carving, just as I am slowly being drawn into its power. Maybe it's the lack of oxygen or maybe there's magic in this room.

"It's a declaration of reverence. Hasculf or someone in his family or some ancestor of his visited Thorvald's Cross and carved this to remind themselves of the trip. And then there's one word I can make out for sure, because it's spelled out here, you see?" He points to very end of the carving and the very obvious runic inscription for R. Then follows what looks a crooked F with the top staff pointing up and the bottom staff pointing down. Then comes the hooked X, then a short staff with a line pointing down and away then the same crooked F and ending with the R.

"R-A-N-A-R?" I ask.

"You forgot the hooked X," he says.

"Yeah, but do you know what it means? I mean I recognize the others. They're Anglo-Saxon futhorc. But Hasculf was a Viking king. Why is the writing in Anglo-Saxon?"

"Who were the Anglo-Saxons?" Victor retorts.

And then I remember my history. Vikings, Angles, Saxons, Jutes, Frisians, Picts, Celts, Britons all became the melting pot that was the British Isles. Why were they writing in futhorc, because that's probably the runic alphabet they knew.

"I get it. Runes were territorial. Futhorc or modified futhorc was what they knew."

"If the hooked X was part of the futhorc it would resemble a very well known rune," Victor responds.

I search my memory bank for the X-rune in the futhorc and then remember the Rune Poem. X was G for 'gyfu' or 'gift'. The hooked X is a G?

"Gyfu, right. Gift. G."

"You remember. And if you put G in there you get Ragnar."

"Well, what's Ragnar?"

"Who's Ragnar, more importantly. Rachel showed you that printout from the Vatican, right?"

It's coming back now. "Ragnar's camp," I exclaim. "Stephen St. Clair was looking for Ragnar's emcampment. Rachel thinks she found the settlement on Lake Champlain."

"Ragnar Thorgillsson was Hasculf's cousin," Victor says. "From what limited knowledge we have, Ragnar was warrior chieftain who got a foothold as a merchant. His camp on Lake Champlain was a trading post with access to the St. Lawrence Seaway." He flips back in the journal to an ink sketch of Lake Champlain and the access point to the St. Lawrence Seaway, easily plausible for a Viking longship to explore.

"So where does that leave us, Victor? 'Ragnar' might be carved on this wall, but what does the rest of it say?"

"I think it says, *Armor of Ragnar.* And that would make sense because the medieval legend was that the third inscription about the actual physical location of Thorvald's Cross came from a suit of armor. Not just any suit of armor, but the Vinland Sentinel. See in the Norse traditions and again this isn't published anywhere, but when you've been reading Sagas for forty years you find the obscure stories. So, in the Norse tradition Thorvald was the first Vinland Sentinel and he had brilliant armor and a helmet cast with his crest then when he returned to Vinland, he was killed and buried. They buried him with the helmet, but the armor got passed down to the next Sentinel."

"So Ragnar was the second Vinland Sentinel?"

"I think so, Rik."

"What about the Vinland crest? Have you ever seen it?"

"Nobody has," he says taking off his glasses and rubbing his nose. "I've been sitting down here for months trying to figure it out. Pouring over everything, every possible algorithim, fraction, literary hypothesis to try and come up with some reason why this inscription is the second marker for Thorvald's Cross. But, I wish I could just get something to stick."

"Ragnar's important, Victor. I'm not there on the Templars yet."

"Well, that's the thing, Rik. The Templars were supposed to have two of the three clues already, this inscription and Lucan's amulet. They knew where to look for Thorvald's Cross because someone told them. Henry Sinclair was the Templar Earl of Orkney and had all kinds of dealings with the Norse. They could have told him what to look for and then they wouldn't need the inscription that's supposed to be on the armor. Problem is now that if you want to find where ancient Vinland might be you have the entire east coast of North America to choose from. Back then, any kind of manmade marker stuck out in the landscape. So, if you had a general direction and the idea to look for Ragnar's encampment or armor, you probably would have eventually found the damn place." He slumps down, almost defeated. "I just wish I could walk out of here right now and say it's real." He exhales in a dejected archaeologist's tone. "I just want it to be real."

"What if," I begin, "What if the hooked X is the Vinland crest? Thorvald's crest from the armor."

"What?" he asks, puzzled.

"I mean, hear me out, it's going to sound simple," but I don't care. I'm getting excited thinking about it. "But what if, the X rune in Anglo-Saxon is acting as a bind-rune?" I'm pointing the carving in the middle of the cross. Bind-runes occurred when two runic characters were amalgamated to form one word or concept.

"Bind-rune?" Victor says putting his glasses back on and squinting at the inscription. "What's it binding?"

"X is gyfu right, gift. So, the hook is pointing left, west. Gift to the west, gift to the left…Vinland."

"Holy shit," he says puzzled.

"I told you it was simple." I'm prepared for the inevitable academic ribbing to follow. I just proposed the answer to a thousand year old mystery by imagining Vikings carving a runic symbol with a finger pointing the way. It's seems ludicrous. But I'm not expecting Victor's response:

"So simple, Rik…it's probably true."

The wooden boards of the steps creak under our feet as we climb out of the basement. Wind, cold and uninviting in the courtyard. Sunlight blinds, blasting home like a supernova. The creaky door outside. The courtyard, echoing with the thousands of nights of music. Pint glasses strewn on the table. Victor trailing closely behind. A deep breath of morning and then the clack of footsteps on the cobblestone. Sergio Leone is somewhere directing, putting me in this scenario.

Kristoph, the Dane, muscles rippling through his shirt stands in the archway leading out. His smile is supercilious and wide. Behind him Tuco emerges, still in the same teal sports coat. Jules Montgomery, the Haitian, rounds out this trio, standing; waiting now for me to act. These faces look through me as if they didn't realize the irony of our circumstance. *Once Upon a Time in the West*. The movie begins and then three hours pass and you feel like it was worth every second. I wish I was Charles Bronson and this smiling Dane was Henry Fonda. The bullets wouldn't be real.

"Lord Lucan will be disappointed you're not dead," Kristoph says already beaming with pride at the fact he might be able to do Lucan a solid and put two in my head.

"Yeah. I'm just a bad penny, aren't I?" My left arm is cast out to my side in a protective gesture for Victor. He grasps my arm and puts it down.

"It's ok, Rik. They need me. They won't kill me," he says trying to move past. But there's no way I'm moving.

"Listen to the him," Montgomery says. "We don't want to hurt nobody. We bring the Professor to Lucan, that's it. We can forget we saw you."

Kristoph looks at Montgomery surprised. Kristoph has no intention of letting me walk from that courtyard and Montgomery has just spoiled his mojo. They're five yards away from me, a quick lunge if I hurry.

107

"If I go with you, you won't hurt him?" Victor asks heroically as I plant my feet and square my body.

"We got orders for you, Professor Meek. That's it," Montgomery says enunciating all of his 'ts' in a Caribbean baritone. Kristoph shakes his head, pissed off. I'm going to acquiesce his request momentarily.

"You shouldn't always follow orders like sheep," I say. "Start thinking for yourselves." And then I charge the five yards forward, surprising the stunned henchmen. I've got a gut punch on Kristoph and a roundhouse to Tuco's face before Montgomery draws the stiletto. I knock away the first thrust and kick him in the balls, buckling him over.

Kristoph is back and lands a one, two combination to my jaw. I block the right cross and land one to his teeth and then go to work on ribs, he doubles over. Tuco, meanwhile, is about to pull a gun. A glint of sunlight bounces off the barrel: Beretta compact 85FS Cheetah with nickel plating. Shit. He's aiming for my chest, smiling and then I see flash of fabric, beard and bluster. Victor charges forward and blasts Tuco in the face with a pint glass left on one of the courtyard tables from the night before.

"Thanks, Victor!"

Montgomery's on his knees. I throw two punches at Kristoph's face and kick Montgomery in the nose sending him sprawling backward. Tuco's Beretta is at his feet and I grab it as Victor and I race through the archway, up the cobblestones and on to the Quay.

Turning left, I hear the first bang of a gunshot. I throw Victor behind a parked car and duck behind the hood. The glass from the windshield above our heads explodes.

"They're shooting at us!" Victor shouts.

"Keep your head down!" I respond, flicking the safety on the Beretta. The clip is full; the compact design allowing only eight .38 caliber rounds. Make them count. The Gardai will be here soon. Dublin doesn't get too many shootings.

The rounds are blasting around my head, but I take a breath and inch up from behind the car hood. In a flash, I see Jules Montgomery's hulking frame running and taking aim with a revolver. Two squeezes of my trigger and he sprawls out on the pavement. Kristoph rushes behind him ducking down next to the wall as he sees Montgomery splayed out catching two .38 rounds in the chest. Kristoph fires in quick bursts, but I manage to keep his head down by emptying the clip into the wall above his head, the stone dust swirling in the air, blinding him. Time to move.

We run, but I can still hear gunshots bouncing against the wall beside me. We dart into an alley in time to hear the first Gardai sirens wailing in the distance. Two quick turns down the side street and we're back on Temple Lane. "I think you're right about leaving Dublin," Victor pants. His midsection and age don't agree with all this trouble.

"They'll be waiting at the airport," I say, grasping his arm and moving him fast, all the while looking over my shoulder.

"How about the ferry to Holyhead?" he says out of breath. "We've got to get to England anyway. Rachel and the astrolabe are in Oxford."

England. We do have to make a stop there anyway. Rachel. An astrolabe in Oxford. Might as well be now that we start the rest of this. I see a cab in the distance and flag him down. My thoughts return to Yeats.

We who still labor by the cromlech on the shore, The grey cairn on the hill, when the day sinks downward in dew, being weary of the world's empires, bow down to you, Master of the still stars and the flaming door.

Weary of empires. I have labored for them and yet it seems I'm still running. On the run, yet again. Another man dead by my hand. It had to be the apocalyptic poem in my head. Couldn't have remembered *Lake Isle of Innisfree* to get

109

through the day? Nothing easy. But who are you kidding? It's the complication that gets you up in the morning. True. But, it's days like today when I wish it wasn't so.

[12]

Crossing

"What the hell, Rodriguez? It's my day off. I just did a forty-hour shift. You'd better be dead or in jail." Jason Brown's monotoned, deadpan intonation brings back a flood of memories from days in the SEALs. Brown was a technology officer and one of the toughest SEALs I ever worked with, now he collects a check from the Central Intelligence Agency in their London post. If anyone can help with this, it's Jason Brown.

"Jay Brown, I'm on my way over for a visit, you game?"

"You out of your mind? Hang up the phone now or I'll have you killed."

Victor let me borrow his cell phone and I'm standing at the ferry railing overlooking the Irish Sea. I can imagine Jay sitting up in bed, eyes still closed, trying to figure out whether he's awake and alive.

"What's wrong Jay, you not alone?"

"No, your sister's here keeping me company. She's fat as hell though."

"Tell her I said hi."

"Will do, now what the Christ do you want?"

"I need you to meet me at Holyhead tonight. I'm heading to Oxford and I need some help for an old friend."

"I'm not your friend. You're a prick and I hate you." He pauses, then: *"What time's your ferry get in?"*

"1900."

"Fine, I'll be there."

"Thanks, Jay."

"Blow me." He hangs up the phone. I imagine him hurling the cell phone across his bedroom and collapsing back into a heap of pillows, blankets and his own sweat. It

111

was good to hear his voice. It's always good to be reminded of proud moments in our past. Jay Brown and I took turns saving each other's lives and I'm fortunate that even if he doesn't want to help me, that at least he'll be around to tell me that my ideas are terrible; yet another one of the moral compasses in my life. Besides, he owes me for covering his ass twice. Once was in Hawaii when he was late for an Op because he was in a sex sandwich with two bikini models and the second time, well the second time I don't count because that Somali informant had it coming for selling us out to his local warlord.

The pain is worse. Pain is always worse when you start to think about it. The sun is fixing to set and the great sparkles are dancing over the Irish Sea. The briny depths below are where I belong. Somewhere in my DNA, evolution didn't take. My thoughts always go back to sea. And now, in pain and out of control, I feel like jumping. That's when Victor sidles up.

"They've got some hot tea inside," he says pulling the jacket he bought at the dock gift shop closer to his body. The salt air in May is still biting out on the open water.

"Not a tea drinker," I say. "Always went for coffee."

He nods and looks out over the water. The sunset makes me think of the quiet moments in the past where the world didn't seem to want to swallow me up. Some of them involve Rachel, some not. Once, when we were staging for a Somali Op, we spent the night in Northern Kenya and I saw the most brilliant sunset of my life. We were running Ops into Somalia long after *Black Hawk Down*. Those pirates aren't anything we didn't know about, it was just like trying to break a hornet's nest with a fly swatter. Anyway, I was sitting in the dust of late afternoon a few miles outside Anjo, the flaming rays nearly scorched my eye, but I didn't care. I sat and stared through Oakleys in dirty BDUs and let everything happen. I let the world spin with me on it. I only wish now that I could have that feeling again. Just let the world spin. Let the ocean carry me. But, pain usually wins.

"I've never been involved in anything like this," Victor says, snapping me back to reality. "I mean, I've had people try and kill me before on digs, but nothing like this. In the Yucatan, they came after us with machetes, but all they wanted was a stone idol." He pauses, contemplating, mulling. "We could still go to the police you know."

"No. I made a call. We'll have help on the other end."

Victor shakes his head impatiently. "I'm just not used to this. I never even cheated on my taxes and all of the sudden I feel like a fugitive."

"You get used to it."

"No, that's just it! I don't want to get used to it!" he implores. "This goddam treasure myth is going to get me killed, Rik."

"Calm down, Victor. That's why I'm here."

He exhales, still staring out over the sea. He hasn't looked me in the eye and I don't expect him to, especially when he asks: "How do you do it, Rik? How do you just act?"

When someone calls up to tell you that a family member has died it feels like you got hit right in the chest. The air escapes, sucked out into a vacuous abyss, a little piece of yourself, your soul, whatever, gone. When your mind finally grasps the concept of things being slowly sucked away, of little pieces of yourself disappearing with every action, the feeling starts to become manageable and then finally you learn to live with it. You learn to live with tragedy ripping away at your core, whether you are the cause or recipient. But, I can't tell Victor that. I can't articulate what it feels like to take a life. He can see my lower lip quivering.

"I don't know anymore, Victor. I thought I had it under control. I was happy for the first time in years. Or at least I thought I was and then somebody brings a goddam helmet into my shop and my universe implodes again." A tear falls into the ocean, whether from the wind in my eye or the tip of an emotional iceberg, waiting to turn all pear-shaped inside my gut. I can feel him put a hand on my bad shoulder. I don't wince. It can't possibly hurt worse.

"You've seen things that I can't imagine," he finally says. He's now turning to look at me, but I can't look back.

"People have always relied on you to save them."

"No. More often that not we were taking lives, not saving them."

"You want to tell me about it?" he asks as the ferry hits a rough patch in the chop sending a faint bit of spray over the railing.

"Nothing to tell, Victor. Whatever I've done, I'll have to answer for it one day." The ugly truth. My name will be read somewhere and I wonder whether the good will somehow outweigh the bad. Not if I keep pulling the trigger. Not if I keep trying to wait out some kind of ridiculous happiness that arrives with angelic choirs. I hate trying to answer these questions. I don't know what's right anymore. I'm still waiting. I'm still wondering if it's possible to be left alone and still be content. All I muster for Victor is, "Until then, I'll keep showing up." I step away from the railing, wiping my eye. Victor remains staring off into the sea. I continue to hope for absolution, but none will come.

Somehow, I feel like things might going to work out with this insanity, especially when I see Jay Brown at the bottom of the ferry ramp leaning against a pole, sipping a coffee. He's built like a Viking: sandy blond hair and beard with a St. Bernard grin. He's trimmed up since the last time I saw him. His suit is slightly wrinkled. It's most likely on its second wear this week.

"You still drinking it with cream like a pussy?" he says thrusting a coffee into my hands.

"Good to see you, Jay," I say as we shake. He slaps me on the left shoulder, nearly making my knees buckle. "Oh shit, sorry. Is that the shoulder where Lucan shot you?"

"How do you know that?"

"Well, when I heard the Atlantic City Police issued a warrant for you on manslaughter charges, I thought I'd give Ski a call and see what kind of mess you got yourself into. Then I read the wires from Dublin and saw somebody went all vigilante on the Quay. Too messy, man. You don't just shoot a guy in broad daylight."

"You're wanted for manslaughter?" Victor intones, ignoring Jay's violent advice and stepping down from the ramp behind me. I suppose I am wanted for slaughter in many forms. But, I don't have time to worry about that right now, so I ignore the question, but Jay politely and quickly answers the Professor's query: "Rik, is that what they call it when you put a corrupt CIA agent's head through a glass display case? Manslaughter?"

Victor is deathly silent but Jay continues: "I say bravo for that move. Joel Molitor was a snowblowing sanctimonious sonofabitch and the world is better off without him."

"Snowblowing?" Victor replies puzzled.

"Nose candy. A bit of Venezuelan pixy dust. Come on, Professor, you were alive in the Seventies."

"Jay, this is Victor Meek," I say, finally interrupting Jay's onslaught of a greeting.

Jay shakes Victor's hand, "Dr. Victor Meek: Graduated Stanford University with a degree in English Lit, MA/PhD in Medieval Archaeology from the University of Virginia, served a tour in Saigon with an Army support unit, published the definitive translation of the Anglo-Saxon Rune Poem and two books on the Viking raids in the British Isles, went loco in the 80s and did a couple digs in Mayan territory trying to prove that there actually was a Sixth Stage to the calendar. Held two department chairs, one at Boston U, one at UVA and is currently retired, living a quiet life in Dublin, reading maudlin Irish writers and drinking Guinness. How's that quiet life working out for you, Professor?" Jay lets go of Victor's flabbergasted hand.

"Jesus. Who is this guy?" Victor asks me, stunned.

"Well, I'm sure as shit not Jesus," Jay says. "Come on."

He leads the way toward the car park. And before I know it, we're flying down the motorway back toward London, Jay Brown our willing chauffeur.

Speeding south, Jay finally quips:

"So you got yourself into a little adventure here, Rik?"

"I don't know what I'm into," I say glancing at Victor's terrified face in the backseat as Jay weaves in and out of evening traffic.

"I'll tell you what you're into, Matthias Lucan is all kinds of bad. When Ski told me he was involved I pulled everything I had on him." He starts digging through papers on the dash, driving with his knees and then pulls out a manila folder. His car is a mess. "This is what I got," he continues, reciting the dossier as he hands me the folder.

"Norwegian mother, English father all that bullshit. Earl of Bingham, la dee da," Jay says finishing the now cold cup of coffee in one gulp. Inside the folder, Lucan's picture is both menacing and cold as if the petty problems of any other mortals were impenetrable to his reptilian skin.

Jay continues: "Decorated SAS operative, then founded Redstone and you know about their track record from the news. The Brits are going to issue warrants for him either tonight or tomorrow for two counts of perjury and obstruction. They can't pin drug-trafficking on him although they've tried. We've got inadmissible evidence, satellite photos of Redstone employees guarding Venezuelan coke plants. Joel Molitor makes a few cameos although the Agency wants to spin it like we had him on the inside the whole time. Stupid bureaucratic bullshit. You can also read in there about a lucrative little business Lucan had going with a couple of Congolese militia groups. Helped put AKs and drugs into kids' hands. You know, those poor bastards they dressed up in wigs and turned loose to rape and pillage? Terrible shit. Hell, at one point I could've told you what Lucan's farts smelled like we had so many cameras and traces on him, but again all illegal and inadmissible, unfortunately."

"You still watching him?" I ask, hoping.

"They dropped the detail last month. Probably when Molitor turned up in the pictures. I wasn't on it personally, but I saw the reports. I also took the liberty of confirming what you probably already know and that is, two Danes named Magnusson were arrested last night trying to break into the Pitt Rivers Museum in Oxford."

"Ski tell you what we're going to be looking for?"

"No. I'm the goddam CIA. I know what you're thinking before you do," he scoffs weaving through traffic and speeding further south toward London.

[13]

English Breakfast

"This is going to be a two-pronged Op," Jay says devouring a rasher of bacon.

"So you're in then?" I ask.

"In? You just worry about your broken down self," he scoffs, "Of course I'm in. I got the day off tomorrow. Besides I still owe you from Somalia."

"And Hawaii," I remind him.

"Oh yeah," he chortles. "That was a damn good night."

We're sitting in Jay Brown's pristine kitchen on the East End of London. The rest of his life is usually a little out of synch, but Jay Brown can cook, there's no denying that. His kitchen is always in perfectly ordered shape and even when he makes a mess in prep, it's gone before the food is served. It's nearing midnight. The five-hour drive from Holyhead to London was destroyed in four by Jay Brown's autobahn mindset. He's fired us up a full English breakfast for a snack, complete with beans in tomato sauce and farmer sausages.

"Wait, wait. I don't understand," Victor says through a mouthful of fried eggs. "We're not going to the Embassy? We're not going to end this whole thing?" He looks at me, almost pleading. "I was all for a treasure hunt, until people started shooting at us."

"People have been shooting at me for two days, Victor. Relax."

"Yeah besides," Jay starts through a belch, "You want some kind of bargaining chip with Lucan right? He's got two hostages."

"You're forgetting," Victor intones, "that his family are the ones who donated the St. Clair astrolabe to the Pitt Rivers Museum. He can get access to it any time he wants."

I take a draft of tea, reminding myself of the menagerie that is the Pitt Rivers Museum in Oxford. Rachel showed me pictures one weekend while we were on the dig in Hunstanton. It's full of long rows of display cases, some artifacts unmarked. It's like a giant building laid out the way a really astute hoarder would arrange his material. Basically, organized chaos.

"That's where you come in, Victor," I begin. "We're assuming he can't access it because then the Magnussons wouldn't be trying to steal it. But you, Victor, you're one of the most preeminent medievalists in the field. If we give a call over there and tell them that Victor Meek requested a private viewing of the St. Clair astrolabe you would get unfettered access. And then…" Victor interrupts.

"Steal it?" he says disgustedly.

"Borrow it, Victor." I say.

"Don't do that, Rodriguez. Just say steal the goddam thing," Jay says finishing some beans.

"This is ridiculous," Victor says putting down his fork. "I can't steal a priceless artifact from a museum."

"Why not?" Jay says leaning back in his chair. "It's not like you'd have to stuff it under your shirt, Professor. Give me a little bit more credit than that."

"We need this, Victor. We might be able to get Rachel back," I remind him.

"And that asshole Nile Donovan," Jay says. "His office released a statement that he's in the Arctic Circle hunting caribou and is unreachable. Washington called us this morning to look into his real whereabouts."

"See, Victor, this is getting to be beyond us. If we can end this now, don't you want to?" I ask putting the pressure on him. It's an unfair move, but I need him to be on board completely or the plan is never going to work.

He finally nods and returns to the slab of bacon on his plate saying under his breath, "This is really good."

"I shoulda been a chef," Jay says sighing. "I'd be Gordon Ramsay by now."

"You got a face for radio, Jay," I kid.

Jay holds up his index, middle and ring fingers and scoffs, "Read between the lines, dick." I have a good feeling this might actually work. Victor even cracks a smile.

Tetley's beer is tasty, but I haven't touched a drink in years. Jay's polishing off a second can. We're buried into his couch watching *Demolition Man* on the flat screen. Nothing like a good/bad action movie in the middle of the night. Victor's asleep in Jay's spare room.

Jay takes a long draft of beer and observes, "I wanted to bang Sandra Bullock for years."

"You and everyone else," I remind him. Neither one of us has the energy to sit up. I know I'm going to have to go and change the dressing on my shoulder eventually, but right now I watch lovely Sandra and her big smile light up the LCD screen.

"So, besides the obvious murder and mayhem how've you been?" Jay asks.

I have to crack a smile. He knows how ridiculous this situation is. "Not bad, Jay. Business could be better. Can't make much money when I'm on the run."

Jay sits up to the put the beer on the coffee table covered in old *Sports Illustrated*, *Daily Mirror*'s and a lone *Playboy* tucked in amongst the mess. "Why did you kill Joel Molitor?" he finally asks after a long pause. "I mean I'm sure he had it coming, but…"

Why did I kill him? I killed Jules Montgomery this afternoon. Did I kill Rhodes when I hired him? Did I kill Joel Molitor or did his greed and betrayal kill him? I'm to blame for all of them and I can take it. I can take it. I think I can take it.

"He comes into the shop and kills this kid I had working for me. Shoots him right in the head. Then he asks me where to find Victor."

"Fucking Joel. I really hated that guy," Jay says. He leans back on the couch letting it process. I killed a guy we both knew, a sworn agent of the United States government. The leather is soft and conforming. My shoulder doesn't hurt much as I recline backward, readjusting my position. Who the hell am I?

"Stealing this thing, that's going to be easy. The hard part's going to be getting into Lucan's compound," Jay says thinking out loud.

"You agree with me, though, that's probably where they're holding them?" I ask.

"Logically, yeah. But if Lucan knows what's good for him, he'd be reading the writing on the wall. Scotland Yard's going to kick down his door any day. He should've hired some more competent thugs than those two winners who tried to get into the museum."

"Yeah, they were shitty poker players too," I add.

"You played poker with these guys?" he asks surprised.

"I had a goddam Royal Flush too. Would've won fifty G's." With that I get up from the couch and head toward the bathroom to attend to my shoulder, leaving Jay on the couch, dreaming about Sandra Bullock.

I had a dive instructor say to me once, *If you're still breathing, then you're ok*. It's meant to remind you to remain calm in tight spots, to keep focused underwater. No matter what happens down there, if you're still breathing, you're ok, you can address whatever the problem happens to be. That mantra repeats now as I'm standing in front of Jay's bathroom mirror, the bloody gauze of a used dressing in his sink, the hole in my shoulder, slowly seeping. Ski's stitch job wasn't bad, but for some reason, as I'm realizing, the wound just won't close.

Sweat. Breathing heavy now. The wound: some truth that wants to break apart before me. Why didn't I tell Rachel everything? Why can't I save her now? Beads are forming on my forehead. And now, I'm inside, completely consumed by subconscious fears and doubts. Images flash like a kaleidoscope: Pop, Rachel, my shop, shattered glass, Molitor and Rhodes dead, Jules Montgomery snapping backwards with exploding .38 rounds, me blasting off M4 rounds years ago like fucking Rambo.

Close your eyes, take thirty seconds and address the problem. Why am I feeling this way? Because someone you trust tried to kill you and the woman you love is being held captive. How can you fix this problem? Find Rachel and Donovan and end this madness. So, that's what you do. Make it happen.

"Make it happen," I say out loud. My shoulder, scalding with pain from the antiseptic I'm now rubbing in, reminds me I'm alive. I'm alive and still breathing. For any good SEAL, that's at least a start, a stepping-stone to solving the bigger issues at stake. New dressing applied. I can hear Jay Brown snoring in the next room. Hours now until we start the two phases of this plan. Steal a priceless historical artifact and then break in to a heavily fortified compound to find our friends. Nothing at all to worry about.

I'm still breathing.

[14]

The Astrolabe

The City of Oxford was built as a monument to education and all that can possibly be achieved through higher learning. There are thirty-eight colleges that comprise Oxford University. The oldest, University College, was established in 1249. The newest, Green Templeton College was endowed in 2008. This city and these buildings literally span the entirety of Western European history. I love the smell of Oxford. It's the smells of great libraries and great museums floating around in the morning breezes. With each windy turn, each twist of an alley, intrepid scholars and travelers find answers in places where they weren't looking. We left before dawn. Jay was pissed but still drove. You can't teach loyalty, even in one of the great halls of this city. Loyalty is found under duress. Where will you be when all the chips are in play? Jay Brown got his ass out of bed and drove to Oxford to help me steal an astrolabe. That's loyalty.

Turl Street runs parallel to Lincoln College, the collection of quadrangular buildings founded in 1427 and alma mater of my favorite novelist, John Le Carre. The cobblestones of Turl are awkward underfoot as I walk towards the entrance to the Covered Market and my eventual rendezvous with Jay and Victor at Brown's Diner, Jay's favorite greasy spoon and not just because it's his namesake. These folks make a better full English than Jay could ever dream to prepare. So, I left Victor devouring another round of rashers and farmer sausages and took a little reconnoiter over to the Pitt Rivers Museum.

The assistant curator, a burbling Oxford don named Plum, greeted me with an enthusiastic handshake, happy to welcome Victor Meek's emissary. "But, where is Professor

Meek?" he asked with rolling jowls. There was a tea stain on his tweed blazer and his portly frame and walk were vaguely Dickensian.

"Professor Meek is running a few moments late. He asked me to come by early and see that everything is arranged."

"Oh quite right. Very good. You know we had a break-in attempt two nights ago, which is why you saw the extra security downstairs. " Plum said with a bluster. "Not sure what they were after, poor chaps," he says with a hint of pity, "but now we're not taking security lightly." I know what they were after and part of me wanted to spill everything to him. He would probably shriek in delight and ask to come along. This guy needed to get out of that museum, but instead, I noded politely at the unfortunate incident and then followed him as he led me back into a modern conference room with a locking door.

First, we had to wander amongst the endless rows of shelves and display cases all piled on top of one another. This museum is a maze of artifacts spanning the entire scope of human history. When you enter through the Natural History Museum, you naturally think that the Pitt Rivers will be laid out in the formality of its parent museum. It's anything but formal. It's an attic, garage sale, consignment shop and exotic haberdashery all mixed and molded together with modern glass cases and a metal detector at the door. A place for everything and everything, seemingly in its place.

There are no windows looking in to the conference room, which for us is a very lucky accident. There is a long bank of windows looking out on to the lane below. We were at the back of the building as Plum turned the key in the door and asked, "How is Professor Meek feeling after his accident?"

"He's doing well I think. His therapy is coming along," I replied. The simplicity of our plan: world-renowned medieval archaeologist Victor Meek was in a horrible traffic accident while on holiday in the Irish countryside. As such, he's confined to a motorized wheel chair for an unknown period of time. This is why there was no way for the Professor to use the normal artifact preservation room to view the astrolabe. He must have wheelchair access. A few calls before noon and Jay Brown had a wheelchair and a van waiting for us in Oxford. Victor had a little trouble with the controls at first, but he seemed to be getting the hang of it as I left to go scout the museum. Plum was happy when I nodded that room would suit the Professor's needs and as we shook hands at the metal detector I promised to return with Professor Meek. Plum, excitable, nearly burbled a yelp.

Inside Brown's Diner, the smell of stale cigarettes and bacon fat is the smell of salvation. It's the kind of place you go on the coldest day of the year to warm your insides. It sits in a little corner of the Covered Market and doesn't boast much room to maneuver. Getting Victor inside with the mechanical wheelchair was a chore in itself, which slightly embarrassed the grizzled Cockney owner working the griddle. He gave us a free pot of tea and promised to rearrange some tables.

The simple chime of the front bell echoes through the quiet diner. It's ten am now and most of the breakfast crowd has cleared out. The road crews will be by for a ploughman's lunch or a few fried eggs in a couple of hours. Victor looks up from the table readjusting himself in the mechanical chair. Pretending to be handicapped is certainly making him uncomfortable and rightly so, but it's the only way we're going to get this artifact through those metal detectors.

"What took you so long?" Jay barks. "I've pissed three times from all the tea we drank."

"It's all set," I say. "You save me any breakfast?"

"No. This guy ate it all." Jay says pointing to Victor.

"When I'm nervous, I eat," Victor says. I do my best to suppress a laugh.

Minutes later, Jay maneuvers the van in front of the Natural History Museum, which allows access into the Pitt Rivers. The streets are busy, as is normal on a typical workday. The University's are almost done for the term and we saw more than a few dons out walking in robes. No sign of men with guns, which is always a plus.

The mechanical device easily lowers Victor on to the ground on the curb and he looks at me, scowling. I see him mouth, "I hate you."

"Not my fault, Professor. You should've been more careful driving," I say trying to make light of this situation, even though it's no joking matter. Victor presses the joystick and swings the chair around three hundred and sixty degrees on the sidewalk, nearly running over a pedestrian. I slide the van door shut and look through the passenger side window at Jay.

"We'll be half an hour, tops."

"Take your time. I had nothing else to do today," Jay quips.

"You know what you're looking for?" I ask.

Jay glances quickly in the rear view mirror then out the two side windows, snapping mental pictures.

"The guy behind me at six in the gray Mercedes is cheating on his wife and trying to convince his girlfriend that he's actually going to bust up his marriage. Nine o'clock: two old bastards just stumbled out of the pub, probably the Eagle and Child and already have half a load on. Three o'clock: Victor's almost hit the Ten in the plaid skirt with the fucking wheelchair and ahead of me at twelve I'm just catching a glimpse of plaid skirt's ass and I must say I want to shove my head in there with a lamp to get a better look."

Sure enough, I glance around to each position and see the middle-aged man in the gray Mercedes slam down his cell phone, the two old codgers who had single malt for breakfast and Victor like Jay staring at the woman in the plaid skirt as she elegantly saunters past. Jay Brown: a master of his craft.

"Not bad. But Lucan's not going have 36Ds and wear a plaid skirt."

"If he looked like that, I'd want to fuck him too. Now, can you go and steal this priceless artifact so we can get the hell out of here? You have any idea how many laws I'm breaking today?"

"Six?"

"Yeah something like that. It's a fucking lot, that's all I know. Good luck."

"Thanks. Half an hour," I say stepping back and joining Victor on the sidewalk. He slowly moves the joystick forward and we make our way toward the museum.

"Professor Plum" as I now like to think of him is there to meet us as we check in at the metal detector. He reverentially shakes Victor's hand, intoning, "It's such a pleasure to meet you, Dr. Meek. I've read all your work."

Victor, ever the good sport, nods and says, "Thank you. It's my pleasure to be here. Thank you for scheduling this on such short notice. I've been looking forward to seeing the astrolabe."

"Not at all. Not at all," Professor Plum says turning to the security guard. He waves Victor and the wheelchair past the metal detector as I step through. Step one, not a problem. We press on.

Plum is talking a mile a minute as we move slowly through the museum to allow Victor's wheelchair to keep pace. The glass cases are filled with rows and rows of antique pottery, weapons and firearms. There's no order but disorder. I'm sure that the giant Alaskan totem in the corner has some reason to be in the same room with an antique washing machine, but for the life of me I can't figure it out. It's still a remarkable museum with many unbelievable pieces and I almost wish I had a few days to wander and get lost, but we've got pressing business in the conference room.

"Can I ask about your interest in the St. Clair astrolabe, Dr. Meek?" Plum says, probably waiting all morning to find the right time in his interaction with Victor to ask.

"Well, I'm not really sure yet," Victor replies. "We think it might have something to do with the early history of North America. Isn't that right, Dr. Rodriguez?" he asks looking up at me.

"Yes. That's the hypothesis," I say.

"Interesting, Interesting," Plum responds. "I believe the Lucan family – they're the ones who donated the piece some years ago – also feel the same way. In fact Lord Lucan, who is more known in notoriety than academia unfortunately these days, has put in a request to purchase the artifact back. Obviously, that puts us in a tight space as it were. We would like to be able to just give back the donated item, but hard times and all." He holds the elevator door and we move inside, Victor just barely fitting with the wheelchair.

Plum continues, "You obviously know that we've had trouble authenticating and dating the item, Dr. Meek."

"Yes, I was aware of that," Victor says. "Everyone seems set against Prince Henry's 1398 expedition from Orkney."

"Well, the old treasure hunter in me would love to believe it," Plum says puffing out his chest, "but the scientist in me just doesn't see it adding up. Too many questions see," he says looking at me. "Too many doubts surrounding the reasons. Risk versus reward don't you know. Why would the Templars, if they were even still in business, set out on a voyage like that when they were perfectly safe assimilating into the populations of Scotland, Scandinavia, Portugal and other such places?"

"How about the old story of Thorvald's Cross?" Victor chimes in, tipping his hand. Normally I would have ended the conversation there, but these two academics are hell bent on sparring.

"Oh the Vikings," Plum says as the doors open. "I love a story with the Vikings involved. Good for the soul. Those old plunderers explored every bit from here to Timbuktu and back again." We move out of the elevator and down the hallway towards the conference room. From the elevated catwalk I can see many of the display cases below. It's impossible not to be mesmerized by the sheer volume of acquired material in this museum; each piece a treasure in its own right, but none more important than any other.

"Would be quite a story if someone found Thorvald's tomb with Templar artifacts inside. Quite a story indeed," Plum quips. "That would certainly put the old establishment into the spin cycle. A few books would have to be rewritten. Lots of bruises to fragile egos. I'd love to be there for the show," he blusters a laugh.

"Indeed," Victor says with a hint of a smile as Plum holds the door to the conference room. Inside on the table sits a brass mariner's astrolabe. Victor's eyes light up. It's all that he was expecting and it seems, much more.

A normal astrolabe is a hanging device with intricate pieces to chart celestial alignments. Astrolabes have been used for centuries and were first thought be used for maritime directional latitudes in the late thirteenth century. The design of the mariner's astrolabe was modified to account for rough seas and resembled a go-cart steering wheel rather than a flat disc. They were made from heavy brass or other metals and usually had a ring in the top so that a captain or navigator could fix a point, line of sight, based off the noon sun and then calculate the latitude of the ship.

The St. Clair astrolabe as it sits before us on a strip of velvet is a weather-worn hunk of brass, and the only distinguishing factor that sets it apart from any other astrolabe in the museums collection would have to be the etched inscription on the outer ring. Victor is carefully examining the inscription with his pointer finger and sounding out the words, "*Aurora, Farsakh.*"

"Cryptic isn't it?" Plum says letting his jowls flop. "If you can figure out the significance of Persian and Latin characters on a medieval astrolabe belonging to a thirteenth century Scotsman then you've certainly cracked the case."

Victor looks up at me like as if he were caught in a maze. "I have no idea what to make of this," he says.

I put a hand on his shoulder, "Perhaps if you had a few moments alone with it you might find some inspiration?"

"Yes, yes, of course," Plum chimes in. "Dr. Rodriguez, let's step out and give the Professor a moment to himself. How's a half an hour, Dr. Meek?" He took the bait and is agreeing with the idea. Perfect.

"Fine, fine," Victor says, still a bit shaky.

I give Victor a nod of encouragement as Plum and I walk toward the door. I can't have him getting cold feet now. He's standing at the altar and the bride is walking down the aisle. Too late to back out without violent consequences. Plum gives me a backslap in the doorframe and says, "Have you ever seen a real shrunken head?"

"No. Can't say as I have," I respond with slight reluctance.

"Well old boy, today's your lucky day."

The way Victor recounts his time in the conference room begins with the twenty or so minutes he spent intricately going over every nook and cranny on the astrolabe, forgetting that in order to pull this off he would have to pop open the compartment on the side of the wheelchair and replace the astrolabe with the five pound plate we had stashed inside. He would wrap the plate in the velvet wrapping that covered the actual artifact and claim to have become ill upon our return at which point I would whisk him out of the museum without stopping to smell the roses.

I hear him curse, "Dammit" from outside the door as Plum and I knock and he quickly responds, "come in!" I've just returned from half an hour of mummified cannibal heads and ceremonial Mayan obsidian knives used to jab a shaman in the dick so he could experience euphoria. Fascinatingly painful.

I've now got even money that he caught a finger on the side compartment while scrambling to make the switch. He lost track of time and just barely got the velvet covering on the five-pound weight. Before I can even get a sentence out he croaks, "Dr. Rodriguez, we need to leave right now."

"What's wrong, Dr. Meek?" I ask playing along.

"I'm not feeling at all well," he says with a little more fervor.

"Well then, let's get you out of here," I say as Victor begins to wheel past and out the door. Plum, like I suspected, follows Victor without even bothering to look under the velvet for the now stolen astrolabe.

Plum, eager to inquire, grills Victor about his conclusions all the way down and as the elevator door opens Victor finally responds, "Well, I have seen it before and each time it gets all the more interesting but truthfully, I really have no idea what its significance is, if any." He looks up at me with a coy grin. He's on to something. Maybe that half hour really did jog something loose.

The rows of display cases stretch out in endless length and depth. This last great pathway is where we must navigate in order to complete the mission. Museum patrons mill about. The Alaskan totem in the far corner looks down on us menacingly, the orca judging our crime. I don't notice at first, but two men move past on the opposite display case near the Zulu spears. It's the shoes that give them away and force me to glance up. The click clack of expensive soles on the museum floor is the sound of violence.

Manuel and Omar, Lucan's Venezuelan mercenaries are scanning the rows looking for us. They're the same idiots from the Harrah's debacle and I freeze as our eyes lock. Omar curls a smile on to his lips while Plum and Victor keep talking, unaware of the danger that just manifested in this museum.

I move fast and they follow up the opposite row. When we reach the foyer, they'll be right next to us and I'm going to have to make a decision. I see Omar reaching in his pocket. Could he have gotten a gun past security? Steps closer now. Moving at 30 frames per second, somewhere a camera assistant is pulling focus. I don't want to be in this movie.

Plum and Victor stop at the doorframe.

Omar and Manuel impeding any further progress.

Plum inquisitively: "Can I help you find something gentlemen?"

My fist sprawling forward towards Manuel's face. Then the pepper-spray. Omar's plastic bottle, undetectable it seems to the museum's security, blasts me into a searing hellhole of horror. I swing wildly and hear Plum' s voice rise three octaves as Manuel falls over Victor sending the wheelchair tipping to the side.

I scream from the anguish of the pepper-spray as Omar punches me in the gut.

If you're still breathing, you're ok.

Still breathing. Address the problem. Fight through the pain.

"Run Victor!" I yell and whirl around with my left fist connecting with Omar's jaw bone. Shaky focus and now I'm tackled by Manuel who sends two punches down on my scalding face. Then someone pulls at Manuel. I catch the smallest glimpse of Victor coming to my aide. Plum screaming, "Professor, you can walk?!"

Kicks. I kick. They kick. And I remember at drill instructor at Coronado spraying Mace in my face and screaming, *Embrace the pain Rodriguez! Fight through it!*

I've been sprayed by this shit before. I can beat it. I can overcome it. Push yourself up. Bad shoulder, more pain. Then another punch. A one two combination from my wild fists and I can see a blazer fall backwards into an artifact case. I hear whistles and a security alarm. My arm grabbed and held and now I'm running. Trying to rejoin the world of sight. Visions blurry against the glasz backdrop. Blue, green and grey. Glasz. Breton word. How the hell did you remember that? Now some red and then yellow. Keep your feet moving. No sounds. My ears ringing. The two punches from Omar. Lips now bleeding.

Light. Air. Tossed into the cab of a van.

Jay's voice: "That went well, huh?"

Screeching tires. Black.

Glass raining down like snowflake shards. "Rik, get up!"

My head rises, eyes puffed out like toasted marshmallows and then a gun falls in my lap. Then a water bottle. Then I hear the shots.

"Rik, would you please shoot back at these cocks!" Jay yells, now weaving through traffic. I'm trying to see. I feel for the water bottle cap, unscrew it and upturn its contents on to my incensed and irritated eyes, the water: a crystalline medicine. Blink now and see what's happening. I can see Victor, head down on the backseat next to me. The back window is blown out and a Mercedes is behind us. It's like looking through wax paper, but I can make out the chiseled jaw of Kristoph the Dane leaning out the driver's side window and shooting at the van. Bullets are clinking around. Why doesn't Kristoph just shoot our tires? Because Jay is weaving so much I feel like I'm back on the *Gina Marie* during a storm.

"Rik, a little help please! This mercenary douche is starting to piss me off!" Jay yells, breaking and then turning on to the High Street. People everywhere. Oh shit. End this now.

I feel the Glock in my hand. It's heavier. Probably a 21. Jay's Agency issue, but instead of the 9mm it feels like a .45. He probably calls it a plastic piece of shit, because that's what it can be sometimes. The symphonic ringing in my ears quiets as I drop the safety back on the gun. Through the film of the wax paper haze, I see the target and squeeze the trigger once, twice and then successive bursts, blasting holes into the Mercedes windshield. Definitely a .45 just by the sound of the report. Thirteen squeezes empties clip. The screech of German breaks and then the grinding of metal as the Mercedes flips on its side. Busted glass on the High Street. Overturned vehicle. Don't know who's dead or alive. I slump over the back seat gritting my teeth as the pepper-spray reforms its attack pattern in my eyes and burns again, ablaze like the car on fire behind us, again and again and again.

[15]

E and E

Lucan's lackeys it seems are like apparitions. They waft in with the fog of uncertainty and disappear with the wind or a flurry of strategically aimed bullets. They have no motivation other than to kill or maim. Their purpose is singular: they must violently prevent us from finding whatever lies at the end of this list of disparate clues. I hope he's paying them well.

The smoke from Kristoph's overturned Mercedes is long gone with the mid-afternoon rain pelting Oxfordshire. We're eight miles away from the city center where the smoldering car wreck has hopefully been cleared. Rain falls on my upturned face, staring towards heaven, standing in the middle of Chaucer's Lane in the little town of Woodstock on the River Glyme. The scorching fire of my peppered eyes is slowly dissipating as each drop falls. Water, my salvation, always and forever.

"Rik, what do you want to do now?" Jay Brown, interrupting my cleansing baptism from the car window. The rain has soaked me through and through, but I have no cares anymore. If enough rainfalls, maybe it will wash us all back into the oceans, back from whence we came.

"Rik! Can you answer the goddam question? Time is not something we have a lot of here buddy."

"Rik, please," I hear Victor plead from the passenger side. But the rain keeps falling and I can hear only the drops on my face.

Victor salvaged the astrolabe. I'm not sure how he got it out of the wheelchair's side pocket, but he got it and hasn't let it go, even as he ducked low to avoid Kristoph's errant rounds. I wonder if that Danish prick died in the wreck? I'm sure he did. If he survived, he's going to be pissed. All the more reason to stand here in Chaucer's Lane and wait for the flood.

"Rik," Jay says now shaking me out of my trance. I turn to catch his eyes and he sees mine. I can read the image off his face. He sees the hollow shell of a once promising PhD, pawnbroker, poker player, whatever I was yesterday and the day before. Now I'm just a killer. Cold-blooded and iced over.

"Rik, get back in the car man, come on. We've got to get out of here," he says through the pelting British rain.

"No. We're not leaving here, not yet. They're here." I point up to the sign on Chaucer's Lane that reads *Bingham 25 km* and the arrow that points east.

"We need a new plan, Rik. We can't get in there now. He'll be expecting us after we shot up half the city. Not to mention the fact that the bobbies have every inch of this country wired with closed-circuit cameras."

I nod. I hope Lucan is expecting us. I don't care much about the cops.

The sign for the liquor store on the corner is inviting and the warmth inside will be comforting. I brush past Jay and walk in there. My skin is clammy and my clothes are now clinging to my body. The bottle of 100 proof brandy in my hand feels natural. A few folded and wrinkled pounds on the counter top, a complimentary book of matches, a "Cheers" and I'm back out the door, back in the rain, back amongst the uncertainties ahead.

"Victor, get out of the van," I say. The Professor, puzzled, complies. Jay Brown looks me over and can see the next few moments playing out.

"Make the call, Jay. Get us some gear."

Jay spits out a few drops of rainwater and ducks under the awning furiously pounding numbers on his cell phone. He knows I'm for real. He knows that any simplistic ideas have disappeared. The time for creative problem solving is at hand. I glance around the deserted lane, unassumingly quiet. Everyone it seems has found their place on this rainy day. Everyone save the three of us.

Victor grabs my arm and forces me around. "What are you doing?" he asks.

But I don't answer. I know what has to be done. The van is not safe anymore. Jay, willingly or unwillingly is going to help me get into Lucan's compound in Bingham and I'm going to end this insanity. I'm going to trade the astrolabe for Rachel and Donovan. I really don't give a shit if he keeps Donovan, but if I get him out it'll be one less death on which to blame myself.

Brandy bottle: upended in the van and over the van. 100 proof, highly flammable liquid settling amongst the rain. Then the matches, lit carefully in my cupped hands. The whole packet sparking to life, then the arching toss and fire engulfing the van. Walking away now. Quickly humming an old Billy Joel song to myself.

It was always burning. Burning always. Chaucer's Lane now alive with a white van pyre sizzling and hissing in the rain.

When a mission goes awry any good Operator will tell you that the next phase is E and E, escape and evade. Finish the job and get the hell out of Dodge. Begrudgingly, Jay called in a favor and had a black SUV with an anonymous driver pick us up on the outskirts of Woodstock. The driver then pulled over, tossed Jay the keys and jumped into another sleek sports sedan that was appeared out of nowhere, a cleverly timed and precisely executed drop. The whole move was cinematically cloak and dagger until Jay cut a loud fart, destroying any trace of Ian Fleming hanging in the air replacing it with the sulfuric aroma of partially digested breakfast.

In the trunk, we found complete incursion kits, right down to the black grease paint, which neither one of us thought was necessary. The jump suits, utility belts, submachine guns, ammunition bandoliers and flash bangs seemed like quite enough firepower.

Jocking up again in the small bed and breakfast on Bingham's outskirts feels like putting on a wet bathing suit. It's uncomfortable and irritating, but it's better than swimming in your clothes. The BDUs are a little bit loose and the boots don't really fit, but it's the best I've got. We surprised the matron at the front counter when we blustered in with duffel bags and bought out all three of her rooms for the night. Thankfully, Jay had some Agency cash and she had no problem accepting a few Euros without asking questions.

Laid out before me on the bed is a HK MP5 submachine gun, two clips of ammunition, three flash bang percussion grenades and the black duffel bag from whence they came. I have to readjust the black cargo pants when I load up the flash bangs in the thigh pockets because the waist is too big. It wouldn't be the worst thing that's ever happened to me on a mission if my pants fell down, but it would certainly be up there. The brown belt from my jeans will have to stand in because the utility belt is proving to be too big as well. Hell with it, I'm wearing my jeans. I'll use the black vest pockets to hold the grenades and the extra mags. I don't need this kind of stress right now.

Victor knocks and barges through the door. Thankfully, I've made the switch before he lumbers in.

"Are you sure about this plan, Rik? I mean are you really sure, because I can see about fifty things wrong with this idea. I think we should just go to the police."

I button up and put the black vest on over my Pocket Aces tee shirt. My shoulder is still throbbing and I could use a shower and some ibuprofen, but unfortunately I've got a world-renowned medieval archaeologist in my face asking me questions.

"Have I gotten you killed today?" I finally respond.

"No," he replies slightly sheepish, "but that doesn't mean today went smoothly! We stole a priceless artifact, shot up Oxford and then set a van on fire twenty yards from Geoffrey Chaucer's house. It's been a bit of a mess if you ask me."

"I didn't ask you."

"Well, maybe you should have, you pain in the ass." He's getting agitated now. I should have rethought my previous comment, but instead I shout back:

"Would you rather be dead right now? Because the minute you told them everything about your theories and deciphered that astrolabe they would've put two in your skull, if you were lucky!"

"You always think you know better, don't you? It's that stubborn, pigheaded Jersey boy that never wanted to hear criticism or any kind of feedback. Rik's way or the highway," he blusters.

"Did you just come in here to break my balls and tell me this is a bad idea or did you actually have something to say?" Now, I'm pissed and without thinking I pick up the MP5 and slide the lever back to open the mechanism, checking to make sure there's no round in the chamber, but Victor jumps back, visibly frightened as if I were pointing the gun at him. His face has a mixture of shame and fear blended with the anger of being completely out of control.

"Victor, it's not loaded," I say calmly putting the gun back on the bed. "I was just checking the mechanism."

The space between us has been compromised and I can see it in his face, in his body language. He's seen the other me over the last two days. He's seen his worst fears through me. I'm just glad I never had to see this look on my father's face. I don't think I would have recovered.

"You know," he begins, "I didn't realize how grateful I am to know you until just now." Not what I was expecting. Then he continues, "I also didn't realize how afraid I am of you until just now." He turns to the door and then turns back.

"Find Rachel. Do whatever it is you do. And don't get killed. I left my credit cards in Dublin. I won't be able to get home."

Victor exits gingerly. His last few words spoken in the choked up staccato fashion of a man chewing back his own emotion as if it were a T-bone steak. His departure now finds me alone with a bed full of gear on loan from the CIA. I repack the weapons in the black duffel bag, stewing a bit from Victor's disapproval. The bag is heavy with all the gear, but I sure can't walk downstairs with an MP5 slung over my shoulder. Wouldn't be proper.

I know that the next person to walk through the door will be Jay telling me that it's time. I owe him for this. He could've been enjoying a day off. Instead, he's helping me break and enter, a B and E. Hell, it could be worse. The treasure could be fake and the story a hoax; all this killing for nothing. How many lives for gold and secrets? Too many so far.

A knock on the door. Jay's annoyed voice: "Rik, hurry up. We've got to go get this horrible plan started and then shoot some bad guys in the face." Hopefully, the matron downstairs ignored his booming voice and off color humor. If not, we'll have some explaining to do on the way out the door.

Usually before a mission like this, any trained Special Forces operator will do three things. The first is to study the mission plan in great detail so that he could draw every maneuver and paint a schematic of any and all buildings he will enter. The second thing is to check and double-check all of his weapons and equipment. The third thing is take a shit. Second and third things done, but we're going into Bingham Castle completely blind. We couldn't even find a gift shop map this afternoon.

The sun has set. Hopefully, Victor is sitting in the little room back in the bed and breakfast translating the words on the astrolabe that he gingerly copied down. I've got the hunk of brass in the duffel that is now snugly strapped to my back. From our vantage point in an oak cluster we can see Bingham Castle below in all its splendor. It's front-lit by big arching lamps. The grounds stretch back for miles. The high stonewalls were laid by some ancient stonemasons long ago. The flying buttresses and winding towers make for a fascinating composition. The only elements that take away from the charm are the huge satellite dishes perched on the battlements. Hopefully with all those electronics up on the roof he's at least picking up the NFL Sunday Ticket. Seems like a shame to waste all that communication gear on illegal activities and whoring out violence to the highest bidder.

Jay, true to operational form, is chewing a big piece of bubble gum. He blows a bubble that sticks to his nose and wriggles it to free the gum. He's already commented twice that it "looks too easy" and in fact he's right. We haven't seen any kind of activity in an hour. There's no sign of guards or any kind of security. There's two big black SUVs parked in the front of the turnabout, but nothing else. No light are on inside the castle at least as far as we could make out. The chimneys aren't showing any signs of life either.

I turn to Jay and whisper, "What do you think?"

He shrugs and whispers back: "Either we go in there and check it out or we stay out here."

"That's all you got? Most of your adult life running covert operations and you're giving me a coin flip."

He contemplates for a moment and then says: "I'm leaning towards going in. I really gotta piss."

"Piss out here."

"It's cold," he says completely serious.

I shake my head and turn toward the castle. The safety switch on the MP5 is palpable under my thumb and I find myself nudging it off. The loading mechanism is in my hand now and I slide the first round into the cylinder.

"I guess, we're going," Jay whispers seeing me lock and load. "Remember the car's two miles back. We're going to have to run like hell coming out. I know you're old and decrepit. Just try and keep up." He jumps up and moves out of the trees. I scoff and follow along, slowly hugging the ridgeline, each step a big closer to the inevitable confrontation with this megalomaniacal prick who seems hell-bent on acquiring a treasure that may not even exist. The astrolabe bounces in the duffel as we press forward through the field grass that separates the oak grove with the castle wall. We finally duck next to the stone and wait for the spotlights to flash on the dogs to be loosed, but there's nothing. It's eerily quiet.

There's a gnarled apple tree near the side of the Bingham Castle wall. The limbs were bent and wrenched over the wall like the arms of a fairy tale witch. It made easy climbing, even though Jay nearly slipped on some lichen. He caught himself, cursed and lost his gum in the process, a bad omen for any operation. We eventually jumped over the wall and inside the compound and still not a lick of movement anywhere.

We're on the east side of the castle. The lights on the south side are vivid. There's a part of me that wants to just bust through the front door and see what happens, but I almost feel like those lights are the fluorescent dots and lines of a giant monster that lulls its prey with the beauty of the lights and then devours it whole. Jay has run around to the north side to see if he could find an entrance, but from my kneeling position, gun poised toward the south side entrance, I can hear him stepping back. I turn my head and stand up to see him shaking his head, "no". Front door it is. Doesn't matter if it's messy. There's no simple way to break into a castle keep except breaking down the door. Good thing Jay brought along some C4.

We sprint around towards the front, our boots now audible on the gravel. I turn my gun around quickly covering the whole area as Jay slaps on a strip of C4 to the heavy oak door. This thing is going to be loud, but it's not going to matter once we're inside. Thermal goggles wouldn't have even worked on this op because the castle walls were presumably too thick. Blow the door then sort it out.

Jay rigs up the detonator quickly like a cowboy tying down a calf in a rodeo. We move quickly out of the way, hugging the wall on either side of the door. Jay counts down, one, two, three on his fingers then hits the trigger. The door blows outward with a spectacular rain shower of shards and we quickly move through, the lights and lasers of our MP5s moving up and through every corner. The blast is ringing throughout the entire cavernous inside. The castle must have been refurbished in the Victorian era because the main foyer has high vaulted ceilings and a crystal chandelier, now damaged by the explosion. To the left is a grand parlor and I make a quick sweep of the room with my gun poised at the ready. Jay has checked the drawing room on the right. The staircase in front of us bisects two hallways. I point left and Jay takes the right.

Oil paintings line the walls as dull moonlight floods the hallway from an unidentified window. In front of me a curtain in front of a doorway is fluttering. I make my way there cautiously. The curtain flaps up and I feel a breeze from outside. Moving the curtain aside I see the palace ballroom and there, sitting back to back in the middle of the room are Rachel and Donovan. The moon is bathing the room with paranormal white light. The double doors leading out to the garden are open. The high hedgerow must have prevented Jay from seeing this way in. We're in now and to my right I see Jay move in to the ballroom, but I'm already running towards Rachel.

She's blindfolded and gagged. Donovan looks like he's in rough shape. I can see the blood on the corners of his mouth. But Rachel is priority number one. She shakes, startled as I fall to my knees in front of her. The gag muffles her scream and I pull off the blindfold, once again meeting her eyes, sleep-deprived and bloodshot. She lights up and I pull down the gag.

"You're alive!" she shrieks.

"I'm alive," I say fighting with her restraints. The rope knots are simple, too simple it seems. And a few flicks of a utility knife frees them from their captivity. Jay pulls up Donovan who moans deeply.

"They broke his ribs this afternoon, for sure," she says helping Donovan up. "He may be bleeding internally. They haven't been back for hours."

Then the world lights up and from above, the balcony that I hadn't seen on the way in becomes a flurry of life. Men who I don't recognize, ten of them in fatigues, lean over the railing and point custom AK-47s down at us. Rachel screams. Jay and I kneel and our lasers move around the balcony like frightened red fairies. We have no idea where to aim. Then I hear a familiar voice bark, "Hold your fire." Lucan steps forward. He's wearing a tan field jacket and black cargo pants. His silver hair and sadistic face appears over the railing as his minions part.

"Dr. Rodriguez," he begins, "You don't mind if I call you 'doctor' now do you? I believe you've earned my respect over the last few days. You're proving very difficult to kill." His voice is still dripping with sinister sarcasm. He missed his calling. He should be on a stage somewhere playing Iago. From this vantage point, he's genuinely terrifying.

Donovan burbles, "I'll pay him. Whatever he wants." Rachel hugs him tight.

"What was that, Mr. Donovan?" Lucan asks slyly.

"He said he'll pay you," I retort, "but I think it'll be easier if I put one through your skull right now."

"Give me the word and we rock and roll," Jay says breathing heavy. "I'm taking at least five of these mercenary fucks with me."

"Why don't you tell your friend to unwind himself?" Lucan quips. "We both know you're not going to shoot. I have the overwhelming chip lead, Dr. Rodriguez, right? No sense going all in when you're holding rags."

"Well, I know I'm putting one in your skull before I'm dead, Lucan," I retort trying to intimidate.

"Gentlemen I believe you came here to bargain," he says leaning farther forward. "You blew my door open so that we could discuss a trade, yes?" And then I see it, hanging from his neck. The amulet supposedly the first or second or third or just one of the many clues that leads to Thorvald's Cross.

"We'll trade, Lucan," I say staring through the sight on the MP5, taking a bead on the amulet hanging on a rope around his neck. I feel Rachel's hand on my shoulder.

"What are you doing?" she asks probably concerned that I might do something crazy. I pull the duffel bag with the astrolabe over my shoulder with one hand, still keeping the MP5 raised with the other, my finger still on the trigger. The duffel slides across the waxed floor with little effort.

145

"There's your astrolabe. Now we walk," I say. Rachel's eyes go bright.

"You got it?" she whispers.

"Stole it. Now let's go." I begin to slowly ease backward toward the open ballroom door. Jay follows. Rachel and Donovan are already shuffling out.

"Dr. Rodriguez," Lucan says full of contempt. "Don't you want to know what this amulet says?" He's holding up the simple stone piece and my eyes are fixed on it through the sight on the MP5. We're almost out, but I stop. I see all the machine guns ready to fire on us and yet the lure of something, treasure, history, enigmatic puzzles of the past has frozen me in my tracks. My mind is screaming to turn and run, but I can't. I can't think clearly.

"You do, don't you?" Lucan says, a smile curling on his lips.

"Rik, forget that. Let's go," I hear Jay whisper.

"Go," I say.

"Rik, forget it. It's nonsense," Rachel pleads breathlessly. I start to step backward again.

"It says *Fire of Ragnar*, Dr. Rodriguez. And it's carved in Anglo-Saxon futhorc. This amulet," he says holding it up, "was given to my ancestor Stephen St. Clair by a Narragansett chief. Ragnar Thorgillsson married into Leif Eiriksson's line. Did you know that? He was made the Vinland Sentinel and knew the location of Thorvald's tomb and all the wealth of the Greenlanders. The Templars wanted to start a new colony there on the foundations of this great line of kings."

"I don't care," I say.

"Yes, you do," he pauses. "You love the idea of treasure. These academics, these professors, they don't understand the lure of adventure. The smell of death and gold. The ghosts of the men who came before you. It's better than any mortal feeling. You *know*, Rik. You know the feeling."

Fire of Ragnar, *Armor of Ragnar*, the clues to this thousand-year-old murder mystery. A dead Vinland chieftain. Thorvald and Ragnar then Prince Henry Sinclair and the possible location of Viking and Templar treasures. Where do all these images earn the right to swirl around in my head and cloud my decision-making? I want to focus and can't. I want to run but I need to know.

"Why don't you join me, Rik? Why don't we all find this treasure together? I know you have an idea. I know you and Dr. Meek have already formulated hypotheses. Let's act on them. Let's find all that money and share it. What do you say?" Lucan's words are like a dull knife in my heart. How could he even entertain the thought that I might join him? It sickens me. The only solace is knowing what's about to happen. Jay hears it too. Wailing sirens.

Lucan's sordid past is finally catching up with him. He did business with the wrong corrupt government and now Scotland Yard is breaking down his gate. I reach down on to my belt and hurl a stun grenade in a high arch towards the balcony. It bursts with a blinding flash and I hear the bullhorns of the police shouting orders to "cease" and "desist". I slide forward, grab the duffel with the astrolabe and jump through the ballroom doors as the glass explodes with gunfire behind me. Jay, Rachel and Donovan are making their way forward but Donovan struggles. I run next to him and in one motion toss him over my shoulder in a fireman's carry. He moans in pain, but I keep moving. Behind me the dull snaps of AK rounds quiet, replaced by the thumping reverb of Scotland Yard sirens.

We run away, embraced by the night.

[16]

No Rita Hayworth

I'm afraid of myself sometimes. I'm afraid that I won't be able to choose inaction when all I've ever been taught requires me to act. I'm caught up in the haze of violence and gold, but all I want to hear is the faint burbling of Nile Donovan draped over my back as we run through the fields adjacent to Bingham Castle.

Rachel and Jay have run ahead. I'm slowly plodding along through the tall grass and Donovan is deadweight on my shoulder. I finally hear him bark, "Stop. Stop, Rik."

"Can't stop," I respond, sweat collecting on my forehead.

"I need a phone," he cries, "I can get us out of here."

We reach the oak grove that Jay and I had used for recon and I gingerly place Donovan down on the ground. Rachel kneels next to him, brushing the hair out of his face. Jay stands up, panting under the weight of the gun and the utility vest. "I hate running," he gasps.

In the distance, the lights and sirens of Scotland Yard have encircled the castle. We've got minutes until the helicopters arrive. We'll have to move quickly. Donovan coughs, his midsection must be aching terribly.

"Does anyone have a phone?" he croaks. "I need a mobile."

Jay takes a compact cell out of the front pocket of his vest. Rachel, still working off adrenaline, is speechless. Donovan lets out a sigh and slowly dials.

"Nile Donovan. KL5717. I need a pickup at," he covers the phone and turns his head to us, "where's the nearest airport?"

Jay thinks for a moment then remembers: "London/Oxford in Kidlington. It's a business aiport."

Nile returns to call, "I'll need a G5 or better at London/Oxford airport in Kidlington, Oxfordshire. Yes. Yes. Three passengers,"

"Four," I interject remembering Victor waiting for my call at the inn a few miles away.

"Right, Right. Four passengers. To the United States. Teterboro, NJ. Thanks." He hangs up. "Rik, is your friend flying with us then?"

I look at Jay. He laughs, "Unfortunately, I've got to be at the Embassy tomorrow to explain our little escapade tonight."

"You won't be in the shit I hope?" Donovan responds

"I'm always in the shit. Just another Monday morning." He turns to me. "Call Victor and tell him to come get us the fuck out of here."

"Victor's here? He's flying back with us?" Rachel asks.

"He's pouring over the inscription on the astrolabe as we speak," I say with a hint of a smile. It's dark but I can see the excitement on her face. I'm sure for the first time in days, Rachel is remembering the possibility of an extraordinary historical discovery. We're close. And hopefully, Lucan will be rotting in jail when we find whatever treasures wait in a sealed off cave somewhere on the Eastern seaboard.

Donovan tosses me the phone. There's audible elation in Victor's voice, when he picks up the call. He's on to something.

Donovan's pissed that they didn't send a Gulfstream 5. All his private transport service could muster was a G450. Still, the G450 is quite luxurious and not to mention these corporate concierge services are known for not asking questions. We're beaten and bloodied, exhausted and sweat-stained when Victor drove into the airport and we were greeted on the tarmac by a uniformed captain and crew welcoming us aboard.

They were quick to arrive with the first aid kit. I wrapped Donovan's busted ribs with an ACE wrap and ice. Rachel quietly fell asleep next to him as we taxied away and Victor, heavily engrossed in his own mental process barely said two words to any of us except: "I'm almost there." I told him about *Ragnar's Fire* and he gingerly wrote it down in the notebook he's been keeping. It's full of wavy lines, arrows and more Xs and Os than a mockup on NFL Sunday. One more clue to this mystery, one more enigma to add to ever-growing list inside Victor's head. He's borrowed a laptop from the cabin crew and hasn't left a little alcove near the back of the plane except to request a double bourbon. He hasn't looked up since.

Saying farewell to Jay on the tarmac was certainly bittersweet. But, in typical fashion he slapped me on the shoulder and said, "We're even, dickhead." I nodded and he continued saying, "Keep your head down when you get back and for God's sake lawyer up." Then, as quickly as he appeared on the dock the day before, he stepped back into the shadows of the airfield and I assume was whisked away in an Agency ride back to London.

I'm certain to be arrested shortly after arriving back in Jersey. I'm going to have to call Ski soon and see exactly what I'm facing. I really don't want to know, but I know he's probably already called Kevin Shipley, my very expensive attorney and another fellow poker player. Shipley rivered trip Queens to my two pair in the World Series qualifier last year at Harrah's sending me home empty handed. Shipley won a seat in Vegas but lost all his chips on the third hand to Phil Ivey. He said it was an honor to give his chips to Ivey, but I still laughed at him.

I don't think he's going to charge me this time especially when he sees the security tape. I may have to give up that '69 Harley in my storeroom that he's been eyeing for months, but I haven't even gotten a nibble at auction so what the hell, it's only my freedom.

I see Donovan wince in the seat and try and readjust. He stands up and walks slowly toward me. I'm in the last row before the bathroom with my feet up between two seats and he nods silently as he steps past me into the bathroom. I want to hate him, but he did just arrange this escape flight and he seems to make Rachel happy. I still really want to hate him though. I scratch at my neck as I hear the toilet flush. I look up to see Victor punching keys furiously on the laptop. The vest I'm wearing is starting to itch and the handgun, a Glock that the Agency has kindly leant me indefinitely, is wedged under my leg. The holster clipped to my thigh has moved. I slide forward to readjust as Donovan emerges from the bathroom, visibly still in agony. He saw me move.

"You all right?" he asks, solemnly swallowing his own pain.

"Fine. How are the ribs?"

"Still broken," he says trying to crack a smile. And then, to my surprise, he sits down in the seat opposite me. "Thanks for coming for us."

"Of course. I couldn't," but I pause before I can finish the sentence. He reads my bad bluff.

"You couldn't leave her? That's what you were gonna say."

I nod, looking away for a split second.

"I understand, Rik. I'd always come for her as well." He pauses, meticulously moving his torso to avoid the searing hurt of his fractured ribs. Biting his lip, he continues, "I didn't expect for her to stay with me this long, you know?"

I do know. I hate that I know. But I'm not telling him that.

He goes on: "She's been the world to me. She's made me feel alive again. I've been spending the better part of the last few years justifying being alive. I've been trying to figure out some purpose. Why I'm here."

"What do you mean?" I ask, genuinely puzzled.

"Well," he starts and then pauses, I suppose trying to find the correct words. "I didn't really make any money till 2002. Stinger was just an idea and then people thought it was good one and then me screwing around with code gave me a winning ticket you see." Stinger data collation allows for super streamlined filing and indexing of complex variables. It's complicated and irritatingly obtuse, but every major corporation and government is using this software now, so go figure.

Donovan, however, speaks with no pretension. His voice is the same now as it was before he was in the Fortune 500. How do I know? Sometimes you can just tell. It's the voice of a kid from Belfast whose check got cashed. All the yachts and private jets in the world can't take that away from you if you always have it. It's genuine gratitude for success. Donovan's got it. It's still so impossible to hate this guy.

"Some people just get lucky. Or they bust their ass. Either way, you're doing pretty well," I say.

"I tell you, Rik, I've just been trying so hard to make it right, you know. I've been trying to give her everything. Because every goddam day is a gift."

"You take a seminar or something?" I ask, trying to bait him.

"No, Rik. No seminar." He takes a long breath. "I spent every day thereafter trying to live well and do something important and I got paid well for it."

"Thereafter what?"

"Do you remember where you were on 9/11?" he asks and I do. I was standing in the middle of Commonwealth Avenue two days into my junior year at Boston University when I was told that the Towers got hit. I got called back to active duty two days later. One month you're living in a dorm room eating late night chicken fingers and trying to understand Immanuel Kant and then two months later you're eating MREs and testing the categorical imperative with live ammunition. Yeah, Donovan, I remember where I was.

"Boston," I respond.

"I was in the World Financial Center. Got all banged up that day. Broke my arm, cut to shit. It was like a glimpse into hell. I don't know how I made it out. A fireman found me under busted glass and carried me out, just like you done tonight. From that day on, I tried to make a real impact. Tried to do the right thing."

A revelation. I really had no idea that he had been at Ground Zero.

"From what I read about you, seems like you've been doing right," I say.

"Just trying to. I've given away my share. But you know I, well, this thing with gold and the tomb, this is what keeps her going, you know? Him as well," he says gesturing toward Rachel's sleeping body and Victor's furious thought maelstrom. "They love this," he continues. "And I love her desperately. So much that it hurts. And so I'll do anything for her. And it appears so will you. In the end, well," he pauses, unsure of what to say next. He finally concludes his thought with a repetition, "in the end," he says and holds out his hand for me to shake.

In the end he wants me to know that he thinks it's been a fair fight. He's tried and he knows I'm now trying. All's fair in love and war and love and treasure hunting. It's a gentleman's move and Nile Donovan is certainly a gentleman. I shake his hand reluctantly. Rachel stirs and I see Victor stand up at his seat and yell, "I've got it!" Rachel's certainly awake now if she wasn't before.

Crowded around Victor's laptop, the astrolabe laying next him on the table, evidence of yet another crime for which I'm wanted, and all I can do is inhale the aroma of sweat and shampoo wafting off Rachel's pony-tailed hair. Victor elbows me, pointing at the screen; a picture of an ornately carved vase from Google Images is glowing on the LCD. The inscription is in Persian and shows one spice merchant pointing towards a citadel, directing a caravan.

"Rik, translate the inscription on the vase," Victor demands.

"What?" I retort. "It's in ancient Persian."

"You speak Persian," Rachel interjects. "You told me you did."

"I don't speak *ancient* Persian," I remind them. "And I can't even speak it very well. I can read a little."

"So read it then," Victor insists.

I lean toward the screen, irritated for being called out. I can understand rudimentary Persian, Pashto and Arabic: times, places, distances, *where's the bathroom?* Things like that. I very much doubt that I'm going to have any luck translating a piece of ancient Persian pottery, but I have a go. The characters look similar to modern characters. There have been changes to Islamic writing over the centuries, but nothing completely drastic. Arabic and Persian have morphed, but again nothing completely off the wall, not like Old and Middle English. The English language lost whole letters and sounds because early typesetters didn't want to spend extra money for the proper molds to put in the printing presses. Scanning the grainy image, I suppose it's not too terribly different. I start to read out loud slowly,

"Paths of enlightenment lead on towards the city of the Prophet. Three miles distance."

"Three miles distance," Victor says with elation.

"Farsakh," I say, "Farsakh means 'three miles' or approximately the ancient Persian equivalent. The word is still used today in rural areas." I've puzzled myself. Why didn't I pick up on this earlier? It was staring me right in the face. "I should've thought of that sooner."

He laughs and smacks my bad shoulder causing me to shudder.

"Yes, you should have. But, people were shooting at us, so I'll give you a pass. Three miles, Rik! That's the second part of this. Now, what about 'aurora'."

"Moon," I respond like student calling out.

"No," Rachel says. " 'Aurora' means 'east' if you take it in the original Latin context."

"Three miles east," Victor says proudly. "I spent all my time trying to figure out if it was an anagram or some type of coded message. It's just a simple directional instruction. Three miles east."

"Yeah, but three miles east of what? And remember the Persians didn't measure in miles, folks. This is a guesstimate at best. Whoever carved that inscription must have had something very specific in mind."

"Of course it's a guess," Victor says, visibly excited, "that's the point. The Templars didn't want anyone to just go looking for their treasure trove, that's why they carved it on the astrolabe. You have to take this thing to whatever place in New Jerusalem that they designated and measure along the exact latitude three miles east and then you'd have your treasure."

"Fantastic," I say, "the only problem is we still have no idea where New Jerusalem is and no idea where to measure from once we get there."

"We will when we find *Ragnar's Fire*," Rachel says making some vast mental connection across the stars and galaxies.

"What did he tell you, Rachel?" I ask, still curious as to the lost days they spent with Lucan.

"He didn't say much," Donovan responds. "Didn't tell us really anything until the night you found us and then he took us in separate rooms. His men beat the piss out of me and," he looks at Rachel, "what happened when they took you? You told me they didn't hurt you, but if they did, so help me."

"No, they didn't hurt me," she starts. Her face tells me different. Her face tells me there something she's not ready to disclose. "He just asked me about the excavations on Juniper Island. But, I didn't tell him anything. I really didn't tell him anything." She's almost convincing herself more than the three of us. She stands and begins to pace, her thinking posture, Donovan turns to her. She brushes him off. He hasn't learned yet to let her go when she wants to pace and think. He'll learn or she'll get rid of him.

"*Ragnar's Armor*, Victor. The armor from the Saga you translated," she reminds herself.

"The inscription in the Brazen Head was *Ragnar's Armor*," Victor begins, "and the Saga said that the location of Thorvald's Cross was etched on to the suit of armor belonging to the Vinland Sentinel. Ragnar Thorgillsson is the only known Vinland Sentinel," Victor concludes. All the cards are on the table now. Wheels are turning inside all of their heads trying to find out the clue they've overlooked, the missing word, phrase, adverbial clause, anything to tie *Ragnar's Fire* and *Ragnar's Armor* together.

"Ok, so hear me out," I finally say breaking the ice. Rachel turns with a look of mistrust on her face. "What does the site Juniper Island look like?"

She looks confused. "It's a waterfront area. We found tools and skeleton beams for a longship. We found a few stones carved with the hooked X but we're not ready to go public with it yet, mostly because the land is privately owned and we've been given special permission, but also, I have no idea who was using it. If it was Ragnar's then we should have found some other elements on the island, like a keep or a storehouse. Something like L'Anse aux Meadows in Canada."

"In all likelihood it was Ragnar," Victor says. "He's the only one we have operating in Vinland at that time."

"What happened to him?" I ask with a smirk on my face. The idea is so simple it's practically comical.

"We don't know," Rachel says.

"He disappears from historic record," Victor adds. "Most likely, he died in Vinland like Thorvald. The Vikings had mixed reactions from the Native Americans. He may have died in battle. He may have just died of natural causes."

I stand up smiling. "So, if you're in Ragnar's camp and your leader dies and you're far away from any sort of supplies or any form of communication, what's the next logical step?"

"You leave," Rachel says.

"Exactly. But what do you do with Ragnar?"

"Well, he's not a Christian. I know that from the manuscript in Uppsala," Victor says. "Most likely they'd build a vessel and set it ablaze."

I let it register with them. Donovan is the first to speak, "A goddam Viking funeral! *Ragnar's Fire!*"

"Have you made any dives around the island?" I ask Rachel.

"No," she says lighting up. Victor claps his hands together.

"The Vinland Sentinel would want to go to Valhalla with his armor on," I say locking eyes with her. She looks at me with a mixture of elation and sarcastic destruction of ego. Good job. Don't let it go to your head.

157

"Well then," she says as Victor nearly skips over to the bar to fix he and Donovan a celebratory drink, "I guess we'll have to go diving again."

"I guess we will."

Teterboro Airport is owned by the Port Authority of New York and New Jersey. It's twelve miles from Manhattan and most of its traffic is made up of corporate executives flying in on the very same type of Gulfstreams that we are currently using. The taxi toward the hanger is slow and measured. Calls were made from satellite phones and Rachel has already arranged for the joint archaeological teams from the Lake Champlain Maritime Museum and Middlebury College to be ready with dive crews when she arrives back to the site.

I called Ski. He didn't pick up. I left him a long message, trying to apologize for my many transgressions over the last few days. I hope he gets it and I surely hope he called Shipley. I've never been arrested. I don't want to start today, but if in the event I do end up in the clink, I'm confident in Shipley's ability to negotiate. I killed Molitor. I fled the country. I'm FFL, but perhaps, just perhaps I might make it out of this. I might be able to go back home to my shop on Morris Avenue right on the edge of the Boardwalk. I might be able to go back to sleepless nights in deep hollows, symphonic with shuffling checks and the raises and calls of the intrepid Texas Hold 'em vigilantes out for their own brand of justice with suited Aces and small pocket pairs. And then again, I could spend the rest of my life in jail.

The dawn hasn't broken yet in Teterboro. It's easy to make out the first whirling flash of police lights through the cabin window. Donovan, Rachel and Victor all lean out to see the armada of State Police cruisers waiting near the hanger as the Gulfstream settles. The engine shuts down and then all is quiet. A flight attendant opens the hatch door and I see the first Suit step through. "Special Agent Dan Desplaines," he says, emphasizing the "Dess" in "Desplaines". He continues, flashing a badge, "FBI. I'm looking for Rik Rodriguez."

I'm not moving. I'm simply letting it all be in my seat. I take a deep breath and answer his question, "I'm Rik."

"You're under arrest for manslaughter," he says matter-of-factly. The silver in his hair makes him look wiser and more experienced than I imagine him to be. Looks are deceiving.

"I've been told that I won't have a problem with you. Your lawyer's already contacted us." His hand moves to the Beretta on his hip. His eyes are locked on the pistol still holstered to my leg.

"I'm going to take this gun out and put it on the ground, Agent Desplaines. Ok?" I respond, trying to control the situation with calm. My compatriots have said nothing. I see Rachel's face as the whirl of lightbars from cruisers outside illuminate and then darken her timorous face.

"Slowly," Desplaines responds.

I comply, resting the Glock on the seat opposite to mine. Desplaines still stands like a wound spring near the door. He's controlling the scene, always keeping the door at his back. He takes a pair of handcuffs out of his pocket.

"Do I need these?" He asks. "You want to surrender under your own accord?"

I nod and stand up. His hand is still on the gun. I walk slowly towards the plane door. Victor and Rachel are both frozen in their seats.

"I'll be all right." I say, trying to be reassuring. "Find the armor," I say to Rachel.

She holds back some sentiment, simply taking my hand as I walk past. The touch is enough to electrify my soul. The silence around is deafening. There is nothing left of the mechanics in the plane. Near the door I hear the faint crackle of a police radio. With Desplaines behind me, I step through the plane door into the blinding spotlights of the New Jersey State Police and FBI. There are more lights and electrical gadgets than a Pink Floyd concert. They're all poised on the plane. Troopers with shotguns and automatic weapons are standing at the ready, just in case, me, the terrifying ex-SEAL suspect decided to pull a Butch Cassidy. I suppose in some twisted way, it's nice to see that my tax dollars are being put to good use.

The Turnpike Barracks just redid their holding cells. They don't smell like piss yet and I'm almost positive I won't catch hepatitis from the cots. The vinyl-wrapped foam is actually comforting when I let myself realize I haven't slept a full night in days. The darkness of the concrete and the metal bars are slightly disconcerting. I know I've slept in worse places, but I don't think I want to get used to it. All they have to do is make an arrest.

When Desplaines led me into the interrogation room a few hours earlier, he made it very clear that they had an ironclad case against me. The Atlantic City Police Department had handed over the case to the FBI shortly after my departure. The Stateys have been kind enough to allow Desplaines to hold me in their Barracks over night.

I responded: "I did it. You have my security tape."

Desplaines sat down, with a notepad open in front of him. I didn't want this to turn into the classic interrogation scene. I was too tired and completely uninterested. Shipley walked in with a bluster yelling, "Rik, don't tell him anything."

"You must be Kevin Shipley," Desplaines responded. "I recognize you from the billboard on the Atlantic City Expressway." It was true, Shipley, against any and all advice put up an obtrusive billboard on the AC Expressway. It's tacky, but he claims his business tripled. I don't buy it.

"Rik, you didn't tell them anything?" he said sitting down, thumping a briefcase on the metal table.

"Yeah, Kevin. I did it. They know I did it," I said.

"Jesus, Rik, what's the matter with you?" he blusters. His speech is staccato and he moves around with a highly caffeinated gusto. He's a damn good trial lawyer. He drinks too much Red Bull when he's playing cards. Always bad to have trembling hands when you make a bet, but again, he never listens to me.

"Gentlemen, if I may," Desplaines began, "I have something I need to put on the table."

"Keep it in your pants, Agent Desplaines," Shipley nearly shouted, "you've got a suspect under duress. You pulled him off a plane. He's not in his right mind. This interview is over."

"I think you need to hear what I have to say." His blue eyes were calming, but the square of his jaw combined with his silver hair gave him the menace of a timber wolf. "I have something to offer you here, Rik."

"I'm listening," I said.

He motioned to the two-way glass divider and another agent stepped in and handed him a file folder. He opened the folder and spread out some pictures on the metal table. The horrific nature of the images reminded me of scenes from a slaughterhouse. The body, dismembered and torn to bits lay scattered all over a room. Blood soaked the walls and it seemed that whoever this was had been destroyed by an unholy monstrosity bent on chaotic retribution.

"These are the crime scene photos from Leonard Leanos's house," Desplaines said. I flashed back to Leanos's twitchy face, standing across my counter, anxiously waiting for me to count out the two thousand he got for the chest, Rachel's treasure chest.

"Lucan told me he 'took care' of Leanos," I said.

"Agent Molitor was there and probably participated," Desplaines retorted. "Between you, me, and your lawyer, Joel Molitor was crooked as a soft pretzel. When you killed him though, you destroyed any chance of us or any other Agency making a case against Matthias Lucan."

"Lucan got arrested last night," I said. "Scotland Yard was in his house after we got Donovan and Rachel out."

"That's what Mr. Donovan and Dr. Hexam told us as well. But, the only problem is, Scotland Yard never got him. He vanished. Gone before they could make an arrest."

My stomach sank. "Not possible," I said. "They had the place surrounded. How the hell could he have gotten out?"

"Not my problem, Rik. My problem is we've got an international fugitive wanted for murder in the US and corruption and perjury in the UK and we have no idea where he's heading. But, we think you and your friends do. This treasure you're after, the next clue is in Vermont, right?"

"Rachel told you?" I asked.

"She did. And she indicated how you broke a few international laws in the process. Seems you're a cowboy. You're messy. You make guys like me clean up your messes."

"You don't know me, Agent Desplaines."

"That's it, we're done here," Shipley said, now incensed.

"I know you, Rik," Desplaines continued. "I know you're not what everybody needs you to be all the time. You're human, just as much as me and your lawyer here. And you know people. You can read people, which is why you're such a good card player."

Desplaines was proving quite the interesting inquisitor. He pressed on, first letting out a sigh and rubbing his hand over his gray hair, "You're looking for gold and

162

you don't know where to find it. You want it. You can taste it. It's the missing piece for you." He kept philosophizing and surprisingly, I found myself still listening.

"But, let me put it out there for you," he paused dramatically, "whatever you dig up is not going to shine as bright as you think, and it's sure as hell not going to fill any holes. You know why? Because you're not Lucan. You're not a murdering piece of shit. But you know his mindset." I did and I do know the mindset. The ecstasy of adventure. The lure of the gun. I can also hear Ennio Morricone cueing up his musicians. Then that devilishly enticing orchestral sound of soul strings pulled taut and then raked over by unwieldy bows leading to the crescendo of death and gold. But how could I ever shout out and tell the truth that I could never be fully human. Desplaines seemed to know this without hearing me say it.

He asked me point-blank, "Do you think Lucan might risk coming after this gold?"

"Don't answer that, Rik. My client is not here to do your investigative work for you," Shipley interrupted.

"Well, then let me ask you this," Desplaines said shuffling through photos and finally producing a picture that makes me sicker than the crime scene. "How well do you know Rachel Hexam?" The picture, date stamped from last year, showed Rachel standing, smiling next to Lord Matthias Lucan. They were dressed to the nines, obviously at an upscale party, and each one held a flute of champagne. They're toasting. Once again, I couldn't find the words.

I have read *Rita Hayworth and Shawshank Redemption* many times. I own the movie. I own the two-disc collector's edition as well. I'm staring at the concrete wall of my holding cell waiting for Rita Hayworth and a rock hammer. But nothing is happening. Stephen King is not writing this story. And

I'm sure as shit not Andy Dufresne. He was innocent. I'm guilty as sin.

Rachel and Lucan are connected by more than just financial grants? Somewhere in the deep I'm lost, swirling through an ocean of sewage in my head. The truth was in the photographs. Leanos, cut to pieces. Rachel, basking in champagne-flavored glee with the man who killed him. How could she do this to me? How could she not be totally honest with me? Because she doesn't love you anymore, dumbass. She's not going to show her hand if she doesn't have to. She'll toss her cards in the muck just like you would. But why? Who knows why we do the things we do? I don't. She doesn't. Lucan doesn't. And that's the very thing, I don't know what Lucan's about or what he's really after. It certainly isn't just gold. You don't risk it all for gold. It's always gold and then you fill in the blank with something else.

I can't sleep in this cell. I can't stop playing the events of the last two days over and over in my head. And now there's a completely different angle. What if this whole series of coincidences and twists was orchestrated? Then I suppose there would have to be one smart-ass maestro.

I've agreed to help Agent Desplaines and the FBI by playing the bait, but first I have to spend the night in this cell so they can clear through any paperwork. On the books, I'm being released on bail, under my own recognizance and all that noise. In reality, Desplaines will lose some evidence (the security tape) if my actions directly lead to the arrest of Matthias Lucan. He is now not only wanted for corporate malfeasance, aiding, abetting and funding terrorism, but they want him for Leanos's murder and illegal drug and arms trafficking through his corporate headquarters in South Jersey. The truth is that I had no choice. No say in how my life will play out until Lucan is arrested. I'm facing serious charges, but Desplaines knows that keeping me in a cell will not bring him any closer to an arrest. I'm the perfect cheese for this rather sadistic rat.

After his revelatory admissions about Rachel, Desplaines showed me all the transcripts from the wiretaps they had on Molitor. Apparently, he was actually more corrupt than I ever thought possible. He shook down drug dealers and was directly responsible for the murder of a witness against Lucan. Desplaines also had the same photos of Molitor at the coke plant in Venezuela. Some bureaucrat would be proud of the inter-agency cooperation. The Patriot Act at work. Unfortunately, I'm in the cell and the man who's responsible for fucking up my orbit is out there somewhere salivating over Templar gold. I guess that Patriot Act is not all it's cracked up to be. And then I think again about Molitor. You never really know a guy until he tries to kill you I suppose. I didn't know him as anything other than a guy with whom I shared a few burgers and some poker. Then he turned on a dime and I took his life. Yet another brick to stack on my wall of regrets and no Rita Hayworth to cover the hole as I try to dig through it.

Still breathing. But I'm feeling oxygen-deprived.

[17]

Conferences

Ski drives fast. The window to the passenger side of his truck is cracked and the faint intimation of salt in the air awakens my sleep-starved soul. The scrub pines of the Parkway zip by in artful succession. Ski hasn't said much since I met him outside the Barracks. He told me Rachel and Victor headed off to Lake Champlain and Donovan was scheduled to deliver a press conference later that morning detailing the whole sordid affair. I stopped him mid-sentence and even though it hurt like hell, I gave him a bear hug, happy to finally return to solid ground. He called me a pussy, told me to toughen up, but the smile hasn't left his face yet even as I fell asleep, miles before we hit the Parkway.

The sun is blasting the Jersey wetlands in metallic orange and sending billions of dancing particles off the water. It's pleasant to awaken to the rebirth of your homeland. Each sunny morning in Jersey promises a complete overhaul of the landscape you knew. No Jersey sunrise is exactly the same.

I hear the faint click of the Ski's turn signal and I see the sign for exit 63, "Long Beach Island". His calloused paw shakes me and now I'm alive again.

"Where we going?" I ask, slightly disoriented.

"The CHEGG," he says.

I crack an elated smile, happy that in a few moments I will be sitting, basking in the fiery smell of *The Chicken or The Egg*. Nothing can penetrate.

The Chicken or the Egg is open all night during the tourist season. The place caters to families in the day and the Jersey shore knuckleheads stumbling out of The Shell or Joe Pop's at night. The walls are decorated in brilliant blasts of color, as if Jimi Hendrix painted it with his guitar. Their wings are legendary, their pancakes are like garbage can lids and the Buffalo fries are a must.

I'm working on an omelet, a short stack and a plate of hot Buffalo fries as Ski shakes his head like a disapproving cardiologist, then steals a forkful of fries to add to his plate. On the side wall, a flat screen TV has CNN streaming the promise of Donovan's press conference delivered live after the next commercial.

Ski takes a long swallow of coffee. His eyes have deep, sunken circles, as if he, like me, got little or no sleep since I stupidly hung onto that hooked X helmet. He's the last bastion of family I have left. I feel like begging him for forgiveness right there; pouring out the last full measure of devotion I have and telling him that I'm throwing in the towel, quitting this stupid business of gold and intrigue and going back to the way it was. Late night card games, wary bartered deals, chasing thieves out of my shop and out onto the Boardwalk and then curling up in my chair in the stuffy apartment reading about the great explorations of the past from a safe distance removed. But before I can say anything, he asks, "So, where are we going to start?"

"Start what?" although I know exactly what he's talking about.

"Start figuring out just what the hell all this killing's been about. Because you know if Lucan's still out there, he'll want to finish what he started. And that means killing you and killing Rachel and killing Victor Meek and killing that idiot Donovan."

As if on cue, Nile Donovan, in casual shirt sleeves strides forward to the microphone. Behind him, the logo of his billion-dollar franchise, *Stinger Corporation*, a name picked to sound intimidating in a marketplace that needs no intimidation, glistens in the spotlights and sparkles in the flashbulbs. The ticker states that he's speaking live in his corporate headquarters just outside of Bridgewater, NJ. The campus is a sprawling green initiative with Segue-riding executives and a pond that generates power with phosphorescent algae.

"Good morning," he begins in his lilting Irish brogue. I reach for another forkful of Buffalo fries and watch him fumble through his notes.

"I, along with my fiancé Dr. Rachel Hexam have recently been the victim of a kidnapping."

Fiancé? He proposed while I was sitting in the fucking clink? Ski looks at me, knowing the word that stung the most.

Donovan continues as photographers clatter and clack the shutters on their cameras, *"The perpetrator was one Matthias Lucan, Earl of Bingham, an international fugitive wanted for drug and arms trafficking and murder."* I can see beads of sweat forming on his brow as the memories begin to resurface.

He shifts his weight at the podium, *"Dr. Hexam and I both owe our lives to the courage and fortitude of two men who risked their lives to save ours. They know who they are and to one in particular, I am eternally grateful. I consider him a friend to both of us."*

Is that supposed to make me feel better? I'm quietly contemplating the word fiancé and how much his genial nature makes me want to throw something at the TV. I see him put his notes down and look directly in to the camera. He's going off script. Somewhere off camera, one of his underlings is freaking out.

"Our kidnapping was not without cause, and I'm sorry to say I believe I can provide a reason. I accepted significant financial backing at Striker's inception from The Navigator Fund, which is a group of international investors based out of Germany and

Switzerland. Lord Lucan, and his corporation, Redstone Security Group, are members."

"Old Nile was cooking the books, huh?" Ski scoffs.

Donovan lets his head drop and presses on, *"I have repaid all of their initial investment, plus interest accrued, but because of Striker's success, this group felt slighted. Representatives from Lord Lucan's firm, the Redstone Security Group personally approached me and threatened reprisal if I did not renegotiate the agreement with The Navigator Fund."* He stops for a dramatic pause. *"It was then I realized that although Navigator has done wide international business with many different governments and corporations, that secretly a large portion of their monies come from illegal activities. I was naïve and young when I accepted their support and I have paid for it with this recent abduction. Lucan is still a threat and is currently an international fugitive. This corporation will personally reward any information that leads to his arrest with one hundred thousand dollars. Thank you and good morning."*

The frenzy of shouts from the gaggle of reporters is slowly drowned out as the CNN anchor takes over recapping Nile Donovan's involvement with The Navigator Fund and how he believes it directly led to his kidnapping. Behind the scenes, production interns are Googling The Navigator Fund so the pundits will be able to hastily banter around words like "secretive", "lucrative" and "undercover."

Ski takes another big forkful of the Buffalo fries and chews sloppily. "Did you hear anything he said beyond the word *fiancé*?"

I nod. "At least he gave us somewhere to start."

"You better call Brown and ask him about this Navigator Fund."

Ski has a point. But, I'm vowing to ignore this latest revealing pile of sordid bullshit until I finish these pancakes.

They all lied to me. What else is new? I've spent the greater part of my adult life bending the truth. Why would I expect Rachel and Donovan to be any different?

"I'll admit I have no goddam clue what he's talking about," Jay squawks from his office in London. *"And truthfully, Nile Donovan's word is not exactly bond in my circles. Not to mention the fact that I'm still trying to clean up the mess we made the other night. I've got internal examiners giving me a colonoscopy as we speak."*

"Keep me posted, Jay," I respond. "Let me know if you dig anything more up about Navigator that's not on the Internet. I'll try and get in touch with Nile or Rachel directly."

"Good luck with that. Donovan's going to seal himself up after this revelation. And you just told me you have no idea what Rachel's really up to. Stay out of it if you know what's good for you. I'm not going to be there to bail your ass out again."

"Good advice. I probably won't heed it."

Ski laughs as weaves in and out of Parkway traffic heading south. My iPhone was lost when Lucan stole Donovan's catamaran, but Ski was kind enough to activate an old LG flip phone for me while I was locked up. It's good to have a friend.

"Watch your ass, Rik," Jays warns as he hangs up. I can imagine him shouting orders to his inferiors around him with deadpan sarcasm. For some reason, I always picture Jay surrounded by a whirling maelstrom of movement and paper.

In the distance, I can see the outline of Atlantic City off to the left. We're crossing the Little Egg inlets. The tide's out and the faint stench of algae and dead seaweed wafts inside as I roll down the window and let the air of my home overtake me.

I slowly punch in the numbers for Rachel's cell phone and hit send. Through the deep reverb of the wind from the window I hear it click right to voicemail. I hang up, wondering where she is and whether I've left Victor with a praying mantis. She will use him up and then eat him? It's too horrible to contemplate. But between Donovan's financial confessions and Rachel's photographs, things are not exactly as I left them hours earlier.

"I got some of your stuff at my place," Ski says. "Closed up the shop indefinitely. You know until we figure all this out."

"We?" I ask hesitantly.

"Of course *we*, dummy. You obviously can't take care of yourself."

I crack a smile. He sees it.

"Shut up," he croaks and then maneuvers right, towards Exit 38 and the Atlantic City Expressway.

[18]

Seafaring Navigators

After a quick shower, a bandage change, and some clean clothes, Ski tosses me the keys to my Jeep, which he has been so kind to collect from Wildwood. I meander down Atlantic Avenue, to the intersection of North Tennessee where on the corner, I spot my destination, the Atlantic City Free Public Library.

I've tried Rachel's cell a number of times. It's quite obvious now that she's either ignoring my calls or something is terribly wrong. Ski is calling north to Middlebury's research facilities on Lake Champlain to see if they can contact her. My attempts to reach Donovan were futile as well. The only one who wants to be in constant contact is Agent Desplaines. I've called in my whereabouts and given him this number. Now, I must sit and read and try to uncover just what the hell all these things have to do with each other.

Four hours and three cups of coffee later, the tiny alcove of the public library feels cavernous. I'm a researcher by nature. It's really what I love about academia. You can sit for hours, finding clues and solving rhetorical mysteries and the outside world can't touch you. They can't get your thought process no matter how hard they try. During SEAL training, I was taught that I could be the toughest guy in the world, a physical specimen, but if I couldn't think my way out of a jam then I was useless to the Navy. Well, right now, surrounded by a stack of books, I'm pretty jammed up.

I've commandeered a computer and the table next to it and I've spread out everything and anything I could think of that might relate to Thorvald Eiriksson, Verrazzano, Vikings, runes, Knights Templar and anything in between. I've even got *The Anglo-Saxon Chronicle* and Seamus Heaney's translation of *Beowulf*. On the plane, we decided that Ragnar's armor might be at the bottom of Lake Champlain and from there hopefully we could tell the location of Thorvald's Cross and New Jerusalem. But, there has to be some other connection. There has to be a piece that's missing.

A canary yellow legal pad, with a plethora of scratches and notes, stares back at me. My watch tells me that four hours has turned into seven and the sun is getting ready to go down. I'm still nowhere and I've found myself repeating over and over the words from an Anglo-Saxon poem called *The Seafarer*: *"Though he would strew the grave with gold, a brother for his kinsman, bury with the dead, a mass of treasure, it just won't work – nor can the soul, which is full of sin preserve the gold before the fear of God, though he hid it before while he was yet alive."*

The poem is from a dusty, translated copy of *The Exeter Book* and tells the story of a wayward seafarer who laments his time away from the shore and then turns to Christianity for salvation. It's the burial and the gold that have caught my eye. These lines seem to describe a similar tableau to the one we all hope to find at the end of this particular rainbow. Nobody knows when it was written but *The Exeter Book* is dated at anywhere from 900-1000 AD. The Anglo-Saxons and the Norsemen living in England traded and intermarried. These "seafarers" were traveling far and wide. Obviously, this poem is not describing the Vinland that Rachel, Lucan and now I seek, but the passage is intriguing nonetheless. As is my memory of the hooked X brooch I pulled from the dirt in Hunstanton with Victor years before.

I stand up and walk around, trying to get the juices going again. Seven hours. Ski called but I haven't called him back. No word from Rachel. No word from Victor. I'm alone, staring down at a collection of notes and dusty books. I have to set aside ancient history and turn my attention back to the computer and this Navigator Fund.

A quick Google search reveals a few interesting hits. The Fund originates in Munich, Germany in 1946. Some believe that they are a few leftover SS scumbags trying to pool money together, but those are listed on the more far-fetched sites. From what I can gather after scrolling around for half an hour, The Navigator Fund is comprised of a group of uber-wealthy European and South American contributors with corporations like Quest Aerospace in Germany, Binary Systems Limited in Copenhagen, Redstone in the UK and US and Banco Bolivar in Caracas. These corporations apart always find their way amongst the most profitable, but together they could be nearly indestructible. My mind races with the idea of international conspiracy theories and I remember names like the Bilderbergs and Illuminati and all that other nonsense until I hit upon a name that's not so nonsensical, Werner Sternbauer.

It's a cool night as I walk slowly out of the library with my collection of notes slung under my arm. I'm not sure if I fully understand the gravity of this new revelation. Werner Sternbauer is one of the highest paid defense contractors in Europe. His sunken cheekbones and designer shades give him away in every photograph and there have been plenty. He has a reputation of corporate raiding by day and adventuring on the weekends. But why do I know him? Well, last year he took third place in the World Series of Poker's European Championship.

He's fifty years old and a legend in European poker. They say he once challenged Johnny Chan to a heads up game for five hundred thousand dollars and when Johnny beat him with pocket sixes, Sternbauer gave him an extra five hundred thousand just for his time. He's a gambler, a manufacturer of weapons both big and small and he's a reported member of the Knights of Christ. There's the connection.

"You spent all goddam day reading through this and all you got is a vague idea that this *might* connect back to the Templars?"

"The Templars became the Knights of Christ in Portugal, you know that," I say as Ski stares off into the night. His front porch has a direct line of sight to the beach. I can hear the waves lapping in the distance. He takes a long sip of coffee from a steaming mug.

"Who said it was a lunatic that always connected everything back to the Templars?"

"Umberto Eco," I respond quickly.

"Yeah, I never read the book," he says. "But, I'm sure the guy made sense."

"He's a good writer."

"I'm sure he is. And I'm sure he would love a piece of this fiction you're crafting right now. Lucan's a psychotic, yes. We agree. But, I don't think he's part of some great international conspiracy."

I lean back on the stoop. I close my eyes for a moment and imagine what could possibly be happening right now. It's been well documented that members of the Knights of Christ were on Columbus's voyages and Verrazzano's. These men were great navigators, apparently working off some prior knowledge of the New World. They said the Order disbanded after World War I, but most would argue that it just went ultra-exclusive and ultra-conservative.

"Listen," Ski starts, "I want to believe that somehow we could tie all this up, you know, but I don't believe these Knights of Christ have anything more to do with the Navigator Fund than the goddam Freemasons. What people do on their own time is their business. And business is the important word. No successful financial endeavor is going to succeed when it's being driven by an ideology that isn't capitalism alone."

"When did you get an economics degree?" I ask.

"It's common sense."

"Common sense? We are way beyond common sense my friend..." And then it hits me like a bolt of lightning. The ring! The ring on Lucan's finger. "Holy shit, Ski!"

"What?"

I turn and rummage through my legal pads and notes and pull out a printout of one of the crosses, reportedly used by the Knights of Christ.

"This is it," I say staring at the picture. He snatches it out of my hands.

"This is what?" he asks staring at the picture.

"This is the same cross that was stamped on Lucan's ring the night I he tried to killed me in Harrah's." I can feel the sonofabitch shaking my hand, with the weight of the gold band on his ring finger. It's like it's perpetually happening, hanging there in time on Ski's porch. I didn't think anything of the stamp on the band at the time. But now, it hits me like a left hook.

"Come on, are you kidding me. You mean Lucan," he stops. "Holy shit. I guess it might be real after all."

"I'm going to Germany," I say jumping up. "Where's your credit card?"

Still staring at the cross on the printout, he tosses his wallet over his shoulder into my waiting hands. Moments later I book a ticket to Munich.

[19]

Knights of Christ

My world has gone dark. Victor and Rachel are both MIA and there's no way of getting in touch with Donovan. They've literally cut me loose. Ski has promised to drive north to Burlington, find them and call me, but part of me wants him to stay out of it. He wouldn't hear of it. He jumped on the Parkway north after dropping me at Newark Airport for the afternoon flight to Munich. I'm sitting near a coffee kiosk outside the security checkpoint in Terminal C, waiting for Desplaines. You can't travel abroad when the FBI has your passport.

I see him slowly amble through the sliding door, gray suit tailored to his frame. He's got the look of a man perfectly at ease with himself and the world. I'm sitting in plain sight and he slowly walks over and sits down next to me. I fold up the New York Times and listen as he produces a plastic tracking bracelet.

"Give me your ankle."

"Don't you want to buy me dinner first?"

"Just lift up your pant leg, smart ass," he scoffs apparently not appreciating my sarcasm. He clips the bracelet to my leg and tucks it into my sock. The seal is unbreakable. I'm now Lojacked.

"I thought those only worked in the USA?" I ask.

"We have a bit more technology in there than the local cops," he says then he pulls out an envelope from his jacket pocket.

"This is a signed statement from the US attorney allowing you to travel internationally." Finally, he hands me my passport. "If you're wrong about this, and I mean if one little thing goes bad while you're over there, I'll spend the rest of my life hunting you down and don't think about trying to outrun me, man. I'm relentless. And let's not forget the CIA wouldn't mind making you go away after you added another star to their wall."

"Point taken." I pause and choose my next few words carefully. "What's the official story on Molitor?"

Desplaines takes a breath and looks away. "Line of duty death. Believe me, it's for the best. Nobody wants a scandal. The world needs the façade of heroes, right?"

"And what about the real ones?" I ask.

"No such thing, Rik. You should know that better than most. Come on, I'll walk you through security."

Somewhere, a Special Agent is watching a blip on a laptop screen. Me. I suppose it's comforting to be walking with someone again.

Gate 19. I've got an hour before we board and the plastic tracking bracelet is starting to itch. I've got one last call to make before we take off and if doesn't work then this whole plan will be for naught. Last Christmas, Ski got me a subscription to *Bluff* magazine. It's like the *Sports Illustrated* of the poker world and despite myself I actually grew to look forward to getting each new edition in the mail. It found a special place on my toilet tank along with *Wreck Diving*.

I recalled a small blurb a few months back about the Kirstenplatz, an ultra-exclusive Bavarian casino on the outskirts of Munich. This was the favorite site of the European wunderkinds and the home game for Werner Sternbauer. The place is supposed to be lush, legendary, and impossible to get into without your name appearing on a list.

I put the phone to my ear and activate one last favor.

"This is Bobby Cusano." I hear his voice, sickly and labored. Bobby C. has seen better days than today, and yet there's still the same bastion of life in his voice that made him such a personable fixture around the casino. I'm sure he has an opinion about the chaos that ensued the other night.

"Bobby, it's Rik."

"Jesus, Rik, I thought you were dead. I had no idea,"

"Bobby, I don't have a lot of time. I know you didn't set anything up."

"I swear to Christ, Rik, I had no idea who those guys really were. I never would have agreed to let that game go on." I imagine sweat beading on his brow. He's telling the truth or whatever truth he's told to himself.

"Bobby, I need a favor." I stand up from my vinyl chair and stare out the window glass on to the tarmac. Planes landing and taking off, heading towards every conceivable destination with wary and intrepid travelers. As I read volumes in the library I came across the origins of "Viking". It was a verb and it meant to go as far away as you could, seeking your fortune. Now, my fellow travelers and I go a-viking in steel ships, uncertain as to where our fortunes lie. Bobby C. can help me rig this journey if he's up for the challenge.

"Bobby, you need to get me on the list at the Kirstenplatz."

"In Germany?" He's flustered. He's not as high in the chain of command as everyone believes him to be. This task might prove above his pay grade. He fumbles his words, *"Rik, I haven't got that kind of pull, you know that. How the hell am I supposed to get you into the Kirstenplatz?"*

"Well, I don't really care how you do it, Bobby as long as it gets done. I almost got shot to pieces because you didn't do your homework. Call in every favor you have."

"Rik, I don't know what to say." In the silence, I can hear the danger floating into Bobby's life like a demonic steam. He, like everyone, is not telling me something. It's an

179

instantaneous flash, like seeing another car's brake lights before it plows into you. There's nothing you can do and in the end it's cruelly sick that you could see it before it happened.

"Say it's done."

He takes a long breath, a deep sigh and finally resigns himself to the inevitable. *"It's done."*

I flip the phone shut and return to my chair, waiting to cross the Atlantic yet again, this time not a fugitive from justice, but a prisoner to a plastic bracelet. Hopefully, this new amulet will bring me some luck.

No word from Ski. It makes me nervous just thinking about it. Everyone I know has gone silent. Even Jay isn't picking up his cell. The East Coast is five hours behind me, just about to contemplate evening. The Munich flight touched down earlier that morning and after a quick jaunt through the city, a gawk at the Glockenspiel and a weisswurst I was back in the hotel room showering and donning a rather expensive knockoff of an Armani tuxedo. The dinner jacket is white. I feel like 007.

The cabbie spoke broken English but he certainly understood what I meant by "Kirstenplatz" especially when he saw my rather uncomfortable penguin constraints. It's 8pm and I fear I might be a little bit early for the high rollers. This is certainly advantageous because my bankroll is nothing special. I've got two thousand Euros that I very quickly have to convert to five thousand so that I can contemplate joining a game with Werner Sternbauer. Five thousand Euros is the bare minimum to buy-in at the cash games inside the Velvet Room at the Kirstenplatz. I'll have to spend a little time out amongst the plebes making these Euros grow. I know this is a dumb idea but, sometimes, dumb ideas are the only ones worth having.

As the cabbie speeds out of Munich proper through the rolling Bavarian hillsides, I'm remembering the connections and trying to gather what I hope to accomplish from a meeting with Sternbauer. I want to know what the Navigator Fund actually is. I want to know what the Knights of Christ have to do with Viking Vinland and I want to know where the fuck Lucan might be. Now granted, he's certainly not going to answer these questions outright. He might not even be associated with the modern Knights of Christ. But, I can be persuasive. And if it comes down to it, I'll just have to beat it out of him instead of beating him on the felt. Bold thoughts and words for a stranger in a strange land.

The Kirstenplatz is a compound built among the remnants of a twelfth century castle. It's a sprawling estate and the main casino/hotel is flanked by two giant spotlights and a red carpet as the cabbie pulls up. I feel like I'm going to the Oscars. But, it's a casino first and foremost and so there is kitch and gaudy architecture-a-plenty.

The doormen, a rather intimidating group of Neanderthals checks each patrons name off of a digitized master list kept on an iPad. Anybody can get a reservation on the hotel side, but to play in the casino you need a credit score and a full background check. It's easier to get a five hundred thousand dollar mortgage in the USA then it is to get in to this casino, much to our chagrin. It's modeled after a venue in Monte Carlo, but copies are not nearly as crisp as the originals, and you can tell this place is trying too hard. Bobby Cusano better have come through for me, because these marble steps leading towards the door do not feel particularly soft and I don't want these masters of the list to put their trade to work.

The thug with the iPad asks for my name and country of origin.

"Rik Rodriguez. USA," I say in the most confident voice I can muster. I can feel the starched collar of this imitation tuxedo strangling me. The thug stares me up and down. I can feel foreboding. But then, with a few swipes from his sausage-shaped finger across the iPad and a nod to his compatriots I walk through the gold leafed door and into the neon-tinted low lighting of Europe's most exclusive high roller casino. Bobby came through.

Everything feels wrong. The chips don't feel the same, the pace of the game is off, everything is stacked against an outsider in this place. I'm languishing, already down one thousand Euros and I haven't seen a picture card in two hours. The good news is, I haven't seen Sternbauer yet either. Still time to make this bad idea work for me.

The table's full of hot shot Germans, dressed to excess. There's an Austrian and three Dubai oil execs who are speaking in Arabic about how much they are willing to spend for an escort later in the evening. The action has folded around to me in the small blind. I look down nervously at my cards, slowly, careful not to snap either against the felt. Finally, something to play with. Pocket tens.

I raise. It's twenty-five/fifty blinds and I make it one hundred to go. The big blind, the Austrian with a bushy white beard and wrap-around sunglasses calls my raise and we see a flop.

King, Ten, Jack rainbow. I flopped a set of tens and a possible straight draw. I check my set to the Austrian who reaches for chips. He tosses two hundred Euros into the pot. I smooth call him, taking a moment for effect.

The turn is a Jack of Hearts. I just made a full house. Tens full of Jacks. This time I bet. Five hundred Euros. The

Austrian smooth calls this time, making me nervous. Could he have Jack/Ten or King/Jack. The river card is a Nine of Hearts. There's three Hearts on the board now and I'm hoping he just made a flush. I push all in. My last two hundred Euros.

The Austrian calls and turns over pocket Kings. Kings full of Jacks, destroying my full house.

"Kings full," he says in Vienna-accented English. The white beard and accent are now reminding me of Karl Marx or Santa Claus. Either way, this Communist Kris Kringle just destroyed my chances of more poker, especially in the Velvet Room with Sternbauer. Defeated, I slide my chair back and excuse myself, moving slowly towards the head, where I hope this piss will clear any remnants of this ridiculous idea that brought me into this casino.

The water from the sink is refreshing. It takes two handfuls to realize what just happened. I pop two Aleve to keep my shoulder from sending me into orbit. What a dumb idea. I mean this might be my dumbest. Reaching for my cell, I have a moment to contemplate what exactly is going on back in the States. Ski could be driving into a trap. Rachel and Victor could be dead and Nile Donovan could actually be the horrible sneaky sonofabitch I always thought he was. All these thoughts evaporate when I feel the hand on my bad shoulder and the voice in Vienna-accented English.

"You were drawing dead, my friend."

I turn and find the Austrian who has removed his sunglasses. His white hair is pulled back in a ponytail and he runs his fingers through the beard.

"What do you want?" I ask. The restroom is empty except for us. He's at least sixty. I'll have no problem overpowering him if need be, but then I see his hand moving through the beard and the gold ring calls out to me like a minaret in some otherworldly call to prayer.

"You came here looking for answers I think. My name is Marten Hering. And your name is Rik Rodriguez, yes?"

"It is."

"Good. You come with me then. Someone wants to see you."

Against any and all judgment I follow Hering out the door and back into the casino. Before I realize it, I'm on an elevator that Hering used a key to operate. We're going down. This is not the way I pictured this going.
As the elevator doors open, I feel the phone in my pocket buzz and I see Ski's number flash in the digital window. I can't answer it now, but at least he's alive.

Hering has beckoned me to follow him down a carpeted corridor. The stonewall is thick and I feel like we're in the castle proper now. This could be the old cellar or catacomb. But everything is brightly lit by grid lights above our heads. I can hear the click of our heels reverberate off of the walls and into my eardrums. Then we come to the end of the hall and a vast iron door which Hering pushes open and now we're outside in a courtyard.

High on the walls spotlights shine down in eerie patterns and Hering turns back to me. He points to a shadow and then I see a match light and a face. The faint aroma of a Cuban cigar. Then Werner Sternbauer reveals himself. He's six feet tall and wears no tie. The sport jacket and suit pants are of the finest Parisian craftsmanship and his silver hair is slicked back taut against his scalp. He is nearly at one with the shadow in which he stands almost as if venturing into the light would cause him some kind of physical pain. Last year in the World Series Europe the announcers nicknamed him, "The Gunslinger". It's easy to see why.

"Why are you here?" His voice is direct and sharp like a hollow point round. The accent is High German with a hint of something else, something Latin, maybe Spanish or Portuguese.

"I came to find you," I say. Hering has stepped back to our left.

"Why?" he asks taking a long puff of his cigar. "I know it wasn't to play cards if Marten there took all your money."

"Kings full versus Tens full. Got to be a bad beat," I quip trying to speak his language.

"If you were an underdog before the money went in, then it's not a bad beat." The statement rings home like Gospel. "I'll ask you again, what are you doing here?"

"Well, let me ask you, how do you know me?"

"You don't get to ask any questions. I ask the questions or this meeting ends with your brains all over this courtyard, understand?"

I know the bullet won't come from Hering. He's probably got a few men lurking out there in amongst the shrubbery, maybe even a rifle up on the wall. Anyway you slice it, he's holding all the cards and if I don't play right I guess I'm fucked.

"Alright," I decide that honesty is probably the best policy in this particular situation. "I want to know about the Knights of Christ. I want to know about Matthias Lucan and the Navigator Fund and I want to know what the hell this all has to do with the Templars and Viking Vinland."

The wafting aroma of Cohiba fills the air around us. I hate tobacco smoke, but a fine Cuban cigar, with the right hint of cedar and earth can make even the cool of a German evening come to life with terrestrial sense memory.

"You certainly want to know a lot, Mr. or is it Dr. Rodriguez?"

"I have a PhD in history."

"Then why the hell do you own a pawnshop?" He's done his homework. My name and my complete dossier were placed in his hands hours before. I really am stupid.

"Family business," I answer. I can feel his temperament relaxing slightly.

"Time for a change, don't you think?" he smiles superciliously. "I mean it seems that the pawn business has brought you nothing but trouble over the last few days. Am I right?"

"How do you know that?"

"I swear to Christ, one more question and I'll stamp this cigar and your skull will be ripped apart by a high velocity round." His anger is now swelling. It's amazing to see him flip on a dime. "You answer me. That's it."

I nod in compliance.

"Now, you want to know about us. Well, you know I'm not going to tell you what the Knights of Christ do or have done. Where's Matthias Lucan? I have no idea. He's one of those people that doesn't understand how to let things lie. He wants and needs and feels something drawing him into the past, when the future is all that is of anyone's concern.

"We are an old order. We are the remnants of the Knights Templar and from them we learned many things including navigation and not just celestial navigation but societal navigation. We've employed these techniques for centuries. We hold many famous and illustrious men in our ranks including Verrazzano and Columbus. But how did they get there? How did they know? Well, I'm sure you have your theories as do we all."

He steps forward and blows cigar smoke in a long arching pattern.

"I can tell you one thing and one thing only. The treasure that everyone seems to be obsessed with it doesn't belong to anyone in particular, but the history, the history belongs to us all. Viking explorers, then Templar Knights, and then the Knights of Christ like Verrazzano and Columbus who went looking for them. It's all there."

"I don't care much about a treasure," I interrupt. "I just want this to be over. I want Lucan dead or in jail."

He nods contemplatively then abruptly changes the subject, "Nile Donovan gave an impressive performance at that press conference. He set about blaming the Navigator Fund for everything. We had no idea what Lucan was doing. Truthfully."

"I don't believe that, Mr. Sternbauer, not for a minute. We're talking about the greatest treasure find of the twenty-first century and you're telling me that you and your little boy's club doesn't want in? You turned Lucan loose on the world and now you're saying he's not your dog."

He chuckles slightly. "The Navigator Fund is worth sixty billion dollars. I don't give a shit about any treasure. And our boy's club has much loftier goals than playing Indiana Jones with some trinkets from our past."

He turns back from where he came. "You go with God, Dr. Rodriguez. Give me a call if you find anything."

"That's it?"

He stops and turns back around. "If I were you, I wouldn't waste my time with trying to read runes. You're not going to find New Jerusalem by trying to extract sentences and fragments from armor or stones. Lucan tried to convince me about Armor and Fire when he first got this idea. The answer's not there." He pauses dramatically and points his hand with the cigar between two fingers at me, "Where do you think Verrazzano got the Viking helmet?"

He knows a lot. He can see the shock registering on my face.

"I don't know," I respond.

"Well, think about it." He turns and walks, calling over his shoulder, "And let me know if you find it, seriously. I'll want to buy back a large portion of it."

His footsteps on the gravel slowly dissipate and I turn back around to find Hering gone as well. I'm waiting for the crack of a rifle. The report leading to my eventual bloody death, but all I can hear are crickets and the faint hum of expensive engines pulling up in the turnabout in front of the casino.

I told the cab to drop me off at the Marienplatz. I loosened the bow tie. I'm pissed. My foray into the world of high stakes espionage ended with all my cash gone and Sternbauer's cryptic question eating away at my brain.

What was I thinking? This billionaire would just confess all the secrets of his order to me. You would somehow get through his security detail and beat it out of him? This isn't the movies. I'm not a superspy. I'm a pawnbroker who once did things in the shadows and now can't sleep at night because of it. I need a strong coffee for the walk back to my hotel.

The deep fragrance of the hot drink sets my soul at ease as I walk through the square. The little bakery directly across from the Marienplatz, the hub of the city, was welcoming and cheerful. My sheepish self needed a bit of bright light. But now my legs are moving swiftly across the cobblestone. The clock chimes midnight but still the city is alive. Munich is bright and cosmopolitan and full of people wondering, wondering about their past, present and futures. Munich's a good city in which to lose yourself, but don't expect to find anything again. The streets are too quick and narrow. It's like swimming in a river. Refreshing, but you'd best be prepared for the ride.

Turning south towards my hotel, I can feel something from the old days. The hair on the back of my neck is standing up. I'm being followed? I don't know for sure. I have to turn and look, but it has to be quick and so I turn my head and catch two suits about one hundred yards back. They saw me turn. They know I made them.

Now, I have to lose them. I finish the coffee in one swig, toss the cup in a waste bin and then dart across the street nearly colliding with a Smartcar. The suits don't expect it and I catch a glimpse of them trying to meander through the traffic. But, I'm already heading back north towards the Marienplatz, the open air of the plaza. I want to get lost in the sea of people. I turn one last time to see if they made it across. I turn back and see the Marienplatz ahead of me, but I decide to turn left, darting towards the Frauenkirche, the Munich Cathedral. The shadows of the side street give me some relief until I see the steps of the church and see a familiar dull light of a cigar. Then the cigar is stamped out on the ground. I stop. It's Sternbauer who walks out of the shadow and down the steps.

"Cloak and dagger tonight, huh?" he says with a devious smile curling on his lips.

The Suits, winded and out of breath, catch up to us. He waves them off and puts one hand on my bad shoulder.

"Come inside with me for a moment, ok?"

We walk up the steps and into the empty cathedral.

The vast expanse of the cathedral is rivaled only by the intricacy of the carved pillars. Our feet echo on the marble and Sternbauer leads me to a pew where we both sit. The dim moonlight filters in through the vaulted windows. He stares peacefully forward as if this place gives him great joy and solace.

"I was hasty before, I think," he says quietly. "I didn't really give you a chance to explain yourself fully. When someone gives you a piece of paper with a name and background, it's easy to get a little impersonal."

"Why didn't you just knock on my door at the hotel?" I ask rather pointedly.

"Because I don't know what kind of man you are. I wanted to be in public, just like you did. You've got see it from my perspective. I'm told that a man is coming uninvited to speak with me and all I know is that he was recently associated with a murder and he's an ex-Navy SEAL."

His point has merit. I suppose everything I've done up to this point has been completely unorthodox.

"Matthias Lucan has been waiting his entire life to take this treasure. Everything else he did was just to keep him occupied, bide his time, before he had enough money and enough power to take it."

"So, he's a total fucking wack job."

"Yes, a total fucking wack job. Well put. He's also a member of our order."

"So if you pay enough, you can get in anywhere?"

"We're not Rotarians, Dr. Rodriguez. The highest echelon of the Knights of Christ is awarded by birth and the lower echelons are more like your Knights of Columbus. A civic and community organization. It's sacred and ancient and something I do not joke about."

"*I would listen to him, Rik.*" The voice is distantly familiar and we both turn to hear the clacking of shoes on the marble. My eyes cannot believe the face, still pock-marked, still deep sunken eyes and certainly not bloodied and hacked to death. It's Leonard Leanos.

"Holy shit!"

I stand and curse in the middle of this Church and cannot believe what in the world is happening. There before me stands a dead man. The man who began this entire insane quest days before when he pawned Rachel's treasure chest with the Viking helmet inside. He's living, breathing and wearing a thousand dollar suit. He looks great for a guy who was hacked to pieces.

"I saw the crime scene photos. You're dead," I stammer.

Sternbauer answers for him, "He faked his death so that Lucan would think he was a nonentity, let his guard down and forget about the real treasure in his possession."

"My apologies for dragging you into this, Dr. Rodriguez. I needed to put the helmet back into play somehow so that Matthias wouldn't see me take what I actually needed." Leanos speaks with erudite precision.

"And what was that?" I ask closing my gaping jaw.

"Evidence," Leanos says. "Rather damning evidence against everyone involved in the Navigator Fund."

"Old fashioned blackmail, Dr. Rodriguez," Sternbauer adds. "Lucan took all our missteps and kept records and threatened to go public. When you're running an international conglomerate, it's not good for business when your client list is posted for all to see."

Dirty. They must have some unsavory names from some unsavory places on that list otherwise he wouldn't have gone through the trouble of faking his own death.

"But how did you do it?" I ask Leanos still in shock. "I saw the crime scene photos."

"There was a CIA agent who was rather cooperative as long as I put him back on the trail of the helmet. He wanted the Vinland treasure just like Lucan and a little bit of money on the side."

Molitor. He had his hands in everything it seems. My guilt evaporates with each new revelation. I hate this feeling. It's guilt mixed with the foreboding that only an empty Gothic cathedral can bring.

"So now, which one of you assholes is going to kill *me*?" I ask almost indifferent to the answer.

They exchange a wry smile and it's then that I catch a glimpse of Leanos's hand. He too wears the insignia ring of the Knights of Christ. Their silence is discomforting. Perhaps they are going to kill me, here inside this cavernous Bavarian cathedral. I suppose there are worse places to die than a church. I know. I've been to them.

"We're not going to kill you, Dr. Rodriguez," Leanos says.

"No, we want to help you," Sternbauer interjects, "When Bobby Cusano, your friend from Harrah's, contacted my associate Hering, I had the idea to give you the information you seek, but like I told you, I didn't know what kind of man you were."

"I knew your reputation," Leanos says. "That's why I brought you the chest. I had to steal it from Dr. Hexam to make Matthias believe my fealty. I knew I had to get it back into someone's capable hands."

They're not *giving* me anything. They don't *know* me at all. I'm bait. I'm a pawn in their chess game with Lucan. They need a guy like me to keep Lucan's mind on the treasure, keep him entertained and occupied so they can keep concocting whatever machinations this Navigator Fund actually profligates. I'm used to it. I'm used to being an instrument in a bigger orchestra, but I don't like these conductors. I don't like what's lying there under their surface. Whatever business they do and whoever they do it with, they don't want anyone to know. It's this kind of bullshit that I hate keeping quiet about, but again I have no leverage. I have nothing except this treasure hunt. I could just walk right now. Throw in the towel for the whole goddamn thing, but there's something keeping me here and there and in this game no matter how foolish I find the rules.

"So Rachel had nothing to do with this?" I ask. This time I know I don't want the answer.

Leanos struggles to find words, but then says, "She's certainly not solely to blame. Her research is fueled by love for Donovan." Love is her gasoline. I'm a piston. Donovan's pushing down the accelerator.

Sternabauer interjects: "Donovan, despite his press conference, is still indebted to our Fund for quite a bit of money. Lucan took it upon himself to call in the markers forcing Dr. Hexam's hand. She was a slave to Lucan's whims about the Vinland treasure. Again, he is a rogue operator, someone over which we have no control. So, I will tell you something now, but it comes with this warning. Matthias Lucan will stop at nothing to find this treasure. You know that. He has nothing now, not even the money to pay the mercenaries to do his bidding. The British government has seized his assets. The Americans are building a case. He cannot run to us for help so you see he has only the prospect of this treasure, which he thinks is his birthright."

A birthright. A right to an ancient stash of loot placed in the ground or in some cave hundreds of years before you were born. I find people's logic completely ludicrous sometimes, especially when that logic has tried to kill me on multiple occasions. I think back to Dickens and the Ghost of Christmas Present. *There are those among you who lay claim to know us.* The zealots: those that do their bidding in the name of whatever dogma they happen to swallow. These thoughts, they swirl around in my head like waves smashing against the Boardwalk during a storm. I try and reorient back to my role in this lunacy and ask, "Do you know the location of New Jerusalem?"

"No," Sternbauer says. "But, I do know that Verrazzano got the helmet from the Narragansett people after exploring what is now Rhode Island."

"How do I know that's true?"

"Because Verrazzano explored Narragansett Bay in 1524," Sternbauer insists, "He labeled it *Refugio* on his maps."

"But that doesn't tell me anything," I press. "You can't say this equals that because somebody might have been somewhere. You need a hypothesis and then you need corroborating findings to back it up. He was also in New

193

York harbor and in the Carribean. You have no idea why that helmet was on Verrazzano's ship."

"Somebody did," Leanos smirks, "because he saw a body."

"Who?" I ask, now irritated.

"Henry Wadsworth Longfellow," he says with authority.

"Longfellow, the poet?" Now this is in the realm of fiction.

"Longfellow wrote a poem called *The Skeleton in Armor*. Read it." Leanos looks at me deadly serious.

"If you know all this, why didn't you just find the treasure? Why didn't you just take it for yourselves?"

"We know bits and pieces from our traditions," Sternbauer says. "It takes a much smarter mind to put all the pieces together. The rest of this quest is up to you." He pauses and adds, "If you want to go?"

Sternbauer stands. He and Leanos and take their leave. I'm alone in a big empty church. I hear the outside door slowly thud closed and I realize that I have to get home. I can only find sanctuary far away from this drafty cathedral. So I go.

[20]

The Skeleton in Armor

I'm being played. I know it, which makes it even worse. I really hate it when things go nowhere near how you planned them. Of course, they're not going after the treasure. Why would they waste time, energy and resources to change the course of Western history? Because they already have a shitload of money.

I'm greeted at the international arrivals hall in Newark by the stern face of Agent Desplaines. It's 7pm and I haven't had nearly enough sleep. My shoulder's killing me and all I want is for this particular insanity to be over, but it can't be because I need to find a book of Longfellow poetry and read "The Skeleton in Armor". The backpack with my meager possessions is heavy and I have to piss and why is no one picking up their goddam cell phone? Not even Ski anymore and the idiot didn't even leave a message last night.

"You eat some sausage?" Desplaines jests.

"My fair share. Made sure it was pork sausage in your honor, Agent Desplaines."

"Can we go somewhere private and you can get this Lojack off my ankle? I think it's giving me a rash," I say. The rash part is true. It now itches like mad.

"Not right now. We're going to offer you protective custody in exchange for testimony. While you were gone, Lucan started cleaning up any and all trace of his goings on here. We think he set fire to his corporate building out in Gloucester County."

"No shit?"

"It didn't burn all the way, but the building's pretty damaged. We're not going to take any chances now. So, yes or no. Right now. Your choice."

"No." I give him a quick pat on the shoulder and walk past him, eager to get to the can and then on to my Jeep in the parking lot.

"Rik, what did you find out in Germany?" he asks.

I sigh. "I don't know. But, you'll know where to find me," I say pointing down to the ankle bracelet. "Have a good night, Detective."

I stop and turn around. "By the way, Leonard Leanos is alive. He's in Munich."

Desplaines shockingly stammers, "What? How?"

"Molitor."

Desplaines shakes his head and takes out his cell phone, quickly dialing numbers.

I walk on. I need a book of poetry. And I need to find bathroom. I see a restroom sign right next to it the arrow pointing toward the parking lot. So far, so good.

It's nearing nine as I pull into the closest Barnes and Noble off the Turnpike. I make a beeline towards the poetry section and find a copy of Longfellow's *Collected Works*. I flip forward and find the poem in question. It's three pages long and tells the tale of a wayward Viking exploring distant lands. It's told from the perspective of one who is actually standing before the skeleton as he tells his story. There's two stanzas that stand out.

The first reads: *I was a Viking old! My deeds, though manifold, No Skald in song has told, No saga taught thee! Take heed that in thy verse, Thou dost the tale rehearse, Else dread a dead man's curse; For this I sought thee.*

The second stanza that catches my eye comes later in the poem and describes the Viking's flight with his bride and reads: *Three weeks we westward bore, And when the storm was o'er, Cloud-like we saw the shore stretching to leeward. There for my lady's bower, Built I the lofty tower, Which to this very hour, Stands, looking seaward.*

He describes a nameless Viking and then talks about him building a tower, but this is all based on a skeleton or a body? I need Meek around. He would know the answer without a pause. I flip to the back of the book and read a few notations. The endnotes for "The Skeleton in Armor" talk about a discovery in Fall River, Massachusetts in 1832. The skeleton, shrouded in brass armor was apparently destroyed by fire in 1843. Longfellow apparently saw this skeleton firsthand and composed the poem for the magazine *The Knickerbocker* in 1841.

I buy the book from a rather exhausted-looking clerk and slowly begin to formulate an idea. The book talks about Longfellow's papers being kept in the Houghton Library at Harvard. I still have my academic credentials from BU in my wallet. They're expired, but I wonder if I could get a look at Longfellow's notes? If the skeleton that he saw was a Viking then perhaps New Jerusalem might be in the neighborhood of Fall River and Narragansett Bay. Maybe Newport? That would explain the Narragansett tribe being in possession of a Viking helmet with a hooked X etched in the side. It could also be a dead end. The café in the bookshop is still open. I'm going to need an extra large coffee to get me to New England tonight. Might have to stop at Mohegan Sun in Connecticut, just to be safe and clear my head with a little poker.

The Jeep is chilly and I'm frustrated. I hear click, click and then voicemail. Ski's phone. Rachel's phone. Nobody. Nobody. I'm alone now. Slam the steering wheel. Shout and scream at this whole scenario. This shitty ankle bracelet itches! Hate this. Hate this. Treasure.

But then, it's always nice to win for a change. Mohegan Sun's Casino of the Wind was opened recently and their state of the art poker room opened with it. It's nestled in it's own cavern, as if cut into the side of a mountain. The swirling lights and flowing metal grating of the walls make you feel like you're in the middle of a tornado, in a cloudburst, on top of an Appalachian peak. Weightless, breathless. I wait for someone to reach out. But, I'm alone in this crowded room. Buzzes and twangs of the casino floor filter in and the reverb of the nightclub permeates the red felt of the 2/5 No Limit table where I sit.

Winning. Ahead. New concept for me this week. The stack of checks in front of me has morphed from five hundred into two thousand courtesy of a turned flush and trip sevens. But, then I'm up and walking away. Cashing out my chips. The flashes and blurring movement of the casino: an organism snaking along, constantly regenerating and yet I am not part of it. I'm set back. Removed. Alone again.

I panic in front of the Krispy Kreme shop near the parking garage. Two glazed and a coffee and my hand shakes. I feel numb. My world, quiet and easy is now completely disheveled and difficult. This didn't used to happen before when I didn't care. I didn't care. I didn't want to be burdened by any other problem except the ones rattling around in my tin can head, echoing with the metallic clinks of pellets pouring from a broken shotgun shell. But now I care. I care. But there's no one to tell.

Donuts and loneliness and the sun is nearly up. Driving north on 95 toward Boston where I think I have a hunch about what I'll find. I know Longfellow liked to sketch and in addition to his correspondence and collected works, the Houghton Library has a few of his sketchbooks. If he saw whatever skeleton he wrote about, he certainly couldn't have resisted a sketch. Then perhaps I'll know what I'm dealing with.

I know Rachel's already diving Lake Champlain and I'm sure Victor's there, excited as ever. I do wish they would call me back. I wish someone would give me updates. Ski probably took Victor out for some drinks over the last two nights and is currently still asleep, happy to have some nights of solitude away from Gina's watchful eye. Hoping that he might answer the phone this morning. For all I know, he's eating maple candy by the fistful and having himself a little vacation. I have no idea.

Harvard. I didn't go here. I stared at them disapprovingly from across the Charles River. We beat them in the Beanpot the year I came back to campus after Afghanistan. Cambridge, much like Afghanistan, doesn't really belong anywhere except where it is. Harvard Square is a complicated mixed grill of trendy shops and anarchy and then there are the shiny brick facades and gated rotundas of Harvard University and my eventual destination, the Houghton library.

Getting in to the library is much easier than I expected. My BU student ID still works after all this time. I tell them I'm writing a dissertation on Longfellow and profusely apologize for not making an appointment to view the special collections. They take pity on me, especially since I look like I haven't slept and they just opened their doors for the morning. They buy it.

I'm whisked into a viewing room, issued a pair of white gloves and wait until the folio boxes from 1840-1850 make their way up courtesy of a graduate assistant with dreadlocks. Unlike the Pitt-Rivers, this viewing room has big picture glass looking out over the library. I'm not in any position to steal anything this morning. I'll have to settle for a photocopy.

Attacking history. Gloves at the ready. I reach through. Sketchbook. Letters. Each one needing ginger attention. A journal. Original notebooks with verse jotted down. Then, next to a pen and watercolor of Narragansett Bay I find a simple charcoal drawing. The title, in Longfellow's own hand reads: *Fall River Athenaeum, December 1840 – The Fall River Viking.*

The sketch is sparsely detailed. It looks like a kid drew a skeleton for a Halloween project and then drew plate armor around it. There's a helmet, but it doesn't look like the one Rachel found. It's rounded and there are no eyepieces. Then there's the chest plate and it's then that I can feel my heart beat a little bit faster. There's a building in the center – the crest. It's rounded and looks to be carved in detail. It has a round roof and round pillions around the outside. It looks like a Scandinavian church. And then there's the stone balustrade. A rudimentary cross carved into the steeple. I've never seen armor that looks like this before. I've never seen anything that looks likes this before. Then I remember the poem – *built I a lofty tower* – This must be the tower. But, it's not a tower. I has all the makings of a church. And who was this unnamed skeleton? Is this rudimentary sketch by one of the great Romantic poets actually a sketch of Thorvald Eiriksson? And could this building etched into his chest plate be Thorvald's Cross, the tomb of the first Vinland Sentinel?

Images, old and new are flying through my head. I'm grasping, trying desperately to find where I've seen anything that looks like this building. And then I remember the qualifying class for advanced reconnaissance at the Naval War College in Rhode Island and drunkenly throwing up in Touro Park in Newport. There on the bluff, in the same park overlooking the city where I lost my dinner during my days of binge drinking, sits the Newport Tower; a round pile of sea rocks with constructed windows, pillars and a second floor fireplace. A building with more theories and stories than it has pebbles in the rock plaster holding it together. Longfellow's sketch of this unnamed Viking had to be one of Thorvald's Vinlanders and the crest on the chest plate has to be the Newport Tower. But again, you can't just say something and it becomes true. If Rachel finds Ragnar's armor and it looks even remotely close to this sketch, then we might have cause for alarm, or celebration. I'm not sure which.

Slyly, I snap a picture of the sketch with the camera on my cell phone. I hope I can sneak out of here before anybody notices. The proof is now pixilated in a digital photograph. I need the astrolabe and a whole bunch of smart people. I can almost see the glistening of treasure, somewhere, close, but still far away.

[21]

Cause for Alarm

North to Vermont and I finally connect with Ski.

"I've been drinking with Victor," he growls, "And there's no service up here. Goddam hippies don't like cell towers."

"You were a hippy once too," I remind him, thinking of the photograph of Ski standing with the .50 cal on the back of a PBR having painted a peace sign on the side of his helmet.

"You got me there," he laughs. "Where are you? You back in the States?"

"I left you three messages. I've been to Germany and Boston while you and Victor were drinking Long Trails. I'm heading north. Tell Rachel I'll be in Burlington before lunch."

"She's already on the boat out to Juniper Island. She's been diving for the past three days," he says, but I know this. She couldn't stay out of the water, not when there's another clue down there. "She's got some good leads apparently. Metal detector has a few hits. Victor showed me two coins she brought up. Silver. Definitely hand struck. If it came into the shop, we'd buy it."

"Is Donovan up there?"

Ski coughs. Morning phlegm. It's only nine thirty. He needs coffee.

"Yeah. He checked in last night. We're right on the water. I wasn't going to stay, but they insisted."

"It's good. You need a vacation. You've had a hard century."

He laughs a throaty laugh.

"What's the ring look like?" I ask.

"You could skate on it," he says and then pauses quietly. "She was really happy though. He did it in New York apparently. The morning I picked you up."

"The morning you picked me up from jail," I say, maneuvering the Jeep to the left lane and hitting the gas hard. "The morning after I saved them from whatever sinister garbage they got mixed up in?"

"Yeah," he says quietly. I'm sure he's got a few comebacks that he'd like to say. A moral lesson, some witty joke, but he keeps quiet, sensing my bitter mood, knowing me too well.

"Tell Victor to call me if you see him before I get there."

"I will. Drive safe," he says.

"Thanks."

I flip the phone shut and toss it on the passenger seat. Don't drive emotional now. You don't care if he gave her the crown jewels. But, I'm driving fast. I ease off the accelerator and realize that I was doing one hundred. Lucky. No swirling lights in the rearview. Drive on.

I'm wasting no time in Burlington. Victor called when I crossed the New Hampshire border into Vermont and told me that he and Rachel were working out of the lab at the Lake Champlain Maritime Museum in Vergennes. Rachel had a relationship with them already and her dig on Juniper Island is in conjunction with their research teams. Victor sounded exhausted. They had been working around the clock.

"I'm sorry we didn't get in touch with you. The days all just kind of blended together," he said this with a hint of such overwhelming guilt that I couldn't press it. His whole life has been turned upside down too. He can't go back to Ireland, at least until Lucan is found. He's caught in that in between space too. I can't be angry with him. It's not his fault. It's the horrible, megalomaniacal, rogue member of the Knights of Christ, Navigator Fund and Redstone Security Group that are to blame for this particularly insane scenario.

Victor's going to meet me at the lab, but I have this overwhelming urge to get back in the water. Rachel's still out on Juniper Island. My dive gear was lost on Donovan's boat, but I grabbed a spare bag with a dry suit, full harness, regulator, fins and a snorkel from Ski's collection before I left for Germany and tossed it in my trunk. I know I couldn't do an Atlantic dive, but it should get me by on Lake Champlain. I guess my dive gear is my security blanket. I didn't feel right about driving around without it.

There's a dive shop right off the Burlington pier and I pull in to the parking lot. The ferry to Juniper Island leaves in ten minutes so the fact that the kid needed three sets of identification and spent an inordinate amount of time counting back my change from the bottle of Trimix I bought has left me a little frazzled. I don't want to miss this boat. The ferry cuts through the calm lake water. The sun is sending tendril rays all over the lake, illuminating a sparkled path toward Juniper Island. The boat is a converted trawler, probably from up north somewhere. Very tiny, but good enough for me considering I was the only one to pay the five bucks to get across. Juniper Island is there in the distance. Half mile from the swirling world of Burlington. To think that one of the great mysteries of North America might be under this dun brown water.

When they leave me on the shore at the rickety dock jutting out I take a long look back at the city and wonder if the intrepid Viking raiders ever thought this place would be a budding metropolis, complete with a university and international commerce. Perhaps they did or perhaps all they saw were trees and deer. I carry my backpack, dive bag and the bottle of Trimix and I can see Rachel's boat, anchored about two hundred yards off the shore. The island is about six acres. Not enough for anything more that a single encampment or longhouse. Ragnar probably liked his solitude or he didn't want anyone to disturb his opulence.

I can't believe Rachel would dive alone. She knows how dangerous it is. But, she's probably too stubborn to let anyone go with her. I'm going to have to swim the two hundred yards out to her boat once I gear up. Swimming with dive gear is never ideal, but I've done worse. I now need to get back in the water.

Surprise. The land drops off. The jutting island gives way to and interesting topographical change right as I arrive at Rachel's tied boat. The swim was easy, but then the bottom just dropped out. I can't see Rachel through the dull, muddy water, but I'm sure she's down there, metal detector in hand. I rinse my borrowed mask, take a breath, check the gas and then descend.

I should've brought a flashlight. It's dark and precarious, but the water is eerily calm. Silt flies everywhere. And then, in the distance I see the faint glow of a work light. It must be forty feet down. The silt begins to break for a moment and I can make out the faint outlines of an underwater archaeological grid. Not as big as the one she placed on *La Dauphine* but big enough for the area where she works.

I can see her now. She's holding a flashlight to the bottom and lightly frog kicking along the perimeter of her grid. The metal detector arcs in long sweeps, ready for anything and everything, ready to find the remnants of Ragnar's funeral pyre and any inscription on armor that hasn't been corroded through the centuries.

Sneaking up on a diver is the worst idea so I slow my kicks down. I reach for a stone on the muddy, muck-filled lake bottom and softly toss the rock towards her position.

The water carries it in a long sweeping pattern and it settles in the mud right by her metal detector. She turns, obviously startled and sees me. All I can do is offer a meek wave. She swims over to me and I can see her haunted eyes. The reflection through the plastic of her mask mixed with the dance work light gives me a dim view of anguish or maybe that's just what I want to believe.

She shakes my shoulder in a receptive gesture. We're there, bobbing, making small kicks with our fins to stay eye to eye. It's a comical dance of two creatures in a world where they don't belong. We're mimicking otters without any sort of grace and sending bubbles floating up toward the surface. I take her shoulder as well and try to offer a faded smile through my regulator mouthpiece. She reaches into the dive sack on her waist and pulls out a tablet with an underwater grease pen attached and begins to scribble a message. She hands me the metal detector so she can get a better grip on the tablet. Holding up the flashlight now, she reveals her words: *I found something.*

We swim back toward the upper right quadrant of her grid, careful to float above and kick out and around so as not to disturb the silt and mud. She takes the metal detector back and hangs it low over the mud. The little LED lights begin to flash and she motions for me to reach down into the mud and extract whatever is in there.

This is breakneck archaeology. Normally, Rachel would do this with a trawl and delicate tools, but today I find myself reaching down into the lake bottom's muck and slime on her command. I can feel metal and when I give a faint tug, whatever was lodged there moves and brings a cloud of mud up with it. When the moment passes and the silt settles, I am holding a piece of green oxidized copper armor. It's a shard and there are black burns on it. Moving my thumb along the ridge, I can see the outlines of a carving and perhaps a rune. I nod to her and exchange the armor for the metal detector, which I now set on the lake bottom. I motion to her for the writing tablet and she hands it over, now fascinated by this shard of copper, no bigger than a dinner plate.

I write: *Newport Tower* and hold it up to her face.

She drops the armor back into the mud.

"I can't believe I didn't see it all along," she says through sips of water from a Nalgene bottle. We're dry now, sitting on Juniper Island's rickety dock where she's moored the boat.

"You're telling me that Longfellow had a sketch of it too?" she gasps giddily. "This is going to rewrite history, Rik." She looks away in ecstatic disbelief. The ring on her finger is conspicuous as she wipes a droplet away from her face. The sun is perfect in the afternoon sky. It's a beautiful May day. I don't want to ruin it, but I have to.

"You used me. You set me up from the beginning, Rachel. That's hurts more than anything that's ever cut me."

"Rik." She tries, but I've got a lot to say.

"No, I know all about the Navigator Fund. I know about Donovan and you and Lucan. I mean how could you do this?"

"Rik, what you found is incredible."

"How does it feel to know he pimped you out when things went bad? You're slave labor to a maniac. You're not going to *find* this treasure. You've been extorted to do it. Say what you want about me, but I would never, ever ask you to do this."

I hear the trees and the water lapping against the shore, meandering in and out of the smooth lake pebbles.

"He didn't ask me to do it," she sears. "You know he didn't ask me. And I'm sorry that I got you into this. But you were the only person I could count on when things went bad. I couldn't do it alone." She wipes away tears from her eyes, but I'm not done. I'm not nearly done with all the things I want to say to her. I've got hundreds of sleepless nights to blame on her. I've got bad beats and stubbed toes and hangnails and gunshot wounds and everything that's hurt me since she's been gone. My pain is her fault or at least that's how I feel as I keep speaking.

"Yeah? And what about me? Then you lie to me. You bring me into this whole mess, get me shot in the process, and you're still lying to me, even right now, you're not telling me the whole truth. Donovan's a scumbag. He borrowed money from the wrong people. He got you into this. I'm here now. I'm here," and then I do something stupid and try to take her hand in mine.

"It's not always about *you*," she screams and with a forceful shove, she pushes me back into the water. Before I fall the five feet off the dock I imagine what it would be like if I had just shut up and enjoyed the moment. Maybe she would have given me another. One of a thousand little vignettes that I took for granted. A kiss maybe? A kiss that I would gladly fall back into hell to retrieve. But, all I get for opening my mouth is a hard splash and the feeling of knowing that when I break back through the water's surface she'll be on the dock, screaming and crying. It's not about me. I'm expendable.

The drive back to the hotel in my Jeep is brutal. She barely speaks. All I know is, Donovan is there and I won't be. I'm going to draw up plans for our eventual trip to Newport and then quietly and stoically lead this expedition of folly so I can earn the right to go back home. Maybe it should be all about the money now? It sure isn't about her anymore. She made it very clear where her loyalty lies. Now, I want my fair share of this treasure and nothing more. Shut up. You don't believe that, not completely anyway. You should.

"Ski should be in there. Nile said he was going to get lunch with him," she says as we snake down the swirling carpeted corridor to the suite where she and her now fiancé have taken up residence.

"I told Victor I'd meet him at the lab," I say.

"Let me change first and we'll all go. You should change too."

I wish she would change not just the damp clothes but her whole icy attitude. Me, I'm still soaked and I left my duffel bag in the car. I was following her around blindly like an idiot. I turn back to retrieve the bag from the car as she puts the key in the door. I get two steps and I feel a hand on my wounded shoulder. Then it crushes. I'm blinded with pain and I turn to find a Beretta shoved in my face and the hollow gray eyes of Matthias Lucan staring right through me. He's crazed, the gray eyes turning to flame red. He's so close to my face I can smell the stale coffee on his breath. Behind him Kristoph drags Rachel into the suite. He's not dead after all.

"Move." He sneers and then I'm shoved through the hotel suite door and a hood is drawn over my head. The blunt thud comes quickly. Dark now. Floating. Quiet.

[22]

The Newport Tower

Dripping. Musty basement. Mold. My fingers work and I feel behind me. The rounded edges of a colonial foundation greet my sensory nerves and the cold of the rocks help me to come around. Chair. Wicker. But it's still dark. Eyes open but there's still a hood draped over my head. Semi-conscious. I can hear nothing else. Alone. Head throbbing. Shoulder, searing, probably bled through my tee shirt. Hungry.

Lights. Steps. One soul and then the hood is whipped off. Hazy focus. A floating light bulb hanging from the ceiling. The metallic slide of a chair on a stone floor and I'm sitting face to face with Matthias Lucan. Haggard wolf. Matted gray hair. Stubble around his chin. A fugitive.

He cracks an ammonia tab and holds it up to my nose and the lifeless chemical punch to my central nervous systems succeeds in bringing me around. He's not an outline anymore. He's a shape. His voice, though dull, rips through me like a banshee.

"You're alive. Talk to me."

My tongue rolls around in my head. My teeth are still there but I can taste blood. I bit my lip sometime in this ordeal. He slaps both my cheeks and I struggle against my restraints. He's got me in plastic police bands, the kind that usually tie up trash bags. They're ripping the flesh from my wrists and ankles as I try to free myself.

"Don't struggle," he says slapping my face again. "Just look at me and answer questions."

"I got an itch. You missed it. Try again," I say spitting blood.

"I'll cut your friends up into little pieces in front of you," he sneers. "You know I will." He's wearing the medallion, *Fire of Ragnar*. I can see it under his jacket. I also felt the sting of his ring on the previous slap. I hate this man.

"What do you want?" I say, the words being forced up from my throat like I've got a bad cold. My face hurts. They must have worked me over. I'm hurting everywhere like I've been in a car accident. Full body bruising.

"You know what I want. I need to know how to use the astrolabe."

"Where are we?"

"Newport. Dr. Hexam gave us that piece of information. Cost Mr. Donovan a few fingers, but…" I can imagine Rachel nearly throwing up at the sight of Donovan being maimed. She told Lucan everything.

"She said you were the only one who figured out how to read the astrolabe. They all agreed. And believe me, Dr. Meek took quite a beating as did your friend Mr. Szelingowski." He pulls out a long dagger, decorated ornately at the hilt. "This dagger has been in my family since the Crusades. And I swear that if you don't do what I ask, I will destroy everyone that is dear to you slice by slice. Your choice."

There's no choice. It's now or never. Find him this treasure or everyone that I love dies in front of me. I feel seasick, but we're not on the water. We're in some nondescript basement in Newport, Rhode Island. I have nothing. I'm helpless. But, even though they all know how to read the astrolabe they put the burden on me. They looked to me to find this treasure and defeat this monster. Called on again to do the right thing and I can't fight it anymore. I throw up in front of me, hopefully on Lucan, but he's up and out of the way, laughing his ridiculously horrible laugh. I spit and let the last bit of bile trickle out.

"Let me ask you," I say gasping for air, "How long before Sternbauer and the rest realize that you're bad for business and come after you with a pro?"

He smirks and adjusts the hanging light bulb that he had bumped when he slid back. "You know Werner Sternbauer?"

"Yes. I met him and Leonard Leanos, who's very much alive. They took all your blackmail material. You shouldn't have sent Molitor to kill a guy if you wanted it done right. Now, you've really got nothing else but this treasure." I'm laughing idiotically. "You've got nothing else but this ridiculous idea," I say spitting.

He punches hard. And the chair tips over. On floor, blood streaming from my broken nose. Then dark, feverish nightmares.

The manta ray. Alone in a vast ocean and I can't breathe. The ray flies forward but stops short. Its gills filter water in and out and it's there looking me over, waiting for me to do something, waiting for me to act. Then there's another ray and another. And then I'm surrounded by them, all waiting for me to move, but I'm stuck to the bottom. As I struggle I'm being sucked down into a vortex, until I can't hold my breath anymore. Then, nothing.

The water bucket wakes me up quickly. And before I realize it, I'm on my feet being held up by Kristoph and Lucan. They march me up the stairs and toss me down on my knees in the hallway of from what I gather is a rather nice colonial mansion. Rachel runs to my side and she holds my bruised face in her hands.

"You're going to be ok. Just trust me." I can see the fear and the hurt and all the conflicted emotions on her face. She: red and puffy. She's been crying hard.

"Where's Victor and Ski?"

"They're ok. They're upstairs with Nile."

"Did they hurt you?"

"Not bad. We've got to move soon."

Their footsteps are deep and hollow like a Johnny Cash song against the tile floor. Lucan grabs my hair and pulls me to my feet. He's got the dagger and points it at Rachel's throat. I push him back. Kristoph drops the hammer on a Beretta and I know this is no time for heroics.

"Alright, where are we?" I ask again.

"Good." Lucan sheaths the knife and opens the door of the mansion and I look out on to Touro Park and the illuminated specter of the Newport Tower. We are right across the street.

Crossing Mill Street now in the early morning haze. At least I think it's morning. Not sure how Lucan had access to this particular house, but now's not the time to ask stupid questions. I'm confronted by the Tower, sprawling skyward like Jonah's Leviathan. It's ghostly ominous. The morning sun hasn't hit it yet and I'm almost afraid of its placid calm. Each stone lain precisely forming a rounded balustrade, the arches cut perfectly with keystones interspersed. The construction: probably a church, maybe a fort, definitely something purposeful. It's a round mystery. And we walk toward it.

Lucan holds the St. Clair astrolabe under his arm. He stops at the iron gate surrounding the Tower and hands the medieval device over to me.

"We're about to continue a quest started over a thousand years ago. Thorvald's Cross, Mr. Rodriguez. This Tower was built by my Templar ancestors on the site of the original monument. The original church had fallen into disrepair when they arrived so they began construction on this. There are stones aligned with Venus. There are solstice illuminations. It's a marvel. While it was being built, they moved Thorvald and all the treasures of Vinland to a spot only decipherable with this astrolabe. Verrazzano wanted the treasure. Columbus wanted it. Now, I will have it for my family and the Knights of Christ."

"You done?" I ask and Kristoph kicks me in the back of the knees sending me down. Rachel gasps and Lucan pulls me up by my bad shoulder.

"No, seriously Lucan, you obviously didn't know any of that until Rachel told you about the Tower. You're a fraud. You don't have any right to this treasure. Your lineage is bullshit. You would've walked past this Tower like the rest of us if we didn't tell you it meant something. Where did you get all that alignment crap? From Wikipedia?"

He sneers. I've angered him. "Now, listen. You're going to climb up this Tower and plot me the direction. You're going to do it because I'm holding all of the cards now. You know what *Farsakh* and *Aurora* mean?"

"I do."

"Good. Now get up there before this town wakes up. And before I start killing."

He shoves the ancient astrolabe in my hand. My shoulder is bleeding through. I can feel it. Rachel cries and Kristoph holds her arm. I nod to her. She bites her lower lip, trying to fight back emotion. I turn to Lucan, "You got a ladder?"

Kristoph slyly brings the Beretta to Rachel's chest indicating that I'd better move and move fast.

"Alright," I say. And with one hop, I climb the iron fence.

Inside the round Tower, I can see the intricate carving and shaping of the rocks. All I care about is finding a ledge so I can climb. There's a fireplace cut into what is obviously the second floor. This must have been a sight in its day. There seems to be little doubt to me now as I look around that this was a Templar round church. Thorvald's followers built him a monument then the Templars came along and built a better one. I wonder how they were connected? Was it just Henry Sinclair and the Orkneys or did the lines of Norwegian kings really interrelate with the Templars farther back? These questions allow my head to reorient from the pain and the constant pounding in my head and see the ledge near on one of the arched Tower legs.

The climb proves to be easier than I anticipated. I've got the astrolabe shoved down in my waistband at the small of my back. My jeans and boots scuff on the seastones, but eventually, I make it to the top and peer out on to the city of Newport. The sun is now working its way over the eastern horizon. I can see down into the harbor and out for a few miles in every direction. This plot will be easy. I need to find the point three miles east with this astrolabe. I need to see where the sun and dial notches match. I swing my legs over the sides and sit on the Tower like Humpty Dumpty on his wall. My head feels like a cracked egg. But now, I have to concentrate.

I face east into the sun and using the astrolabe I can see the Sachuset Bay near Middletown. That's the most likely place.

"It's the Sachuset Bay. *Aurora Farsakh* is three miles east. That's about three miles."

"Good. Get down and we'll plot it on the map," Lucan says in a raspy croak.

The climb down is much more precarious and I have to work to not fall and break my neck, especially toting the cumbersome astrolabe in my back waistband. But, I finally put my feet down on the grass again, secretly hoping that at any moment we'll hear the whirl of police sirens and this whole mess will be over. Then I remember that I'm still wearing the plastic bracelet tucked into my sock. Desplaines. The FBI. Hopefully, the cavalry's not far away.

[23]

Purgatory Chasm

The morning sun is giving way to clouds. We've set out at gunpoint, this time carrying Victor, Ski and Donovan in tow. Donovan's got a shot of morphine on board to deal with his severed fingers. He hasn't come around yet.

The drive across Memorial Boulevard and over into Middletown was uneventful and it starts to rain as we reach Purgatory Road, a dead end. Lucan steps out and orders me to get out. Rachel, Victor and Ski then follow us down a footpath with signs leading towards *Purgatory Chasm*. The path is dirt, with smooth rocks on either side. The scraggy trees hang over in a sickly looking canopy. It begins to rain as I step forward. And then it starts to rain hard.

"Anybody got an umbrella?" Ski jokes.

"Shut up and keep moving," Lucan snarls as we keep walking further. "Suchuset Bay is going to be right below us according to the map."

"What is it exactly that you think we're going to find, Mr. Lucan?" Victor asks. He's visibly shaking, not doing well with the rain or the torture or any one of a hundred little things that have gone wrong since he left his house in Dublin.

"You know just as well as I do, Dr. Meek, that the Templars most likely had a cache or a hoard cut in the rock face or some sea cave…" Lucan responds.

"…And now it's under water for sure," I add coming to end of the footpath and a huge rock cavern dropping down at least sixty feet into the choppy ocean below. This is Purgatory Chasm and the horrible echo and reverb dancing off the rock faces make it certainly worthy of its naming. Lucan steps up next to me. With a quick side step I could shove him into this crater and be done with him forever, but he seems to sense this and steps back.

He looks out over Suchuset Bay and scans the horizon. "Dr. Meek, how far do you think the ocean advanced in seven hundred years?"

"What do you mean?" Victor asks puzzled and shivering. The rain is now pounding down.

"I mean that this chasm could have very well been part of the shore line originally and would prove a perfect hiding place for a cache of treasure, don't you agree?"

"Lucan, this is stupid," I yell through the rain. "You're never going to find anything. We've got a vague idea where we are. We're about three miles from the Tower but who knows. These assholes didn't exactly leave detailed instructions."

"It's over, Matthias," Rachel pleads. "Let us go."

Lucan weighs the decision. He seems to mull over every bad decision he's made up to that point. He's got the faraway look of a man wrestling around with deep understanding and then a lack there of.

Thunder. Lighting.

A look in my direction. "We're going to get you some scuba gear and the you're going to dive this chasm for me," Lucan says.

"What? Are you crazy? You want me to dive in this? There's no way we can get a boat out there. The chop is too much. And besides I don't have nearly enough equipment for a cave dive. I don't even know where the bottom is down there."

Lighting. Thunder. A gun. He places it on the side of Rachel's temple.

"Still feel the same way, Rik?" he asks with a supercilious smile. It's then that Ski decides to be a hero. He rushes Lucan, who whirls and fires, hitting him in the side of the abdomen. He collapses in my arms as Rachel screams.

He's breathing. He's alert and oriented, gurgling.

217

"I'm alright. I'm alright," he says through pangs of pain. The 9mm slug went right through the side of his abdomen. I'm frantically feeling the wound and I don't think he hit any vital organs. Enraged and covered in Ski's blood I stand up and face Lucan who points the gun at my head.

"You want to be a hero, too?" he says, with the smiling hatred of someone devoid of any spark of decency.

"You're going to die very soon, Lucan."

"We all die," he pauses cocking the hammer back on his Beretta. "I want to die surrounded by gold."

A boat. A bad idea. Victor keeping pressure on Ski's wound. Donovan profusely apologizing to me while he fought the pain in his mangled hand. Rachel, Lucan and me moving slowly out into the choppy sea of Suchuset Bay. We left Kristoph holding our friends hostage and by the time we arranged for a boat and dive gear it's been nearly two hours. Ski doesn't have much time.

Rachel drives, hitting every breaker. "I hope you know how exceedingly stupid this is, Matthias!" she screams over each wave.

"Sail on, my dear," he shouts frenzied. "Bring us to our fate!"

Lucan holds the gun over me as I make myself ready for this cave dive. The rain is teeming now. Where the hell is the Coast Guard when you need them? I surely hope Desplaines is arranging something based on my current position in the world. The plastic ankle bracelet still hasn't fallen off.

She pulls the skiff near the cove by Purgatory Chasm. She's in the trough now, rocking in between the breakers. She can't seem to find a way to steady the skiff. Then the wind kicks up bringing the rain crashing down around us.

Thunder. Lighting. Wind. Lucan.

"Get going, Rik! Explore that chasm and come back before your friend dies!"

I want to kill this man more than I could ever imagine. I see Rachel's face as she tries to right the skiff. Rain is bouncing off her yellow rain jacket. She's tough. She's the woman that I loved. The past tense. Gone with each moment that she struggles on with the wheel of the skiff.

I check the regulator. Gas ready. Rented dive gear uncomfortable. Rachel looking. She nods a sympathetic yet understanding nod in my direction and then goes back to work on the skiff. Rope tied off with plenty of slack. I'm not diving into a cave without a lifeline. I look at the devil behind me and fall backwards into the water ready to face whatever devils are in front.

Diving in a storm is the worst idea. Above me, the chop is flowing but below the currents are surging in and out and around. The undertow is fierce and I fight for control. There's zero visibility and the cheap dive light is not much help.

The bottom is thirty feet down and I swim towards the opening to the chasm unsure about what I'll find. The fierce crashes of the waves above remind me that yes I am mortal and currently all of my friends are in danger. Make this quick.

The chasm. A deep trench and what looks like a rising shoreline. This must have been beach a long time ago. The current behind me now surges forward and I'm already plunged into the chasm, letting out rope as I go.

Ten feet from the mouth. Then twenty feet. Then a rush of water around me and I roll, tangled in my own rope. Desperately kicking now, trying to free myself from this web. And then the light falls to the bottom, slipping out of my hand. I can feel the tug of the rope from the skiff. Could they be moving? If so, I'm fucked.

Maneuvering now and I slowly free myself from the entanglements. I can see the faint sunlight above. My light on the bottom and I have to softly flutter kick down. Grasping the light in my hand along with a fistful of sand I shine the light to the left and then I see the mouth of the cave.

Nearly out of rope as I swim forward. There are steps cut into the rocks. Carved steps. Human steps. Manmade. This cave was made! And then in front of me, three huge boulders blocking an entrance. All the while I feel the tug and pull of the skiff and the currents. This is a bad spot, but I kick on and see that over the years, the rush of ocean has dislodged one of the boulders, just enough that I might sneak through. No time. No time for this and yet I have to. No. Swim back. End this insanity.

So I swim back through the chasm, tossing and jostling all around. Hitting the side of the wall a dozen times. The rope still feels taut. I wonder how far out they drifted. The chasm disappears around me and I surge straight up and break the surface. The boat is one hundred yards away. I wave them down.

"Rachel!" I scream through the rain. She and Lucan stand. "I found something, Rachel!"

She slowly moves the skiff over and I'm careful to avoid the boat.

Thunder. Lightning. Waves crashing around and on the rocks. I can't last much longer treading water here.

Lucan stands on the edge of the boat. He looks down at me. "What did you find?" he shouts.

"A cave. With stairs," I yell back.

220

"That'll be it then." He smiles. Then he pulls the gun and points it down at me.

The end.

I'm ready.

But Lucan's chest explodes instead. He falls forward into the sea in a dramatic splash of body and blood. Rachel looks up at the chasm and I turn to see Rhode Island State troopers with flashing lights up above us. They're waving their hands gesturing and then I see why.

The wave. Bearing down on the skiff.

The boat overturns in dramatic fashion. It flips and turns in the wash and Rachel and I are both flung into the chasm. I'm still lashed to the boat and once I realize that my fate lies with it, I frantically cut myself loose. I have to find her.

She's bobbing under water. I'm got a spare regulator and I take her in my arms, putting the regulator in her mouth. The surge of Trimix opens her eyes. But we're blind. I can only see the faint slivers of sunlight cutting down through the chasm. I can tell how far we're in. The wave sent everything crashing into the chasm in apocalyptic splendor. The skiff has shattered on the rocks into a thousand splendid shards above our heads.

Then I see the cave and the stairs cut into the rock face. Maybe, just maybe it hasn't flooded. I take her in my arms. I know we can't get out through the cave entrance. The sea is too rough, so I try one last bit of effort. One last move. The cave.

Boulders. She can't see anything and I can barely see either even through my mask. I devise a ridiculous idea. I hold her head in my hands and look at her. I unhitch the regulator and harness from my body and set about strapping it on hers, all the while sharing the nozzles. I lift her up and hoist her through the crack in the boulder. Now I'm without air. If there's nothing on the other side of this boulder, then we're dead.

221

Last bit of energy. Kick forward. Up, over, in. Surface. We break the surface, both of us.

"What the hell are you thinking giving up your tank like that?!" she screams hitting me with the mask. "You know I never would've done that to you, dammit!"

I'm coughing and trying to pretend she's thanking me for saving her life instead of scolding me. We're in a cave. It's pitch black all around us. But there's oxygen. We're alive.

"What the hell is this?" she asks looking around in the dark.

"There were stairs cut into the rock surface and the three boulders were blocking an entrance way."

"This is manmade?" She coughs and laughs at the same time. "Please tell me you've got a light? Any light?"

I reach into my wetsuit belt and pull out a pack of waterproof matches. Then I strike one, sending light bouncing all over and around the sides of the cave. It's abundantly clear to us where we are. We're not in a cave. We're in a tomb.

Rachel is elated. I can hear the music swelling in her head. There, before us, carved into every nook and crevice of these rocks are shelves and chests and carefully ordered and catalogued treasure!

"Rik, this is it! We found it!" She wades slowly up on to the gravelly rock. She's shivering cold. I follow. I'm destroyed as well. Every ounce of me. All I can do is drop to my knees. She's moving. I'm stationary.

Before me is the sarcophagus. The runes are everywhere. Front and center: the hooked X. "Old Thorvald," I mutter as Rachel holds up a rather ornate gilded cross.

Templar treasures and the gold of Vinland all resting in the same place. All surrounding the Viking king. Such is the stuff of legend. Ours are the first faces to look upon these treasures in centuries. We are a part of history now.

Her face: beautiful against the match light. She throws her arms around me in a stunning embrace. It's hello and goodbye. I know I've served her well.

[24]

A Treasure

The stony floor of Thorvald's tomb kept us safe for six hours. By then the Rhode Island State Police with the help of Agent Dan Desplaines organized a rescue mission into Purgatory Chasm after the storm had cleared off the coast. He never told me if he was the one who picked off Lucan, but I have a feeling he's just not sharing. Kristoph cried all the way into custody. Victor and Ski were elated when the Agents and Troopers knocked his head against the roof of the cruiser.

They found Rachel and I shivering, huddled together among the third largest cache of medieval gold and artifacts to ever be pulled from the earth.

Rachel, Meek and her team of archaeologists went to work cataloguing and organizing the find and separated the various crusader gold from the older more fascinating tomb of Thorvald Eiriksson.

His men buried him with his armor intact in a stone coffin. The scholars from Norway and Sweden are still sending Victor for the antacid bottle every time he tries to re-decipher the inscription. History is being rewritten now by my friends.

I suppose I was proud to be a part of this claim although the legal hassle that is currently underway between the federal government and the state of Rhode Island is quite legendary. I believe we as the treasure hunters might see some money from this find, but I'm certainly not holding my breath.

Donovan paid an exorbitant fine for his dealings with the Navigator Fund, but gave Interpol some very good information about Sternbauer and his compatriots. The indictments are still pending last I heard. He did, unfortunately, make good on his promise to Rachel and married her in spectacular fashion. She wanted to have the wedding on the beach in Wildwood at sunset. It was quite a breathtaking sight. She kissed my cheek in the receiving line after the ceremony and I knew then that she would be happier than I could ever make her with the man standing to her left. I shook his hand despite myself. His missing fingers are still something to get used to. Such is life when you borrow money from scumbags.

Ifiok, the new kid I hired last week, wants me to bring him takeout sushi while he's working the graveyard shift at the shop. Depending on how this particular hand plays out, I might do just that.

I couldn't sit through the reception. I had put on my best suit and tried to put whatever best face I could forward, but I knew I'd either say something stupid or not say anything at all so I got in my Jeep and drove north from Wildwood. I think she saw me go. I took a final moment in the parking lot, wishing and wanting that stupid, smiling groom to be me. But then, I watched the wind whip through the sea grass and the long expanse of beach with fresh breakers falling with precise rhythm. Things were right for the moment. I'm out here and they're supposed to be in there. I know my place.

I offered Victor a chance to escape with me, but he was having a rather interesting conversation with the associate dean of Princeton. Perhaps he might get back into teaching? Would be good to have him around.

Refocus now on the immediately important. It's nearly nine o'clock and I'm down two hundred. The Harrah's poker room is alive with a flurry of action tonight. The talk is of the next World Series of Poker event coming to town.

I'm last to act and I glance slowly down at my cards. Pocket Aces.

I'm ready to take some money back. Maybe severance for these last few months. I suppose I'm happy now. Back again to the quiet nights along the Boardwalk. The summer crowd roared in and then whimpered out. It'll be getting on to winter soon and the cold will creep back along the Boardwalk and into my life. It'll remind me about the empty spaces in my apartment and around the shop. The cold will furrow in to every crack and crevice around me and make me realize that time is indeed pressing on, moving faster with each passing hour or second. And then I'll be faced with that awful, inevitable question that faces us all: was I significant? These beautiful lofty things: questions for smarter men like Yeats or sunny days with no chance of rain. Me, I'm just a busted up SEAL; a pawnbroker who dabbles in history and diving and a man who hopes to one day make a serious study of Texas hold 'em.

"Your action, Sir," I'm told by an impatient dealer. He's been impatient all night. He should know that poker, like life, is a game of sizing up opponents and if I'm going to get any callers I'm going to have to Hollywood my hand for a little bit. I look again, this time with a machine-gun snap against the felt.

Pocket Aces.

Still there.

I'm still breathing.

I raise.

ACKNOWLEDGEMENTS

This is my first novel and it would not have been possible without the love and support of my parents and sister: Steve, Diane and Ally Carr. You've been a constant source of inspiration over the years. To Joan Carr, who showed me how to be "Indiana Jones". To Daisy Savage, who so graciously edited the manuscript and offered insightful commentary. To James McManus, who worked diligently on the cover design. To Janet Steen, who navigated me through the ins and outs of Microsoft Word. And to everyone who took time to give valuable feedback especially: Steve Carr, Christine Meek, Janet Wolter, Zach Laverty, James Wujciak, Tim Calotta, and the Spring 2010 Fiction Workshop at William Paterson University. I thank you all.

This book hinges on the tireless research of two friends, Scott Wolter and David Brody. They have showed me a world full of treasure and possibility and their various publications, including *The Hooked X: The Key to the Secret History of North America* and *Cabal of the Westford Knight* have been eye opening throughout the writing process. I appreciate your encouragement and your friendship, gentlemen. You gave me the most valuable piece of advice when it comes to understanding controversial and debated historical artifacts: "when you walk into a room and there's a bunch of empty beer cans, chances are there's been some drinking." It's a dynamite aphorism. I cite you both with thanks.

My poker habits are anything but "fixed" as most of my buddies know. Thanks to Zach Laverty, Jason Brown, Dave Chakrin, Dan Szelingowski, Dave Szelingowski, Rob Flynn, Nick Linfante, Kevin Shipley and Dan Desplaines. You guys taught me how to lose my money graciously and inspired Rik's poker prowess. To Jay, Desplaines, Chakrin,

Shipley and the Ski brothers: thanks for the use of your names! Guys who didn't make the cut, wait for the next book. You'll be there.

To Ron Rodriguez and Rik Dugan: two amazing educators who amalgamated in my imagination to become the poker-playing pawnbroker with a PhD. Thanks for everything over the years.

And of course, no writer can thrive without a Muse, and a constant source of wonder and amazement. Chelsey, my heart and my words belong to you.

13993236R00134

Made in the USA
Lexington, KY
02 March 2012